The Midnight Rapist

The Midnight Jogger had struck again, but once more his victim had escaped with her life. The next girl might not be so lucky. That was what he feared: the Jogger would kill . . .

Lt. Victor Lolo stood at one of the open windows of his Parker Center office, overlooking the distant streets beyond Main Street. The ugly tenements and aging commercial buildings of Los Angeles had disappeared behind the smog and, in his mind's eye, he saw dark caves where animals slept during the daylight hours. Animals that came out at night to mug and murder. And rape . . .

LIMBO

Other Books by Vincent McConnor

＊ ＊ ＊

The French Doll
The Provence Puzzle
The Riviera Puzzle
The Paris Puzzle
I Am Vidocq

LIMBO

VINCENT McCONNOR

THE MYSTERIOUS PRESS

New York • London • Tokyo

MYSTERIOUS PRESS EDITION

Cover design by Irving Freeman
Cover illustration by Nancy Stahl

 Mysterious Press books are published in association with
Warner Books, Inc.
666 Fifth Avenue
New York, N.Y. 10103

A Warner Communications Company

Printed in the United States of America

Originally published in hardcover by The Mysterious Press.
First Mysterious Press Paperback Printing: April, 1988

10 9 8 7 6 5 4 3 2 1

For
Muriel and John Bertucci
who prefer Paris
to Los Angeles.

LIMBO

One

1

He saw the girl's red hair shining in the moonlight as she came out into a grassy open space between the trees.

She was wearing the same jogging suit she had worn the night before and the night before that.

Kneeling in the crotch between two thick branches, peering down through the leaves, he held his breath as she jogged closer. Grasping a bough, he balanced his body as carefully as that wildcat he saw in Mexico when he was a kid, preparing to spring onto an unsuspecting rabbit.

He felt like that wildcat as he watched her and was aware of the easy way her legs were moving back and forth.

He'd been watching her for several nights, at first following her in his car; then, last night, he selected this tree and climbed up here to plan what he would do.

Tonight, for the first time, he wondered who she was and why she came out alone at this hour. What was she thinking . . .

She was, at the moment, considering this miserable day that was coming to an end and the dreary week ahead that wouldn't be any better. She was unhappy with what was happening at the office since Harrison and Myra split. Until then her boss had always been involved with models. Tall, blank-faced blondes, posing and preening for television commercials, who were in and out of the sound stages.

Old man Conroy owned the studio but Harrison had run the operation, with her help, since his father had a second heart attack and retired to Palm Springs. She always knew which models were sleeping with Harrison because he gave them his unlisted number and she had to put their calls through, going along with the lie that they were phoning about future jobs.

But when he broke with Myra, after twenty years of marriage and two monstrous children, the phone calls stopped and he had turned to her. His secretary of five years! As though he wanted the security of her familiar face and body . . .

This girl, apparently, wasn't afraid to jog alone at night because she didn't look back as she ran and never turned when headlights flashed at her. He slowly revolved his torso, swiveling on the branch, as she passed underneath him. . . .

Maybe she'd better start looking for another job. Except there were so many girls her age—some even younger—desperately hunting positions in Hollywood. It wouldn't be easy to find one as good as the job she had. There were dozens of executives she knew, through her work at the studio, but she couldn't think of one for whom she'd care to work. They were all jokers or creeps. Even worse than Harrison . . .

He glanced up and down the traffic lanes, on both sides of the center islands, one stretching toward the beach, the other pointing back through Brentwood. No cars visible, in either direction. He grasped the branch firmly, with both hands, and swung down onto the soft grass. . . . .

She heard a faint thud behind her but didn't bother to turn. Another dead branch falling. She'd been jogging for three months now. Ever since Harrison asked her out to dinner the first time. She had accepted his invitation, somewhat reluctantly, and met him at a dimly lit Russian restaurant on Sunset Boulevard. The food was incredible and nothing happened that first night. Harrison only wanted to complain about Myra and tell her his troubles with the children. All of which she already knew or suspected. They had continued those pleasant dinners in the same discreet restaurant, at least twice a month, but she knew what was coming, recognized the warning signs. Harrison stroked her hand as they talked after dinner, and kissed her good night on the cheek before they got into their separate cars. She had begun to sleep badly, twisting and turning until three in the morning, before falling into a restless sleep broken by nightmares. She also started to lose weight, but in spite of that decided to start jogging and found that it did help her sleep better.

Now, as she ran, she became aware of another jogger behind her. This happened nearly every night. She enjoyed running a few blocks beside some attractive young man—all of them said they were college students—who would dart ahead, after a brief conversation, quickly leaving her behind. This guy was coming closer, his feet striking the ground lightly, so he couldn't be such a big one. She didn't look around. Better wait until he was beside her and said something. The different ways joggers tried to start conversations! Some were brash and macho, from their first word, others seemed shy. . . .

He saw that they were approaching one of the flower beds. Some kind of white and yellow blossoms. The white stood out in the moonlight against the dark green leaves. He quickened his pace until he heard her breathing. She had a good figure under that jogging suit. Short and plump. Not too muscular, like some . . .

She was aware that he was running beside her, slowing his stride. Probably staring. She felt his eyes on her flesh but wouldn't turn unless he spoke. . . .

He, as usual, avoided looking at her face. "You always jog this late?"

"Why not?"

"Isn't it kinda dangerous? All by yourself! Not much traffic. No people walkin' . . ."

"I like jogging when there's nobody to bother me." She turned her head slowly, and saw that he was younger than she had anticipated. "Earlier in the evening they slow their cars and whistle." She was surprised to discover, as the moonlight hit his face, that he was sort of attractive. His skin brown from the sun. Eyes so pale they were almost invisible. His curly hair, cut short, was an odd brownish-blond, almost the color of his tanned forehead. They were approaching one of the big flower beds that were planted on some of these grassy islands.

"You jog a lot?" she asked.

"All the time. How 'bout you?"

"Most nights. Except weekends. You live 'round here?"

"Yeah. With my folks."

"I share an apartment with a girlfriend." She glanced at the flowers they were passing and inhaled, but like so many other things in Los Angeles, they seemed to have no perfume.

Suddenly he grasped her arm.

His hand on her arm was hard and surprisingly cold through the sleeve of her jogging suit. "Hey! Leggo of me!"

"Be nice," he mumbled, pushing her toward the flowers.

She tried to free her arm but his grip was firm.

He covered her mouth with his other hand as he thrust her between the flowers.

She struggled, frantically now, but was unable to escape. One of his hands was pressed across her mouth and the other, holding her arm, shoved her back. She screamed but the sound died in her throat as her legs collapsed.

He pushed her down, falling with her into the darkness, green leaves swaying around them on long stems.

"I won't hurt you," he whispered into her ear.

Then she realized who he was and the knowledge terrified her.

The hand moved away from her face, but now his open mouth covered her closed lips.

Pounding him on the back with her fists, she sensed how useless it was. And only a moment ago she'd been worrying about Harrison Conroy! As he pulled back, she was aware of the clean scent of crushed grass and felt the earth under her shoulders.

"Be nice. . . ." Fumbling between their bodies with his right hand, he found the zipper of her jogging suit.

"No! Please . . ."

He slapped her across the face.

She moaned as he arched his back to open the zipper and felt the cool night air on her breasts as she begged him not to hurt her.

He struck her again with his closed fist, across an ear, and pain exploded, rocketing through her head.

He felt her collapse beneath him and knew that, like the others, she had fainted.

Springing to his feet, he whipped out of his trunks, and dropped them on the grass. He sank onto his knees, astride her hips, ripping the jogging suit away from her body. A sob came from his throat as he eased himself on top of her again. "I love you," he whispered. "I love you. . . ."

His body undulated, snakelike, legs thrashing like twin tails.

2

The long white corridors echoed with the constant summons of buzzers and bells. They were duplicates of every impersonal hospital corridor he'd seen from Pago Pago to Los Angeles. Sunlight poured through a row of windows, but the air was sickening with disinfectant. Barely glancing at the scurrying nurses and blank-faced orderlies, or the slow-moving patients in their pajamas, robes, and wheelchairs, he found the numbered door he sought and entered a white box of a room with one window. The slats of the Venetian blinds were closed, but he could make out a small figure in the bed. Barely able to see the face, he noticed only a mass of dark red hair like a drying bloodstain across the white pillows.

"You're the detective?"

He turned to see a faceless young woman rising from a chair in the corner near the window. "L.A.P.D.—Special Investigator Victor Lolo."

"You're Mexican?"

"No. I'm not."

"Somebody called from the desk. Said you were on your way up. You don't look like a detective."

"Sorry about that. We're supposed to look like average human beings. Not pretty-faced detectives on some lousy television show."

"I can't really see your face."

"That puts us in the same league. I can't see yours."

"You look Mexican. . . ."

"I'm Samoan."

"Greek?"

"I was born in American Samoa."

"Oh! Now I know."

"Pago Pago. They told me downstairs you live with the victim."

"The victim's name is Zena Casparian. We share an apartment in Brentwood."

"Zena sounds Samoan."

"She's Greek. Her family lives in Sausalito, and they're flying down this afternoon. Such a frightening thing to happen to a girl . . ."

"How old is she?"

"In her twenties."

"When did you learn what had happened?"

"Middle of the night. Police phoned. I thought Zena was asleep in her room, but they said I should bring a change of clothes and money. That she was attacked while she was jogging. When I got here they told me she'd been raped. But I'd already guessed that."

He moved closer to the bed. "How long has she been like this?"

"They said she was in shock when the medics brought her in. Came out of it while they had her in Emergency. They'd given her sedation before I arrived, but she recognized me. Grabbed my hand and wouldn't let go! . . . Even when they brought her up here. But then, pretty soon, she fell asleep. I stayed the rest of the night. Went down to the cafeteria and called my office. Told them I wouldn't be in today because of family illness. I couldn't say it was rape. Called Zena's boss and her folks. Told everybody there'd been an accident. She can tell them what she pleases. . . ."

"Why was she jogging so late? The report said it was nearly midnight."

"She claims jogging helps her sleep. There's no traffic at that hour. Nobody bothers her."

"Somebody was waiting last night to rape her," Lolo said, almost to himself. "Read the report when I got to my office this morning and came straight out here. I'm based downtown. I get all rape reports because I'm working on the Jogger case. Newspapers call him the Midnight Jogger."

"You think he did this?"

"Looks like one of his jobs. Did she tell you anything while she was conscious?"

"Not really. She was trembling and sobbing the whole time."

"They all react the same way."

"Kept begging me not to leave her . . ."

"That shot they gave her ought to be wearing off soon." He turned to the bed and looked down at the sedated girl. His eyes were adjusting to the faint light and he was able to see her face. More attractive than her friend, and several years younger. Eyes closed, long lashes resting on her cheeks. Eyebrows hadn't been plucked to make her look like one of those skinny sticks in the magazines. "You say she's Greek? She's got red hair."

"It's dyed."

"How long has she been jogging?"

"Maybe three, four months . . ."

"This guy's probably been watching her for several nights. Did she say what he looked like?"

"I already told you. She didn't say anything."

"If it is the Midnight Jogger—I'm starting to call him that myself—this is the first time he's turned up in Brentwood. His last appearance, a couple months ago, was Beverly Hills. Before that it was Burbank and Culver City."

"He gets around."

"That's what makes it tough to catch him. Never hits the same area twice. We think he's been operating for six months. Gotta hunch that's when he came to L.A.—six or seven months ago. Another victim turns up nearly every month. I've been expecting him to strike again. Any night."

"You have any idea who he is?"

"My personal hunch is it's some college kid. One of the other victims saw his face. She says he's young. Not bad looking. Whoever he is, he's sick in the skull. Your friend's lucky. So far this guy hasn't killed anybody. I gotta find him before he does."

"What're you doin' about it?"

"Checking every lead but getting nowhere. You haven't mentioned your name. . . ."

"Wanda Higgins."

"What sort of work do you do?"

"We're executive secretaries. Both of us."

"Same office?"

"I'm with a television producer in Studio City and Zena's boss is head of a Hollywood studio. Rents office space and shooting stages to independents. That's how we met. My boss rented from her boss to shoot a TV pilot. The stupid series never got off the ground, but Zena and I have been friends ever since. Hey! She's wakin' up."

Lolo snapped on a shaded table lamp beside the bed and saw that her eyes were only partially open, the lashes quivering, one cheek wet with tears.

"Ms. Casparian . . ."

No reaction.

"It'll take another minute." He turned back to Wanda. "I can see your face now."

"You still don't look like a detective. Much too handsome."

"Wanta see my I.D.?"

"Don't bother. You've got an honest face."

He leaned over the bed again. "Ms. Casparian . . ." Keeping his voice down in order not to frighten her. "I'd like to have a little talk with you."

She moaned softly.

"Ask you some questions . . ."

The eyes were opening slowly.

"I want to help you. I'm a detective."

She frowned. "Detective?"

Her friend moved closer, on the other side of the bed. "It's okay, honey. Everything's okay."

"Wanda?" She reached out, groping for her.

"I'm right here." Taking Zena's hand in her own as she sat facing her on the bed, Wanda said, "You're going to be fine, honey."

Zena clutched her hand. "I was . . . raped!" She began to sob quietly. "All those stories I've read . . . in the papers. This time . . . it was me! It was awful! Just awful . . ."

"I've got to ask you a few questions, Ms. Casparian," said Lolo. He edged closer as she stared at him. "Did you get a look at your attacker?"

"He was running. Behind me at first . . ."

"A jogger?"

"Yes. I thought . . . he was . . . a college kid. . . ."

"Tell me exactly what happened."

"He grabbed my . . . arm. Knocked me . . . down . . ."

"Could you see his face?"

"He had . . . blue eyes. They were . . . kinda weird. . . ."

"In what way?"

"So . . . pale . . . I could hardly . . . see them. Like he didn't have any eyes . . ."

"Was he tall or short?"

"Kinda . . . tall . . ."

"Taller than you?"

"Two . . . three inches. Maybe . . ."

"She's five feet four," Wanda explained. "With shoes on."

"So this guy's five feet six or seven. One victim claims he's six feet. Another says he's short. What color hair? Could you tell?"

"Burnished blond. Almost . . . same color . . . his face. Kinda . . . bronze . . ."

"Bronze?"

"Like from the . . . sun. Even his . . . hair. Bronze . . ."

"Straight hair or curly? Long? Short?"

"Short . . . and curly. I think . . ."

"That's what one of the other women said. Short and curly. But you're the first to say his eyes are blue."

"Pale blue. They frightened me!" She began to sob. "I hate him. . . ."

"How was he dressed?" he persisted, aware that he wouldn't be able to question her much longer.

"Gray . . . sweatshirt. Darker gray . . . trunks . . ."

"How old would you say this guy is?"

"Maybe . . . twenty-five . . ." She turned to Wanda. "It was awful! What am I gonna do?"

"You'll be okay, honey. I already phoned your family. They'll be here this afternoon."

"No!" Her eyes were closing. "Don't want—see . . . anybody. . . ."

"I won't bother you any longer." Glancing at Wanda as he moved away from the bed, Lolo said, "Tell her, when she's feeling better, I'll need to question her again." Heading for the door, he realized that as usual he'd learned very little from the victim—only that the Midnight Jogger had pale blue eyes. That was one new piece of information.

As he strode down the corridor he considered what she'd said about the guy's hair. Burnished blond. Same color as his tanned skin. Kind of bronze . . .

One of the other victims had said something like that.

Maybe it was the moonlight that made his hair look bronze. The moon did strange things to colors and it had been bright last night. Almost full. He couldn't recall whether there'd been a moon when the others were attacked.

This girl was the Jogger's fifth victim.

So he had to look for a guy with pale blue eyes and bronze hair.

"Good luck, Vic!" he whispered.

He wondered if the bronze-haired blue-eyed bastard was sleeping late this morning. . . .

3

D on waited at the front of the cluttered souvenir shop, standing on a folding metal chair near the closed glass doors. He was peering through a narrow vertical opening into the display window, watching people passing on Hollywood Boulevard. He always did this before any job, willing himself to be calm, freeing his mind of everything— as that yogi in Frisco had taught him—eliminating all that wasn't essential to the moment. He could feel his body temperature dropping, the palms of his hands cooling inside the rubber gloves he had on.

The boulevard was like an immense television screen when you saw it from here, framed by the big window, flashing with reflected rays of sunlight from passing cars. People walking on the sidewalk looked like actors with their painted faces and crazy clothes.

He wouldn't enter the window until there was no one passing and he could see in the reflection of the other display window, across the entrance walk, that the boulevard was empty toward Vine Street.

"Mornin', Don. Watchin' the weirdos? You can't tell the freaks from the creeps."

He had sensed someone approaching behind him, but didn't bother to turn. From the high-pitched voice he knew it was the skinny old salesman with the long scaly fingers like bird claws.

Morning jobs were not his favorites, unless it was standing in front of a theater, but shop windows and supermarket jobs filled in when no new movies were opening. This store paid only twenty bucks an hour. He was now getting fifty to stand outside a first-run theater. That was a lot harder, of course, because some of the stupid kids would pinch him to find out if he was real and try to push him off his platform. Sometimes they did.

"Business ain't good," the salesman whined. "Was surprised when I seen you come in this mornin'. Guess the boss hopes you'll pull in the tourists. They look, but they don't buy."

He saw no approaching figure reflected in the other window and nobody passing on the sidewalk. Moving quickly, he pushed the plywood partition back and stepped from the shaky chair into the window. He made his way cautiously along the narrow path between rows of bright-colored boxes containing magic tricks and a display of rubber noses, ears, and feet arranged against the window pane, extending from the entrance out to the street, across from the other display window.

"I'll come in every hour, as usual, and dust ya off, kid. Unless we get busy."

Don heard the partition close behind him as he reached the front of the window. From a low table crowded with pink and white plastic figures of Marilyn Monroe, he picked up his white baton and stood facing the sign he'd set up before going into the office to change into his clown costume.

Now he was alone. . . .

None of the people, hurrying past, had noticed him yet.

He could see his own reflection in the plate-glass pane. His spiky orange wig. The big red mouth of his rubber clown mask. The enlarged holes around both eyes, the exposed flesh painted white, then powdered so you couldn't tell where the rubber ended and the flesh began. His clown costume looked fine. Not the clumsy kind worn by circus clowns, but scarlet and white tights with ruffles and pompoms, neat scarlet leather slippers, and white cotton gloves covering his gray rubber gloves.

Velma made all his costumes from the sketches he drew.

This outfit was copied from pictures of European clowns he'd found in a library book.

Miss Edith, his art teacher in Texas, always said he had talent, but she'd be surprised if she knew what he was doing for a living. If she went past this window right now, she wouldn't recognize him. . . .

A dirty-faced boy, maybe ten years old, stopped to stare at him and was sticking out his tongue.

He eased into one of his less difficult poses. Awkward, so he looked like a mechanical figure, but easy to hold. He'd begun to fade the present from his mind. Soon he would be floating. Somewhere between conscious and unconscious.

Moving clumsily but with purpose, jerking only a few inches at a time, raising his right hand with the shiny white plastic baton, then suddenly swooping down toward the window. Rapping sharply on the glass with the scarlet tip of his baton, startling the boy and making him pull back. Now he pointed the baton toward the sign. Big red letters on white. He could see them reversed in the plate-glass window.

K O K O
MAN OR MACHINE?

A gray-haired woman had joined the boy and was staring up at him, mouth ajar, showing cheap false teeth. She looked like a tourist. Why did female tourists have such wrinkled necks? He jabbed his baton toward the entrance and was surprised when she nodded and went inside.

The boy, meanwhile, had gone on his way unnoticed.

"I'm nobody," Don whispered, his lips barely moving. "Nobody . . ."

"What's your name, boy?" Miss Purdy smiled down at him. "You must tell me while they've left us alone. Your name, boy. Your real name."

"Don't have one." That's what he wrote on the pad with the stub of pencil she gave him. She had tried to trick him into talking while the others went to lunch, but he hadn't been fooled. He never trusted Miss Purdy after that.

She had looked shocked when she saw what he'd written. "But everybody has a name."

"Not me," he wrote. "I'm nobody."
"Everybody is somebody."

As Don recalled other memories from his past he began, without consciously planning his motions, to perform one of the routines he'd perfected for store windows. Not so elaborate as those he did at private parties. Here, where nobody could touch him, he didn't have to avoid inquisitive hands or be distracted by wisecracks.

He couldn't hear what people said on the other side of the window. It was as though he'd lost his hearing. Even the traffic noises were muffled. A passing ambulance, siren screaming, filled the enclosed space briefly with throbbing sound that penetrated the rubber mask covering his ears, but after that passed, the silence was even more noticeable.

He'd been performing his mechanical-man act for two years, in store windows and at private parties, and his routines were worked out to fit each. He didn't have to think about what he was doing anymore but could let his thoughts wander. . . .

His flesh felt cool now, in spite of the heat in this cramped display window. His pulse was slowing even more.

In the past six months, he'd reached a point where his act had become automatic. It was as though an unknown power entered his body and controlled his arms and legs. He could let his mind wander back through his life and relive the things he'd done.

He liked the good times best. When Ella had been young and pretty. Before Tomas, his father, left them for good.

Those shrinks had questioned him about his childhood. Tried to find out what happened to make him stop talking. Who his parents were. Where he'd come from . . .

With all their tricks they couldn't make him tell them a damn thing. Couldn't make him talk about anything.

What was the first moment in his life that he really remembered?

He'd never wondered about that before. The very first thing he could recall . . .

It would have to be something to do with his mother. All his early memories were of her. Especially Ella laughing. If she was unhappy, in those days, he hadn't known.

Ella told him, much later, that his father had gone to

Mexico before he was born to look for work and hadn't shown up again for three years. Walked in one night, as though he'd never left them, angry because his dinner wasn't ready.

He'd often wondered how his mother, alone with a baby, had managed. Were there other men then? Like the ones who visited her, later on, every night in Texas, after Tomas left them for good. He'd been too young to know if all of them were her lovers. . . .

What was his first memory? Those shrinks never asked him about that. What could it be? If it wasn't Ella . . .

His white-enameled crib? Or did he remember that because he saw it constantly, long after he'd stopped sleeping in it? That crib had remained in a corner of their shack—always piled with junk—until he and Ella moved again. . . .

His earliest memory . . .

Maybe it was the first time he saw Tomas. The night his father came home from Mexico. Although he had no idea where they were living or how Tomas had found them. Ella must've cooked a big dinner that night. He could see them eating. Candlelight on his mother's red hair. Or was that a different night, maybe Dallas or San Antonio? . . .

He was three years old when Tomas came back the first time. So he couldn't have remembered that. Must've been the second time . . .

More pictures floated through his head, like scenes in an old movie. Other dinners and one meal the three of them had eaten on the bank of some river. He could see Tomas playing a guitar and singing, throwing his head back and laughing, long black hair twisting like snakes around his shoulders. He had no idea why they were eating outdoors or where that was. Mexico or Texas? They'd driven back and forth in that old Chevy so many times when his father wasn't working.

There was much he couldn't remember. And never would.

Those shrinks said there were holes in his memory caused by some of the bad things that had happened to him. Black empty holes. They claimed that was why he couldn't talk. He didn't want to remember the past.

He had foxed them!

Even then, in his early teens, he'd been a pretty good actor. Before he really knew what an actor was.

That's what he wanted to be when he first came to Hollywood. A movie star. Like Jimmy Dean! He'd worked hard for a year, taking lessons and trying to find an agent, but the only work he could get had been as a stuntman.

He'd enjoyed that at first, the excitement of watching the real actors and working at the big studios, but the danger had begun to worry him as he saw friends injured, and finally, when Pike Splain was killed, he had no more guts for doing stunts. Velma had begged him to give it up.

It was the year after Pike died that he moved into the Coop. Since then his life sure had changed. Thanks to Velma Splain.

He was making a pretty good living now. Even had some money in the bank, for the first time—more than three hundred bucks. He could never have managed that if Velma hadn't made him save money every week. Especially with his costumes.

She put this clown costume together with the help of her friend who, like Velma, had worked in wardrobe at Paramount before she retired. The other woman had made it at home and hadn't charged him too much.

Velma took care of all his costumes, repaired them when they were torn and had them cleaned for him. A terrific dame, as long as he could stay out of bed with her. She claimed she was thirty-five—Pike would be forty-two if he was still alive—but he suspected Velma must be close to forty. Her blonde hair was dyed and sometimes, when she went to a movie, she wore an even lighter blonde wig.

The one night she'd gotten too friendly, soon after he moved into the Coop, he had ripped her dress when he pushed himself away from her. They were alone on the living room sofa (Lori-Lou had been sent upstairs to bed) and Don had managed to escape Velma's wet lips and clutching hands, fleeing from the house to the Coop in the back.

He hadn't meant to tear Velma's dress. Worried all night about what he could say to her next morning, but she was the first to speak. She apologized to him! Told him she'd been lonely. She hadn't meant to upset him. Knew he was much younger . . .

He'd explained that he had a steady girlfriend and wasn't

interested in anybody else. Which, of course, wasn't true. He'd never had a girlfriend.

Velma never mentioned that night again. He was glad she didn't because he liked Velma and was happy living in the Coop behind her little house on Poinsettia Place. She still asked questions about his girlfriend, who, he told her, lived in the Valley and never came into Hollywood.

He'd admired Pike, enjoyed eating dinner with the Splains when Pike was alive, although their daughter, Lori-Lou, was a pain in the rear. Now that she was eleven, however, she wasn't so bad. Still a pest, at times, with her constant questions, but she went off to school before he was awake and he only saw her at night when Velma insisted he have dinner with them. That happened at least once a week. Home cooking, but not as good as his mother's . . .

It was weekends he had to avoid Lori-Lou—always hanging around the Coop while he worked on his cars, eating candy bars and asking questions. All that junk she ate was making her fat. Velma complained and threatened but never did anything to stop her, like cutting her allowance. Lori-Lou needed a father.

He thought of himself at Lori-Lou's age. Making a fool of himself, hoping people would like him. The shrinks said he acted that way to get attention, because he needed a father.

Every kid needed a mother and a father. One alone wasn't enough.

"Come to dust ya off, kid."

The old salesman's high voice, whispering in his ear, brought him back to the display window and he saw that half a dozen people were watching him through the glass.

"Business ain't no better t'day. Boss is complainin', as usual. Hold still, kid. This won't hurt none."

He watched the staring faces react as the orange wig was lifted, revealing the shiny white skull of the rubber clown mask. His body stiffened as the salesman picked up a feather duster and flicked it across his head. The stupid fool was even dusting his face. When he could see the window again all the people were laughing.

"Now I'll put your hair back on."

The wig was pulled down over his head.

"And wind you up for all them nice people."

He felt the pressure against the center of his back as the idiot cranked the noisy metal ratchet attached to his scarlet leather belt. He began to move again, jerking his arms and head, taking another position.

"See ya later, kid. . . ."

He swooped toward the glass pane, tapped it with his baton, and pointed to the entrance. Saw several of the watchers make their way into the shop.

There weren't too many people yet, but there would be more in another hour. Out of each group a few always went inside. Mostly tourists. Smiling and innocent looking. He could always tell them from the sharp-eyed locals.

His muscles were relaxing into another easy position.

He noticed a ratty guy with mean little eyes edging between the others. One of the plainclothes characters from Hollywood Division who wandered up and down the boulevard day and night, looking for pickpockets and pushers.

The beady rat-eyes glanced up and at him and one eye winked.

When Don finished here he would have a quick hamburger, then drive down to Santa Monica, spread a towel on the sand, and stretch out in the sun. He never went to the beach on weekends, when thousands of noisy people made it impossible to relax. Weekdays it wasn't so crowded. He liked it when all you heard was the distant surf. . . .

When he left the beach he would drive up the Coast Highway past Malibu. That always relaxed him. He'd drive as far as Zuma Beach.

Tonight, maybe, he would catch a movie. Not one of the first-runs. They were too crowded and noisy. He liked small neighborhood theaters better. He would lose himself in the darkness and become a part of what happened on the screen.

"I'm nobody," he whispered as he withdrew deeper into himself, no longer conscious of eyes staring at him.

His mind was returning, as always, to Tomas and Ella. That night his mother was killed.

"I'm nobody. Nobody . . ."

4

The Midnight Jogger had struck again, but once more his victim had escaped with her life. The next girl might not be so lucky. That was what he feared: the Jogger would kill. . . .

Lieutenant Victor Lolo stood at one of the open windows of his Parker Center office, overlooking the distant streets beyond Main Street. His usual view of the city was missing, the ugly tenements and aging commercial buildings of Los Angeles had disappeared behind the smog and, in his mind's eye, he saw dark caves where animals slept during the daylight hours. Animals that came out at night to mug and murder. And rape . . .

That wasn't really how it was. He was aware of that. All the same, that's how he thought of this city: a hiding place for criminals, some of whom were hiding from him.

On a clear day he could look down at the only tree in the neighborhood, a ragged palm sticking up from a backyard piled with parts of cars, wrecked in long-forgotten accidents, rusting behind a crumbling stucco house that had been empty ever since he had moved into this office. The opposite corner had been bulldozed, leaving a vacant lot that had become overgrown with weeds, where a Mexican woman sat every day on an overturned basket, waiting for customers to come and buy the small packages of marijuana hidden under her skirts. One day a pair of her customers would kill her. But she wasn't one of his problems. He was assigned to special investigations. . . .

Some days he watched the Mexican woman through binoculars he kept in the bottom drawer of his desk, but today he hadn't bothered to take them out.

This morning he could barely see the woman hunched on her basket or glimpse the ghost of that dying palm tree. A haze of smog, from traffic in the busy surrounding streets, covered everything, which was just as well, because when he could see the palm tree and there was even a small patch of blue sky, it always reminded him of tall green palms swaying against pure blue sky above a long stretch of clean white sand.

Except there had been smog in Samoa, long before he left. What would Pago Pago be like today? More high-rise hotels? More tourists and more noise?

Lolo sighed, remembering how it had been when he was a boy.

Yet he knew, in his heart, he would never return to the islands.

He was doing what he had wanted to do, working as a cop in this funky city he'd dreamed about since the first time he heard of Hollywood. This was the life he'd hoped for. He'd read every detective novel he could find in Pago Pago, especially Hammett, Chandler, and Simenon. . . .

Turning from the windows, he stared at the three file folders spread in a row across his desk. Each one contained a single current investigation. They had come from every division. Cases that needed expert assistance. There was a disappearance in Beverly Hills that he had a hunch would turn into murder. Next to that was the file concerning a rock star savagely beaten by intruders in his Malibu estate. He swore he didn't recognize them and nothing had been stolen. That could be another crime involving drugs or gays. Gays he understood, but he was getting damn sick of drugs. Narcotics were turning up in nearly every new investigation. It disgusted him that human beings were destroying themselves—mind and body—with heroin and cocaine. He had too much respect for his health and his body ever to touch drugs.

He wondered if the Midnight Jogger was on drugs. . . .

These three folders held every known fact on each of his

current assignments and he hadn't come up with a solution, as yet, for any of them.

The Midnight Jogger file was the thickest. It lay open on the faded green blotter where he'd been checking over its contents again for the past half hour.

Another girl raped last night. Zena Casparian.

Lolo sat down again and stared at the open folder.

That was his urgent case at the moment. There'd been no fresh developments in any of the others for several days.

And it was the Jogger who interested him the most. He was curious about what went on in the mind of a rapist. Especially this one.

Who was he? Where was he hiding?

Right now, as he sat here, dozens of detectives were out working on all three cases. Chasing after fading leads, asking the same questions again and again . . .

While he sat here staring at an open file folder.

He'd gotten some of his best ideas doing this in the past, but he'd come up with no fresh ones today.

He seldom ate at noon, trying to hold his weight down. He liked to sit in this silent office studying his current cases, searching for some piece of evidence he'd missed or overlooked.

Today's lunch hour had been devoted to the Midnight Jogger.

After questioning Zena Casparian at the hospital, he'd gone to the police lab and was shown an impression of a shoe print found under a tree where the rapist had, apparently, dropped from a branch last night. The earth had been moist because leaves shaded the spot during the day and gardeners had recently watered the grass.

The print had been made by a shoe with a ribbed rubber sole, which the lab identified as a brand of running shoe worn by many joggers.

They had an earlier print left behind by the Jogger in January, at the edge of a lane behind a shopping mall in Burbank. It was the identical shoe with a small tear in the rubber at the back of the heel. Depth of print indicated the wearer was the same weight he'd been four months ago.

They would have to find him, with that shoe in his possession, before the prints could be of any use.

Zena Casparian was the Jogger's fifth victim.

Who would be the sixth?

Lolo glanced toward the open windows again.

Where was she at this moment? That next victim . . .

Working in an office? Taking her lunch break? Gulping a hamburger before she did some shopping?

She could be anywhere. The other victims had been found in widely distant areas of the city. That's why he'd been called in to coordinate the investigation.

Odd that the rapist never picked a victim in Hollywood . . .

He hadn't thought of that before.

Could it be because the Jogger lived in Hollywood and didn't want the police looking for him where he might be recognized?

There were several small parks in Hollywood, many dark streets where he could hide in a tree or behind shrubbery. . . .

Had he finally hit upon something important?

Did the Midnight Jogger live near Sunset and Vine? Or Hollywood and Western? Better give a little thought to that . . .

The police artist was revising his earlier sketch of the Jogger, changing the color of his hair and eyes to match the Casparian girl's description. Pale blue eyes and bronze hair. Maybe that would lead to something.

Lolo frowned at the assortment of documents and transcripts in the open file. On top was a report he had dictated this morning to a police stenographer after he'd returned. There was nothing in that or any of the other pages that added up to a goddamn thing.

He'd checked the dates of those four earlier rapes and found, after contacting a pal at the Weather Bureau, that the moon had been full only once before. The night of the third rape. So there were two rapes when the moon was full and three when it hadn't been.

Which proved absolutely nothing.

Except it was that girl in Burbank who was raped when the moon was full—the third victim—who said the rapist's hair was "dark blond, almost reddish." So the guy's hair might only look bronze or brownish blond when seen in moonlight.

Women were known to be inaccurate about the color of

anyone's hair. For that matter, both men and women were notoriously unreliable when asked to describe a suspect's appearance. A dozen people could witness a bank robbery and you'd get twelve different descriptions of the robbers.

The single word typed on a label pasted at the top of the folder was RAPE. He had printed MIDNIGHT JOGGER in black ink, underneath, after the newspapers gave the guy that name.

Lolo fingered the typed pages until he found a list of the first four rapes. He ran his eyes down the names and checked where each attack had happened.

The first was a residential area in Culver City. He remembered that dark street with its row of old trees. Next was a shopping mall in Santa Monica. Another shopping mall, this time it was Burbank. The fourth rape was in a back alley of Beverly Hills where residents like to jog late at night.

He checked all the dates again.

The first rape attributed to the Jogger was last November, the second was December, and the third was January. The fourth wasn't until March and the fifth was last month. May . . .

No rapes in February or April.

Had he been out of town? Behind bars for some other crime?

Or had there been rapes, both those months, that weren't reported?

More likely they'd been reported but had gotten lost in the flood of memos and paperwork, never noticed by anyone who would relate them to the Midnight Jogger. . . .

Lolo snatched up the phone and punched a button.

"Yes, Lieutenant?"

"Take a memo. Send to all divisions. Ready?"

"Ready, sir."

"Check for any report of a female raped in your district during months of February and April this year. Contact me personally if you come up with anything. . . . Got that?"

"Yes, sir."

"Sign my name and have it sent out at once. Marked urgent."

5

Don locked the heavy door of the Coop, as a matter of habit, slipped his keys into a hip pocket, and headed down the drive toward the front of the property.

Velma had phoned right after he'd gotten home—she had seen the Honda pass her open side windows—and insisted he have dinner with her and Lori-Lou, so he'd decided not to catch a movie tonight. The hot sun at the beach had made him drowsy. After a fast shower, he put on a clean sport shirt, Levi's, and huaraches.

He liked living here because the Coop was his private territory. Nobody bothered him, and Velma couldn't get inside when he was out. He'd changed the locks after he moved in, and she'd never asked for a key. Anyway, Velma wasn't the nosy type. Even Pike used to say that.

Glancing back as he walked, he saw that the Coop was hidden by dark green vines that covered its sides and spread across the flat roof. From the street you couldn't tell it was there.

To his right was a rectangle of cement, a metal pole at each corner supporting clotheslines for Velma's laundry. There was always something hanging there. This evening it was a row of Lori-Lou's short white socks.

On the other side of the drive was a high wooden fence extending all the way to the street, hiding the ground-floor windows of the next house and shutting out most of the noise from the neighbors' loud parties. He'd never seen any of the people next door but Velma said they were trash and she was always warning Lori-Lou not to speak to them. But then, Velma called most people trash.

Her kitchen windows were brightly lighted and dinner should be ready—one of Velma's big meals, Don hoped, like she used to cook for Pike. Good thing he only ate a hamburger this afternoon or he wouldn't be able to do her cooking justice, and Velma would pretend her feelings were hurt. Pike always ate everything, and before he died it had begun to show. He'd gotten a belly and his stunt work had slowed down.

Pausing under the branches of an overgrown avocado tree, he saw cars passing on Poinsettia Place, behind the steel-mesh gate that was locked, day and night, to keep intruders out.

There were lots of prowlers in this part of Hollywood, but Velma had never been robbed. She claimed it was because Kong, the black Doberman that Pike had raised from a pup, ran loose here all night. His deep bark would scare anybody away.

He noticed that the garage door, behind the house, was padlocked. Velma wouldn't be going out to play bingo with Pete Pottenger.

There was an old Jimmy Dean movie on television Don wanted to see, which began at eight, so he would leave right after he finished eating.

His own cars were in the garage Pike had built for himself behind the Coop. Don kept the doors locked even when he was home.

Music coming from the new building, south of Velma's property. Five or six Koreans crowded in each two-room apartment. Their cooking smelled rotten and their music was like the screeching of wild parrots he'd heard, long ago, in Mexico.

The air was warm tonight, like the middle of summer. He got a sickening whiff of jasmine as he walked. That big bush, across the street, must be blooming again. Somebody should poison its roots.

He went up the outside steps, the rope soles of his huaraches making no sound, and saw Velma through the screened windows, moving around the kitchen, a white apron over her bright-colored muumuu. She reminded him of Ella, always cooking. Only his mother never had a real kitchen like this and she was a lot thinner than Velma. Younger and prettier.

He knocked on the screen door before pulling it open.

"Wish you'd stop knocking, honey. Told you a hundred times. Just come right in." She turned, smiling, from the stove. "You're family."

"I know, Velma." The air in the kitchen smelled good enough to eat.

"Gimme a kiss."

He kissed her on the cheek.

"We're eatin' late t'night. Didn' have any appetite earlier."

"Where's Lori-Lou?"

"Glued to that damn TV set. Where else? Inform her majesty, for me, it's time to eat."

"I'll do that, Velma."

She turned back to the stove. "Don't like you knockin' on the door like a stranger. Salesman or somethin' . . . You pay rent here! This is your home."

"Sure is." He heard the television blasting rock music as he crossed the dining room where the round oak table had three places set for dinner. Hung over the table was a copper lamp with lighted electric candles under a shade covered with pictures of cowhands on horses chasing a steer.

Kong crept out from under the table, sleek as a snake, stretching and nudging Don's leg with his nose.

"Hi, Kong. How's the boy?" He stooped to scratch behind one pointed ear, as Pike had always done, and the dog's tail wagged in response. "Only three places for dinner? Where's Pete tonight?"

"Ain't heard from the bastard all day," Velma responded. "Drunk again, I s'pose."

The music from the television set got louder as he passed under the archway into the living room and saw Lori-Lou curled up on the big sofa staring at some singers with orange faces. He couldn't tell whether they were girls or guys. Passing behind the sofa he saw that Lori-Lou was munching a chocolate bar. "Whacha eatin', kid?"

Blonde pigtails whirled and the hand holding the candy vanished. "You scared me!"

He saw that her round face, in the flickering light from the big television screen, was getting to look even more like Pike's. "Does Velma know you're eatin' candy before dinner?"

"Nope, and you're not gonna tell her." She crammed the last of it into her mouth. "Are you?"

"How many you had since you been watchin' TV?"

"Only two . . ." Chewing furiously.

"You'll be sick again."

"I will not."

"When you don't eat dinner, Velma always knows you've been piggin' candy bars."

"You won't tell her, Don! Please . . ."

"Do I ever?"

"Okay . . ." She swallowed the last morsel of candy.

"Stinkypie!" Velma called from the dining room. "Turn that damn TV off. Salad's on the table."

"Yes, Mommy." Lori-Lou pushed the remote control, which was sitting on the arm of the sofa, and the orange faces faded as she scrambled to her feet.

"C'mon, Cricket. Time for dinner." Don placed an arm around her affectionately as they went toward the dining room.

"When ya gonna stop callin' me Cricket?"

"Soon as you stop talkin' so much. The only time you don't chirp's when your mouth's fulla candy."

"I do not!"

"I've heard a whole field of crickets chirpin' that made less noise than you."

Velma hurried in from the kitchen with a napkin-covered breadbasket. "Okay, folks! Sit down and eat your salad." She placed the basket in the center of the table. "Stinkypie, you didn' have any candy this afternoon, I hope."

"Now, Mommy . . ."

"Okay. You'll eat your dinner an' enjoy it." Velma

collapsed at her usual place, and Don sat on her right across from Lori-Lou. "Dive in, kids!" She snatched up the breadbasket again, pushing the napkin back to reveal split sesame rolls. "Toasted these with cheese an' garlic," she said, offering them to Don. "The way Pike always liked . . ."

"Thanks." He took half a roll and set it on his butter plate.

"They're my favorites, too!" Lori-Lou peered into the basket to see which roll had the most cheese and grabbed one before her mother moved it away.

Velma set the basket down, selected a roll for herself, and covered the others with the napkin. "Made guacamole tonight. My own recipe."

"Looks good." Don reached for his fork and began to eat.

"Never seen a recipe but I've eaten guacamole, you know, enough times in Mexican restaurants. How's that taste?"

"Just like I used to get in Mexico." It wasn't bad but something seemed to be missing, though he had no idea what.

"And how was your day, Don?"

"Had a window job on Hollywood Boulevard. Went to the beach after that, an' sunbathed."

"But you never swim!"

"I just like to stretch out an' relax in the sun. Too many people usin' the water."

"Was there a crowd?"

"Hardly anybody."

"An' you still didn' swim?"

"Nope . . ."

"You are a character. Pike always said you were." She turned to her daughter. "What was that you were watchin' on TV?"

"Don't remember."

"But you only just saw it! Not two minutes ago."

"Didn' see the start. So I don't know what it was."

"No point in watchin' TV unless you know what you're lookin' at. People who watch anything that comes on the screen are morons," Velma said, glancing toward Don. "Don't you agree?"

He shrugged, avoiding an argument. "I watch mostly old movies. But I like t' catch 'em from the start."

"I'm the same way. Unless I see the beginnin' I never understand what's happenin'. . . . You see the newspaper this evenin'?"

"Nope."

"There's another piece about that Midnight Jogger."

"What's he done now?"

"Same's before. Raped another one."

"Yeah?"

"Last night. This time it was in Brentwood."

"They caught him?"

"They'll never catch the guy. Somebody found the girl unconscious an' called the cops."

"I know what rape means," Lori-Lou announced.

"Do you, young lady!" Velma faced her. "An' what, exactly, does it mean?"

"Some of the kids were talkin' 'bout rape today in school."

"That's a fine subject, I must say, for eleven-year-olds to be discussin'. Were you one of those involved in this conversation?"

"It was Betsy Hoffman an' two of the older girls. They were all gigglin' an' Mrs. Pringle asked what they were talkin' 'bout, an' Betsy said they were talkin' 'bout rape."

"How'd Mrs. Pringle react to that?"

"She told Betsy to stand up an' tell the rest of our class the meanin' of the word rape."

"Did she?"

His salad finished, Don put his fork down, aware that Lori-Lou was desperately trying to think of what to say.

"Go on!" Velma ordered. "What did Betsy tell you?"

"She said that rape was like when a boy wants to kiss a girl but the girl doesn't want him to kiss her. . . ."

"That's all?"

"Well . . . "

"Tell me the rest!"

"Betsy said rape was when a boy makes you let him kiss you. Holds your arms while he does it . . . "

"An' that's the meanin' of rape?"

"Yes, Mommy."

"Have you ever been—raped?"

"Oh, no, Mommy! I won't let any boy kiss me."

"I should hope not. What did Mrs. Pringle say to all this?"

"She said girls mustn't ever let boys kiss them. We should slap them whenever they try."

"Good for Mrs. Pringle." Velma turned to Don again, raising her painted eyebrows and smiling. "Now we've settled that, I'll bring the rest of our dinner." She rose from the table and reached for their empty salad plates, which she piled on top of her own. "Rape is not a subject to be discussed by eleven-year-olds." She carried the plates toward the kitchen. "When I was eleven I never even heard the word. Much less discussed it."

Don grinned as he looked across the table at Lori-Lou. "You've got some chocolate smeared on your upper lip," he whispered.

She ran the tip of her tongue around both lips.

"Ya got it."

"Thanks. Mommy didn' notice."

"What're you two whisperin' 'bout?" Velma called from the kitchen.

He raised his voice. "She's tellin' me 'bout her music lessons."

"Well, you're old enough to hear 'bout them."

Don smiled at Lori-Lou. "Can you play a tune on that flute yet?"

"Not really . . ."

"Well, work on it, kid. You've had it since Christmas."

"My teacher's gonna gimme a piece by Mozart to study."

"Who's he?"

"He's the one in that movie. Lived hundreds of years ago."

"That stuff's for squares. You like school any better?"

"Better than I did last year. How 'bout you? Did you like school when you were a kid?"

"Not much. Mostly 'cause I hadda go to so many different ones."

"Why was that?"

"We moved all the time. An' later, after my mother died, I lived in a lotta different places. Always went to a new school."

Her eyes were round with shock. "Your mother died?"

"Yeah."

"I remember when Pike died. . . ."

"That's only a year ago."

"My Mommy's never gonna die." She stared at him, wide-eyed. "Is she? Mommy can't die! Can she?"

He thought of himself, the night they carried Ella away to the hospital. "Of course not."

"You swear?"

"I swear. Not ever . . ."

"Hope this turned out okay." Velma hurried back with a large tray holding three dinner plates. She put it down on the table and set a plate in front of each. "They had fresh shrimp on special at Ralph's."

"I love shrimp!" Lori-Lou inspected her plate, hands clasped, with an air of rapture. "But I don't like potatoes with their skins left on. They're groady! Isn't there any spaghetti an' cheese?"

"You had pasta last night." Velma rested her empty tray on the old-fashioned sideboard and returned to sit at the table. "These are new potatoes, young lady. You'll eat 'em an' like 'em!"

Don saw the curried pink shrimp and crusty-skinned potatoes with a mound of snow peas and strips of zucchini. "Hey! This looks great!"

"Hope you're both hungry." Velma snatched up her fork and speared a shrimp. "I forgot to fix any lunch, so I'm famished," she said, chewing the shrimp. "Tastes pretty good."

"We used to get Gulf shrimp when I lived in Texas," Don said. He was eating his second shrimp. "But I never ate potatoes cooked like this. Best I ever tasted!"

"Fried 'em in peanut oil. I was tellin' you 'bout that Midnight Jogger. . . ."

"Yeah?"

"This girl's in the hospital, but the paper says she'll be released t'morrow. Doesn't give her name, as usual, or tell exactly where it happened in Brentwood. They never name the streets anymore. This time the girl was able to give the cops a description of the guy."

"She saw his face?"

"Not too well, I guess. The paper said she only saw his eyes an' the color of his hair. Claims his eyes were sorta pale blue . . ."

"Pale blue?"

"An' his hair's kinda dark blond. Sorta bronze colored." He laughed. "I never hearda bronze hair."

"I bet she didn' say any such thing. Some reporter put words in her mouth," Velma said, chewing as she talked. "Crime gets worse every day. Especially here in Hollywood. Checker I know, at the Safeway, was tellin' me 'bout the robberies in this neighborhood. Apartments right here on Poinsettia! Muggings on Fairfax! Whores an' pimps on Sunset! Cops gotta protect people better. An' the judges gotta put the punks behind bars an' keep 'em there! Not let 'em out to mug an' rape again. Ya know? Somethin's gotta be done. . . ."

As Velma talked they cleaned their plates, except Lori-Lou, who left one potato untouched.

Don held the last of his sesame roll under the table and felt it pulled away, gently, from his fingers. He heard Kong crunching the crust as Velma collected their plates, glaring at the uneaten potato.

"I worry 'bout Stinkypie walkin' home from school every day."

"Aw, Mommy . . ."

"Never know who's waitin' in a car to pounce an' grab her . . ."

Don glanced at the old wooden clock above the sideboard and saw that his Jimmy Dean movie would be starting in fifteen minutes.

Velma continued to chatter as she arranged the dinner plates on her tray. "You never know who's lurkin' 'round a public school. Dope peddlers an' perverts!" She carried the tray toward the kitchen. "I worry every afternoon, till Stinkypie comes home. . . ."

"Will that girl be sick?" Lori-Lou whispered, leaning across the table toward him.

"Which girl?"

"The one that was raped."

"She probably wasn't hurt bad. Maybe frightened. You shouldn't ask questions about such things."

"That's what Mommy says."

"She's right."

"I stewed fresh peaches for dessert," Velma called from the kitchen, slamming the refrigerator door. "Made custard to go over 'em. Remember last summer, Don? You said you liked peaches in custard."

"I remember."

"Mommy! Can I have my peaches plain? I loathe custard."

"This restaurant aims to please every customer." Velma talked on in the kitchen. "What you doin' t'morrow, Don? More jobs comin' up?"

"Shop window in the mornin'—a bookstore in Beverly Hills—to promote some science fiction, so I'll wear my spaceman outfit."

"You're doin' okay, kid." She brought their dessert on the same tray. "Pike sure would be happy if he knew," she said, handing a bowl of peaches to each and putting one down at her own place. "He always said you'd make it with your mechanical-man routine. Encouraged you for a year before you decided to try it." She carried her empty tray to the sideboard, then sat at the table again. "All because you were waitin' for him that day at the studio, an' fell asleep."

"I wasn't asleep. I'd been sittin' on that bench so long I went into sort of a trance."

"Pike said you were sittin' there like a dummy, eyes wide open."

"What's a trance?" Lori-Lou asked.

"It's like you're half asleep," her mother answered.

"I've been able to do that since I was a kid," Don explained, hurrying through his peaches and custard. "Shut things off. Close out all sounds."

"Pike thought you'd had a heart attack," Velma continued as she ate her peaches. "He had to shake you."

"Takes me a coupla seconds to come outta it."

"Was almost a year after that before he convinced you there was money in doin' a mechanical-man act."

"Didn' think I could do it with people watchin' me."

"We never know what we can do, do we? I remember years ago . . ."

The telephone shrilled in the front hall and Kong growled under the table.

"That'll be Pete." Velma put her spoon down. "If he's lookin' for dinner, he can try McDonald's." The phone continued ringing. "Answer that, Stinkypie, like a sweetheart."

"Okay, Mommy." She gulped her last stewed peach. "You wanta talk to him?"

"Only if he's sober."

Lori-Lou jumped up. "Can I turn the TV on?"

"If you must." Velma watched her hurry toward the hall. "Don't know why I put up with Pete Pottenger. Except he's like a part of Pike. They'd been pals for so long—like brothers. Did all those stunts together." She folded her napkin automatically. "How 'bout coffee?"

"Not tonight, Velma. I'm goin' to bed early an' rest up for tomorrow." He dropped his napkin on the table. "Thanks for dinner."

"Maybe dinner Saturday night? Pete should be here."

"If I'm not workin' . . ."

"Mommy!" Lori-Lou called from the hall. "Pete says he's sober. He hadda work late at Universal."

"In that case, I'll talk to him." Velma jumped up from the table, breasts bouncing under her muumuu.

Don rose at the same time, eager to leave. "Thanks again for a swell dinner."

"My pleasure, honey." She hurried toward the hall. "Let Kong out as you go. He's had his dinner."

"Here, Kong!" Don said, snapping his fingers. "C'mon, boy."

The Doberman shot out from under the table, followed him through the kitchen and out the door.

Kong trotted with him, all the way back to the Coop.

Don went straight to his garage, behind the compact one-story building, and checked the two doors. Both were padlocked, as he'd left them when he came home. He always checked again before going to bed. Lots of cars got stolen, every night, in Hollywood.

That done, he circled the Coop to the front, Kong padding along beside him. He unlocked the door and reached in to snap the wall switch, lighting a lamp on his bed table.

He leaned down to stroke Kong's head. This was another nightly routine. "Okay, boy, you're on guard till mornin'. Give 'em hell!"

The lean black body streaked down the drive.

Don waited until he heard Kong barking, when he reached the locked gate, giving notice to Poinsettia Place that he was on duty.

Glancing overhead he saw that the sky was bright with stars.

He went inside, into silence, closing the heavy reinforced door and securing the dead bolt. Only then did he inspect the small space that was his home. He did this every night, no matter the hour, whenever he returned.

His home! The only real home he'd ever known.

This was a chicken house when the Splains bought the property. Pike had cleaned it out, enlarged and rebuilt it for himself. He'd installed a john with a stall shower and put in electricity.

Don's eyes slowly checked his possessions as he sank onto the narrow bed. Pictures of young movie stars, guys and gals—dozens of them—in neat rows on the white-painted walls.

One whole row of Jimmy Dean.

In a minute he would turn his TV set on for that movie—*East of Eden*—one of his favorites. By then the stupid commercials should be finished.

Most of his furniture he'd picked up at a garage sale, but the studio bed, with its brown-and-white-striped spread, had been given to him by Velma when he moved in. A large calendar hung on the closed door to the john with a color photograph of some Mexican mountains. Some day, when he saved enough money, he would go back to Mexico and look for his father's mountain.

He peered at the open skylight above the center of the room, which he'd cut into the roof after he boarded up all the side windows. The skylight gave plenty of air and light to the Coop, and in hot weather he covered it with a bamboo blind on pulleys. The small air-conditioning unit he bought last summer was set against the wall near the head of his bed.

The windows were boarded over, covered with plywood

on the inside, hidden under ivy, morning-glory vines, and rambling roses on the outside.

His eyes moved over the big cupboard—closed now—at the end of the room, where he kept his clothes and costumes. Pike had built that for the cowboy outfits he used in his stunt work. When Don moved in here the whole place stank of horses and sweat from that cupboard.

Pete Pottenger had taken all of Pike's stuff. They were the same size, tall and muscular but overweight, both of them bowlegged.

Don had spent a week cleaning out the Coop, painting the walls white and laying black linoleum on the floor.

Pike had built the Coop, he confessed one night, to get away from Velma. She was always complaining about how his cowboy wardrobe smelled up her house, so he had moved everything into the Coop.

This was also where Pike would escape to spin yarns and tell lies with Pete and his other studio cronies. They drank here for hours and swapped stories about their experiences as stuntmen. Velma brought them food and coffee but never came inside. She had given the place a name—The Coop Club—but Pike and his pals never called it that. To them it was always the Coop.

Don had been invited to some of those drinking parties. Sat in a corner with a can of beer listening to their lies. He was the youngest and had been working less than a year as a stuntman. Didn't smoke and he only drank two cans of beer all evening, but he told them stories about Mexico. Mostly lies. They treated him like a mascot.

It was after he'd been doing this for a while that Pike brought him home for dinner, and he met Velma and Lori-Lou. Little did he suspect he'd ever be living here and Pike would be dead.

First thing he'd done, before painting the Coop, was to clean out the empty bottles: Scotch, vodka, and wine. And beer cans . . .

The phone rang, startling him out of his reverie. He snatched it up from the floor, rested it beside him on the bed, and lifted the white receiver to his ear. "Yeah?"

"Where ya been, kid?"

"Harry! Just got back from dinner."

"Been callin' since 'round seven."

"I was in an' out." His agent's whiny voice always annoyed him. Whenever Harry Sneal said "Nice day!" it sounded like a complaint.

"Gotta job comin' up for ya. Another pree-meer! The new Carlo Dario pitcher at the Dome."

"Terrific!" He glanced toward the actor's picture, thumbtacked to the wall.

"They wancha two hours, six to eight, front entrance. Hundred bucks an hour. The check to be mailed to me. They wancha in an' outfit like a Mexican cowboy."

"Got just the costume! You've seen it."

"Pitcher opens next week. Thursday night. You did that winder job this mornin'?"

"Two hours."

"They pay ya?"

"Cash."

"Don't forget my ten percent."

"I'll stop by in the mornin'. 'Round noon." He checked the electric clock on his bedside table. "It's eight o'clock. Doncha ever go home?"

"Not if I can help it. The wife's always there. See ya, kid."

"Yeah." He rested the phone on its cradle and lifted it to the coffee table near the small TV set. He thought of Harry Sneal in his creepy office overlooking Vine Street. Harry was a mean little twerp. Not much larger than a midget. But he knew everybody and he was agent for a lot of stuntmen and some of the old character actors as well. Harry had been Pike's agent. That's how he'd met him. Through Pike Splain . . .

So he was going to do his act again in front of the Cinerama Dome!

He got up from the bed and walked toward the far end of the Coop, pulling a ring of keys from his pocket. Found the right one and opened the lock of the carved cabinet that filled up most of this side wall. Velma gave him the cabinet when he was hunting for furniture, said she and Pike bought it in Mexico.

Better hurry or he would miss the start of that movie.

He swung the double doors open, pushing them back out of his way.

Just then he heard a faint scratching overhead, on the roof. One of the neighborhood cats. Happened all the time. Sometimes during the day he saw their faces peering down at him from the edge of the skylight. He'd put up a heavy section of chicken wire and nailed it on all four sides to keep them from falling inside.

He pushed a button inside the cabinet, lighting a row of bulbs set into reflectors around a hinged trio of mirrors. He'd gutted the original shelves and installed everything himself. This was much better than the portable makeup tables they used at the studios.

For a moment, as always, he studied his reflection in the mirrors: the short black curls that covered his head, black eyebrows, and eyes with pupils so brown they were almost black.

"I'm here, Mommy," he whispered. "I'm here. . . ."

He looked a little like Carlo Dario. The actor had always reminded him of his father. . . .

The last time he saw Tomas he must've been around Carlo Dario's age. Maybe even a little younger than the actor . . .

Moving quickly, he unlocked and pulled out a shallow drawer under the center mirror. He picked up the tiny suction cup from a small white plastic box and removed the contacts from both his eyes.

Then, very carefully, he removed the curly black wig, fitted it over a padded wooden block, and set it between the two blocks holding his long-haired black wig and his other curly one.

He unscrewed a jar of cold cream and, with his fingertips, worked the cream into his eyebrows and lashes, then wiped them clean with a tissue.

His eyebrows and lashes were dark blond now.

But the pupils of his eyes were gray, not pale blue.

His mother always said they were hazel. Like hers. Although her eyes changed color.

And his hair was light brown. Not bronze!

He stared at his hair in the mirrors.

Bronze?

That was stupid.

Two

6

Don parked his old black Honda on a side street behind the Cinerama Dome because by the time he was finished here the theater parking lot would be too crowded for him to get his car out. Mercedes and Rolls bumper to bumper and the parking jockeys would be nowhere in sight.

Checking the mirror, he saw that his wig was fine. Long strands of straight black hair hanging down both sides of his face from under the sombrero, and with his contacts in place he looked more Mexican than Carlo Dario. After all, he was part Mexican. Carlo was Italian.

He wore no makeup, except on his eyebrows and lashes. His suntan would be dark enough, even under the glare of spotlights in front of the theater.

Opening the glove compartment, he brought out two pairs of gloves, one plain gray rubber and the other soft black leather gauntlets. Rested the gauntlets on the seat beside him, while he pulled the rubber gloves over both hands. Tugged them up, under the ruffled cuffs of his embroidered Mexican shirt, then put the gauntlets on over them.

He got out and eased his wheeled platform down from the other side of the car onto the sidewalk. The platform had been his invention, for movie openings like tonight, private parties, and sidewalk performances. He had designed it himself, but turned his sketches over to a carpenter he knew at Columbia, who built it for him. He gazed at the compact platform, proud of his creation.

It was low and rubber-carpeted, its wooden sides lacquered black with a coiled red snake painted in the center of each.

An aluminum handrail around three sides of the platform at waist level, supported by steel rods at the four corners. The whole thing was so light he could carry it with one hand, yet strong enough to support his weight and, with its four ball-bearing wheels locked, nobody could move the platform unexpectedly while he was doing his act.

He locked his car and, shoving the platform ahead of him, started up the street toward the rear of the theater.

The arc lights fingered the blue sky above the dome in the front, and there was a steady hum from their big generators.

As Don came closer he heard the voices of the crowd that already was lining up along the red carpet spread across the pavement from Sunset to the theater entrance. Many were teenagers who didn't have tickets for the performance. A few wide-eyed tourists who'd been wandering past stopped to gawk, along with the usual Hollywood crazies who turned up for every picture opening.

He swung the stage door open and lifted his platform into the air-conditioned corridor. A uniformed guard, seated beside a sliding inner door that led onto the stage, looked up from the newspaper he'd been reading.

"You again!" he said, folding the paper and lurching to his feet. "Been six months or more."

"Yes, sir." Don smiled, turning on the charm. "Sure has."

"They told me you'd be here tonight. Last time you was dressed like an Indian. In full war paint."

"That's right."

"Kinda early, aincha?" He glanced at his wristwatch. "Only five thirty."

"Always like half an hour of quiet before I start, so I can clear my mind an' meditate."

"I remember last time you sat at the back of the stage in the dark."

"Thought I'd do the same thing today."

"No room. They brought in a truckload of sound equipment. Crew's in there now, still workin' on it. Why don't you sit in the auditorium?"

"That'll be fine."

"Nobody to bother ya. Maybe a coupla ushers wanderin' in an' out." He motioned toward a side corridor. "I'll show ya the way. . . ."

"Thanks, pal."

The guard went ahead. "Need some help with that contraption?"

"It don't weigh much," Don said, pushing his platform toward a metal fire door at the end of the corridor.

"You kinda look like the star of this here pitcher. . . ."

"Think so?"

"Of course he's older than you. Met the guy this afternoon. He's makin' a personal appearance tonight. After the pitcher."

"Yeah?"

"Come by to test the mikes an' check where he has to stand." Swinging the door open. "I'll hold this."

"Right." Don lifted his platform, swung it into the lobby, and set it down on the thick carpet.

"Ya know this here Dario guy's 'bout the same height as you."

"That right?"

"I thought, from his pitchers, he was taller. Nice fella. Not like some of these snotty actors we get. Think they're big stars."

Don followed him through the curving lobby, where a huddle of short fat men in dinner jackets had gathered near the entrance doors and a line of uniformed ushers stood guard.

"Here we are, kid." Pushing an inner door open. "Make yourself at home."

Don rolled his platform into the silent auditorium, dark except for hidden bulbs making a pink glow around the edge of the ceiling.

"Sit anywhere. See ya later."

"Right." He heard the whisper of the closing door as he shoved his platform toward the center, then turned down a long aisle sloping toward the stage.

The curtains were closed but he could hear men's voices shouting orders backstage and there was a distant sound of hammering.

All the seats in the auditorium were empty.

He sank into a deep seat on the aisle, third row from the rear, facing the closed curtains.

So he was as tall as Carlo Dario! He'd never known that.

People said he was too short when he was studying to be an actor, but if you were a star, it didn't matter how tall you were.

Look at Jimmy Dean and Dustin Hoffman. . . .

This job tonight should be easy. The teenagers would stay behind the ropes and the people passing close to him, on their way inside, wouldn't stop for more than a quick look. Still, there was always some lush—man or woman—who tried to pinch his arm. He handled pinchers by lunging forward suddenly and startling them.

His eyes focused briefly on the curtain as they trembled in a gust of air from backstage.

He was beginning to relax. Mustn't fall asleep . . .

He'd wanted to be an actor. That's why he came to Hollywood. Studied acting and dancing . . .

As a dancer he'd been a dog with too many feet and he wasn't much better as an actor.

His teacher—that phony, Jonathan Harrigan—told him so in front of the whole class. "Sorry, Mr. Geraldo, you show no evidence of any talent. None whatsoever!"

That was the name he'd taken. Used his real first name, Geraldo, as his last. Rick Geraldo! Not a bad name for a movie star . . .

"You don't have the temperament, Mr. Geraldo. An actor—every actor—must have temperament. You, apparently, have none."

He could still see old Harrigan's stuck-up expression. Nose in the air, eyes flashing, double chins quivering.

"You're wasting my time! And taking precious time from my other students, who do have talent. One or two of them . . ."

Don had stood there, in the center of that low platform they used for a stage, with tears stinging his eyes.

"How long, may I ask, have you been studying, Mr. Geraldo?"

"I—I'm not sure. . . ."

"Not sure! I knew you were with someone else before I made the error of accepting you as a pupil. How long have you been trying to become an actor? Surely you can recall that, even if you are unable to memorize the brief scene you were told to learn for today. . . ."

"A year, I guess."

"One year! And you've learned absolutely nothing. I am totally unable to teach you anything."

"Yes, sir."

"Don't bother to come here again."

"No, sir."

He had never returned to that bare room, above a vacant shop on Melrose. Never took another acting lesson from anybody . . .

Mrs. Hobson, in Bakersfield, had warned him about wanting to be an actor. He could see her spectacles gleaming when she shook her head. "Such a difficult profession! I've always felt sorry for young people who aspire to acting. Most of them never succeed. . . ."

"I know, Mrs. Hobson."

"And you're still determined to go to Hollywood, knowing this?"

"Yes, ma'am."

"Acting's so precarious, even if, by some miracle, you do become one. I wonder what will happen to you. . . ."

After leaving Harrigan he had gone from agent to agent, but nobody would handle him without experience and credits.

He'd worked as a box boy in a supermarket, made deliveries for a pizza parlor at night and parked cars on weekends for restaurants.

At the same time he'd continued to look for an agent and finally got one through an actor he'd known while studying with Harrigan.

The agent rented space in an office on the third floor of an old building on Sunset. He'd sent Don out on a few interviews, mostly cattle calls, where a long line of kids would wait for hours and when you got inside the guy never gave you more than a minute.

"Name? Who sencha? Whatcha done?"

That last question ended the interview.

All those guys who interviewed him had looked alike. Small and skinny with long hair and owl eyes behind spectacles. Some had beards.

The only one he remembered—would never forget—was the last.

That creepy guy with the husky voice.

The address was a one-story building on the Strip where two secretaries were typing in a windowless central corridor with bare walls and four closed doors, two on each side, names lettered on them in black. As he headed toward the nearest secretary, he saw MARK MORTON PRODUCTIONS on one door. " 'Scuse me, miss . . ."

She looked up from her typewriter.

"I'm Rick Geraldo."

"Oh, yeah. I'll see if Mark's free." She rose from her desk and swayed toward the door he had noticed. Went inside, leaving it open, returning at once. "He'll see ya. . . ."

"Thanks." He went past her, across an inner waiting room barely large enough to hold four empty folding chairs, two on each side, and through another open door.

The sunglasses worn by the man behind the desk watched him enter. "Shut that door, kid."

"Yeah, sure." He closed the door.

"Rick Geraldo?" His voice was hoarse, like he had a cold.

"That's right."

"I'm Mark Morton." He held out his hand.

They shook hands, across the desk. Don was aware that Morton's hand was perspiring.

"Sit down, kid," he said, motioning to an armchair.

Sinking into the chair he sized up the skinny little guy in the light from a pair of windows. Venetian blinds were slanted up so nobody could look in from the street. Morton had a pink baby face and his hair was too black, probably dyed. He was wearing a sport jacket over a Hawaiian shirt.

"How old are ya?" Morton whispered.

"Nineteen."

"Look younger. Wish your hair was blond."

"It is, sort of. I dye it."

"What for?"

"I like the Latin look." That was before he bought his wigs. "My father's half Mexican."

"Whatcha done on TV?"

"Nothin' . . ."

"Movies?"

"None. I worked on the stage in New York." He'd been told that couldn't be traced. "Couple of shows Off-Broadway."

"Stage experience is the best. I like to work with stage actors. They know how to take direction. Young actors don't learn nothin' workin' in TV or movies. There's never enough time." He rose from his desk as he talked, and wandered around the small office. "This part's in a new TV series. Not big, but people will notice ya. . . ."

Don turned his head, awkwardly, following him.

"Still gotta find a name for the lead." Morton sank onto the center of a big couch that was placed against one wall. "You done much swimmin'—athletics?"

"Ever since I was a kid."

"Take your shirt off. Lemme see what kinda body ya got."

"Sure." He struggled to his feet, peeling off his shirt and T-shirt, then dropping them onto the chair.

"Lotta muscle for your age."

"I've always worked at developin' my body."

"Ya look good." Morton patted the couch beside him. "Sit here. So we can talk."

"Okay." He sat down, not too close, feeling awkward and exposed without his shirt.

"I think you might be okay for this part. . . ."

"Yeah?"

"First we gotta get to know each other a little better." He reached out slowly and stroked Don's bare arm.

"Wha'cha mean?" He knew what the guy meant. He'd heard about men like this from students in his acting classes.

"This part could start ya on a big career. I'll do everything to help ya. . . ." He took hold of his hand, lifting it from the sofa seat suddenly and kissing Don lightly on his bare shoulder.

"Don't do that!" He jerked his hand away and got to his

feet. "I've been told 'bout creeps like you," he said, snatching his T-shirt from the chair and pulling it over his head.

Morton rose from the couch. "Look, kid, I wanta help ya. In return I won't ask much. . . ."

"I don't want your lousy job!"

"Without a guy like me, you don't have a chance in this town. Kids like you come a dime a hundred."

He put on his shirt without responding.

"I'm a good guy," the husky voice continued, pleading now. "Never hurt nobody. I'll give you a break. Be your friend." He placed an arm around Don's shoulder. "More than a friend . . ."

Suddenly, knowing what he had to do, he put both hands under Morton's arms and lifted him off the floor.

"Hey! Lemme go!"

He carried Morton across the room and set him down beside a closed door.

"I'll fix it so you'll never work for nobody!"

Don opened the door and, as he suspected, saw it was a closet, empty except for a pile of old phone books in a corner. He shoved Morton inside and took the key from the lock.

"Stupid bastard!" Morton screamed.

Don slammed the door and locked it.

Not a sound came from inside the closet.

He was laughing as he hurried back to the secretary. "If you ever want your boss, I've locked him in the closet."

"Locked him in—" Turning to the other secretary. "He's locked the queen in the closet!"

When he reported back to his agent what he'd done, the guy laughed until he was red in the face, but then he stopped, abruptly, and told him to find himself another agent.

Don never looked for another one, never went on any more interviews, and it was another year before he got his first job as a stuntman and met Pike Splain. . . .

The slowly parting curtains drew him back to the present and he reached down to touch the handrail of his platform.

The curtains pulled back to reveal the huge screen.

He could see himself up there in front of that wide screen—where Carlo Dario would stand tonight—saw himself bowing and smiling, receiving applause from his fans. Rick Geraldo's fans!

The thought made him shiver.

This empty theater was like a spaceship. That big dome overhead rising through the darkness toward some unknown planet. No one at the controls. All the crew had been killed. He was the only human left alive and he must go up to that big control panel with its hundreds of flashing lights and steer the ship to a safe landing. He would save the world and be a hero!

This domed auditorium with its rows of empty seats was more like a church or a tomb. A tomb waiting for the dead to arrive. The living dead! He'd seen them in some movie. Coming down the aisles in silent processions wearing long white robes. They would sink into all these seats without a sound.

He was startled by a hand touching his shoulder, looked up to see a smiling usher in a fancy uniform.

"Evenin', sir. Publicity guy says it's time to do your act."

"Sure." He lurched to his feet.

"I'm the one who pushed you outside last time, sir. Want me to take this thing now?"

"I'll roll it out myself." He clicked the lever releasing the wheels and shoved the platform up the aisle behind the usher.

In the lobby all the ushers were still gathered near the glass entrance doors.

Passing a mirrored wall he glimpsed himself pushing his platform. Saw the bandolier packed with fake wooden bullets draped across his shoulder, the snakeskin band around his sombrero, leather thongs tied under his chin, and the fake gun in its leather holster.

"You can push me from here," Don said, slowing the platform to a stop as the usher turned.

"Where you want me to put it, sir?"

"Same's before." He whirled the platform around and hopped onto the rubber-padded rectangle, clutching the handrail with both gloved hands.

"Open those doors, you guys!" The usher shoved the platform toward the entrance.

The other ushers looked around and two of them sprang

toward a pair of the glass doors, swinging them back to let the platform roll through.

Don glanced at the crowd behind the red velvet ropes, on both sides of a wide red carpet that stretched out to the boulevard where limousines would soon deliver the stars. The murmur of voices faded as people saw him but grew louder again as they resumed their conversations. Spotlights aimed down on the area where men and women in evening clothes, from the networks, were waiting to interview the celebrities. Guys with hand mikes and portable cameras darted in every direction trailing their snaky cables. A big orchestra, booming Mexican music, poured from hidden speakers.

The roar of the generators, visible on Sunset, was much louder here and the arc lights continued to rake the sunny sky.

Several policemen had gathered around a traffic cop astride a horse.

The usher slowed the platform to a stop, facing the crowd in a glare from the overhead spotlights. "How's this, sir?"

"Fine."

"I'll lock these wheels for you."

Don heard the lever snapped.

"Good luck, sir! I'll roll you back inside when you finish."

"Thanks."

Don was aware of the usher returning to the lobby, where he would join the others. Any minute now they would fling all those glass doors open and people would start going inside. The invited guests never showed up before seven-thirty and none of the stars would appear until just before eight. Then there would be a stampede, everyone trying to get interviews for the TV cameras. That's when Carlo Dario would appear. At the last minute . . .

Don raised his arm slowly, a few inches at a time. Then he moved his head awkwardly, eyes wide, inspecting the nearest line of people before blotting them from his consciousness.

He noticed several familiar faces. Teenagers who turned up at every opening, arriving early to get a place in the front row behind the ropes. They were the ones who hopped up and down, squealing and screaming, when each star appeared. Several crazies from Hollywood Boulevard mixed in with them. One old dame, face painted like a mask, wearing a big hat trimmed with flowers and a long pink dress that was faded and torn. Somebody said she'd been a star in silent pictures.

His hands, under the double covering of rubber and leather, were getting cold and heavy. Feeling was draining out of his arms as their actions became automatic.

He realized his stomach was growling. He always did a performance on an empty stomach. Instead of eating lunch he'd seen two movies this afternoon. After he finished here he would go back to the Coop, take another shower, and get a late dinner in Hollywood.

Chauffeured limousines pulled up to the curb, and people in evening clothes got out. Most of the early arrivals were executives and their wives. Others came on foot from bus stops or after parking their cars on nearby streets. These were people from all the studio departments who had worked on the picture. None of them would be dressed up. He knew some of them, but nobody had ever shown any sign of recognition when he was doing his mechanical-man act.

This was nothing like that first night he'd done his routine at a theater—the first time he'd done it in public.

He'd rehearsed for weeks, over and over for the Splains, after Lori-Lou went to bed. The whole thing had been Pike's idea. . . .

Pike had seen a mechanical man at some carnival back in Montana, where he'd been making a picture on location. He'd wanted to do such an act himself but never got around to it and, as he said, he'd gotten too fat. He described in detail the guy he'd seen perform and acted it out for Don until he got the idea.

Velma had helped with Don's first costume, after many long talks. Pike thought it should be a cowboy outfit like that guy in Montana, but Velma insisted it be all white or all black because that would catch people's attention. Finally they agreed that a white outfit would get too dirty, so, with Velma's help, he'd put together a black outfit, piece by piece, from Stetson to boots.

The Splains never suspected he wore a wig. He had only one wig in those days but now he had three. All of them black. Two curly ones with short hair which he wore most of the time, and a long, straight-haired one he'd gotten much later to use in his act. The Splains thought he wore it over his short black hair. Nobody knew that was a wig, too. . . .

Except for the old man in Hollywood who made all three and took care of them.

Don had a final rehearsal for the Splains before his first public appearance, with Lori-Lou staying up late to watch. She screamed when he swooped down toward her, then ran out of the room with Kong yelping after her.

That same week Pike arranged for him to do his act outside a movie house in the Valley that showed nothing but old Westerns. The theater owner was an ex-cowboy who had worked with Pike as a stuntman. He agreed to let Don test his act beside the box office while they were running a revival of *Shane* with Alan Ladd.

Pike and Velma had sat across the street in their car, Lori-Lou between them, and watched him.

Compared to the routines he did now, that first public performance must've been terrible but he didn't realize it at the time. He'd been promised five bucks, but so many people stopped to watch him and bought tickets for the show that Pike's friend had paid him ten.

He'd taken the Splains to a bar in Studio City to celebrate, leaving Lori-Lou asleep, locked in the back seat of their car.

He still had that black costume and used it for shopping mall jobs.

Pike Splain had been like a second father to him. Guiding and encouraging. Never getting angry or putting him down . . .

There was an announcement—a man's voice from the speakers—and the teenagers were jumping and screaming. Somebody's name, but he hadn't heard whose.

Everyone was looking and pointing at a skinny kid with blond hair hanging below the shoulders of his white leather jacket. Probably some rock star. He was being interviewed for television with all the mikes poking at his face. A blonde in a skimpy red dress that seemed to be made of shiny beads posed beside him. She was laughing and doing a little dance as the guy talked into the mikes. Now they were moving away from the cameras, coming toward the entrance, the rock star waving to his shrieking fans as he and the blonde walked between the rows of ushers.

They were heading straight for him!

He began to move, more abruptly than before, making his body look even more off balance.

The girl squealed as they paused in front of his platform. "He's cute! I wanna take him home."

"Yeah?" The guy moved closer, squinting up at Don's face. "Is it real or a bloody machine?"

Don swooped toward them, one arm jerking up, pointing toward the girl.

She caught his gloved hand between her fingers and tried to pinch him. "Oooh!" She pulled back. "He's got a wooden hand."

"To clonk ya over the noggin wiv, ducks."

"It's a machine! Not a person."

"Fink so? I could make 'im squeal wiv one kick in the balls."

Don pulled back quickly as they moved on, then continued his routine.

His double gloves had worked again. Anyone who touched them thought his hands were artificial. He'd discovered that little trick for himself.

The voice kept crashing from the speakers with each new arrival but he was no longer listening.

The spotlights on the red carpet seemed to get brighter, but the faces of the crowd behind the ropes had blurred. People were passing more quickly. Couples and groups. More stars were being interviewed, all of them in evening clothes. The men tanned, with sleek hair, their faces shining like they'd been sprayed with oil. The women sparkling with diamonds. Some wore long metallic coats that glittered under the lights. The stink of their perfumes—wave after wave—was sickening.

He heard the voice again, saying now that the man being interviewed was the producer of *Vaquero*—a fat little man in a dinner jacket, wearing spectacles, with a fat little wife beside him, also wearing spectacles.

The Mexican music continued without interruption.

Don had seen all of Carlo Dario's pictures. One day, when he was working as a stuntman, he'd passed him, walking across the parking lot, laughing and joking with a couple of girls who looked like secretaries.

Maybe tonight he would get a chance to speak to him. Ask for his autograph.

More people hurried past, into the lobby, most of them barely glancing at him. He withdrew again, into his own silence, blocking out the uproar of music and voices. His routines only lasted fifteen minutes, so now he was repeating them. Another half hour and he would be finished here.

He wouldn't go inside, wearing his costume, to see the movie but would come back next week and buy a ticket when there wasn't such a crowd.

Didn't like Westerns as much as movies about crime and detectives. They were his favorites, although when there was lots of blood and violence, he always got up and went out to the lobby.

"Carlo Dario!" The name exploded from the speakers and spread in a pulsing wave of sound from a hundred throats.

Don turned his head as the star's name vibrated in his ears and saw him standing in a glare of light, bowing and smiling, surrounded by the television people, all of them trying to get his attention.

"Our star of the evening!" The voice from the speakers was booming.

"Carlo Dario—in person—ladies and gentlemen! The star of *Vaquero*—Carlo Dario!"

The crowd was going wild, screaming and pushing. Some of the teenagers ducked under the ropes but were stopped by the ushers who formed a solid wall around Carlo.

He noticed people waiting behind the actor as he talked into the microphones. They must be friends—two men and three women. One woman, an attractive redhead, small and plump, was in front of the others.

Carlo looked younger in person—and much handsomer! He had thought the same thing that day when he saw him at the studio. . . .

Don had stopped doing his act and now stood staring at the actor. Nobody would notice because all eyes were on Carlo.

He'd like to hear what Carlo was saying but his voice was low as they taped the interview for television and radio.

Maybe they would have it on the late news tonight. He would turn it on before he went to bed. They might even show him, standing here on his platform, doing his act.

Now all the television people were speaking into their mikes.

The interview was over.

Carlo turned to leave, waving to his fans as he joined the redhead. She must be Carlo's wife, or his girlfriend. . . .

Don resumed his act as they came toward him, arms and legs moving, to attract their attention. Maybe Carlo would stop and talk to him.

That's when he'd ask for an autograph. Before he left the Coop he'd slipped a pad and pen into one of his pockets. He'd gotten several autographs from stars in the past when he performed at premieres.

They were passing his platform now.

Carlo was talking to a man in a dinner jacket.

The redhead left the others and came close to Don's platform, and stood there looking up at him.

He realized she was smiling.

Their eyes met and held.

Don, in spite of himself, smiled.

Her smile became more pronounced.

She looked like Ella. His mother had been about that height, short and plump, with the same kind of red hair. About the same age. Ella was only thirty-three the last time he saw her. That night she died . . .

The moment was broken when Carlo turned from the man and called to the redhead. She took his arm as they went toward the lobby.

Carlo hadn't even looked at him!

Don forgot his routine as he watched them go inside. It didn't matter. Nobody was watching him. Everybody was rushing to get in before the picture started.

He began to move, automatically, without thinking. Twisting and swaying.

Damn Carlo Dario! He hadn't even glanced at him.

Lousy bastard . . .

7

Victor Lolo saw the slanting fingers of light sweeping across the darkening sky—pale yellow against purple—as he followed Sunset toward Hollywood.

A new movie must be opening. Didn't happen much anymore. The big studios were making fewer pictures every year.

When he was a kid the word Hollywood meant a magic kingdom, on the other side of the Pacific, where handsome guys and beautiful dames lived golden lives in strange places called Malibu and Beverly Hills when they weren't posing in front of cameras. He and his friends read the latest fan magazines every month.

Since coming here he'd discovered that much of Los Angeles was like a Hollywood version of Pago Pago, especially the decaying areas around some of the old studios and near the beaches.

He'd learned that the personal lives of movie stars weren't anything like those fan magazines had reported. Some of them were well known to the police. They were involved in auto accidents, some were on drugs, others were being blackmailed. They even got themselves murdered. . . .

The actors he'd met, in line of duty, certainly had nothing even slightly golden about them, but were frightened human beings in serious trouble.

Slowing his car on the overpass above the Hollywood

Freeway, he glanced south toward that little church where
Samoans gathered every weekend to worship. Impossible to
see it through the twilight. On Sunday you'd probably be able
to hear them singing all the way from here. Nobody could
sing hymns like Samoans. They had sturdy lungs under their
fat and muscle.

He'd gone there many times when he came to Los
Angeles, but after that first year he'd gotten too busy with his
law studies. He should get up some Sunday morning and join
those happy voices again.

Lolo began to sing softly, an old Methodist hymn, as he
drove down Sunset.

He'd called Morita from a pay phone, after dinner in a
Chinese restaurant. Told her he would see her around nine.

Thursday was the night he usually spent with Morita, but
last night he'd been involved with a series of raids in the
Valley. Another disgusting child-porn case. He'd phoned
Morita yesterday afternoon and told her he wouldn't be free.
It was long past midnight when he got to his apartment.

This had been another day when little was accomplished.
Nothing had developed on any of his current investigations,
including the Jogger.

He would question this Lansing girl on his way to
Morita's. Maybe she'd be the one to come up with something
that would lead to the Jogger's capture. The police report said
she had red hair. Like all his other victims . . .

He thought about Morita as he drove.

Their relationship was the best he'd found since coming to
Los Angeles, the first that seemed permanent. Before
meeting Morita he had picked up girls in the more expensive
Beverly Hills singles bars, then had to listen to their endless
complaints—all of them variations on a theme of loneli-
ness—before laying them. That was all he wanted, a good
lay, with a minimum of conversation.

Morita, on the other hand, said very little about her
personal life or her past. He knew only that she was born in
France and had arrived here several years ago. There were
three other men in her life at the moment, and she saw each
of them one night a week—Monday, Tuesday, and Wednesday. He had checked them out. All of them were married.
One was vice-president of a television company, another was

a famous attorney who specialized in sensational divorce cases, and the third was a Beverly Hills surgeon. She kept Friday night open, in case one of her four men happened to be free, but Saturday and Sunday nights were her own. She never saw anyone those two nights.

He was Morita's Thursday-night man, but since he couldn't make it last night, she was seeing him tonight. She had dined alone at her apartment, and the rest of the evening was his.

He had no feeling about her other three men, had never seen them and felt no jealousy.

She was his Thursday-night woman.

Sometimes he took her out to dinner at an expensive restaurant, and at least once a month he sent her flowers from a florist in Beverly Hills, but nothing more. Morita knew he couldn't afford expensive presents. She also knew that, if possible, he would protect her with all the power attached to his job as a cop, but he doubted she would ever need that. She was too smart to become involved in anything dangerous.

Morita was one classy lady! In every way. Sophisticated and educated. Completely honest. What's more, she was the most beautiful woman he'd ever known. He'd never seen a woman like her, even in the movies.

She once told him she lived the life of a high-class Parisian whore in the United States. Which was what she'd been before she left France. She made no pretense about it. She laughed and called herself the last of "les grandes courtisanes."

He'd read about them, back in Pago Pago, when he discovered French novels. Especially Balzac . . .

Before turning his gray Plymouth up Vermont, he glanced toward Hollywood again and saw that the arc lights seemed brighter because the sky was getting darker. He wondered what new movie was opening. Or was it another shopping mall?

He turned west on Franklin, slowing as he checked the street numbers. The building he sought turned out to be a large apartment complex. This afternoon's police report said Lisa Lansing lived here with her mother.

He pulled into the first vacant parking space, locked his

car, and hurried up the walk to the elaborate entrance, which led to a mirrored lobby with no attendant.

Tenants were listed in gilded letters on a framed wall sign. He found MRS. J. LANSING in apartment 39, which would be the third floor.

The elevator was silent and fast.

No name card appeared on the apartment door, only 39 in polished metal under a grilled peephole disguised as a knocker. He pushed a button to the right of the door but heard no bell or buzzer inside.

This upstairs corridor was brightly lighted.

He wondered, as usual, how they secured such a large building. Did they have many robberies?

Turning back to the door he jabbed the button harder and heard two locks snapped.

The door was opened by an attractive honey blonde in a long robe, white with gold stripes, holding a crystal goblet in one hand.

"Yes?" Her blue eyes brightened as she inspected him. "Who might you be? Shouldn't have opened this door without asking who you were through the squint-hole. But I'm glad I did. I was expecting another gentleman."

"I'd like to see Lisa Lansing."

"Lisa isn't here just now. I'm her mother. Who are you?"

"Special investigator Victor Lolo." He pulled out his wallet and showed his ID.

"You've finally found that creep who raped my sweet daughter?"

"No, ma'am. But we're still looking."

"Then I suppose you've more questions to ask. Come in."

He moved past her, into a small foyer fragrant with her perfume.

"I thought all detectives wore hats."

"Not anymore. I've never owned one."

She closed the door and floated through the foyer ahead of him. "We can chat in the living room."

"Your daughter has red hair."

"That's right."

"But you're blonde."

She laughed. "Both dyed."

Lolo saw that she moved with grace. Tall woman with a

nice figure. Not thin but slim. Hair freshly brushed, in soft waves. He glimpsed golden slippers on her bare feet. Probably in her forties, but could easily pass for thirty.

She sank onto a low chair without splashing her drink and motioned toward a sofa upholstered in pale green. "May I offer you something? I've made a pitcher of sangria. I prefer it with white wine."

"No, thanks. Just had my dinner."

She lifted her goblet in a friendly salute and took a slow swallow of the sangria. "Is that good! My first today. Only just out of the shower."

"Sorry to bother you at this hour. Phoned earlier, but got no answer."

"I worked late."

"You don't look like a working lady."

"I'm an extra. Movies and television."

"An extra?"

"Dress extra, and a damn good one. I've put two kids through college. My son—he does something with computers in San Diego—and my dear daughter, who, unfortunately, has decided not to graduate."

"I'd like to ask your daughter a few questions."

"You'll have to go up to Pacific Grove. That's where she lives now. Ever since that unfortunate incident in Griffith Park."

"That's what I want to talk to her about."

"But that happened three months ago!"

"I didn't find out about it until this afternoon. You see, Mrs. Lansing, I'm trying to catch this Midnight Jogger."

"You think he's the one raped my daughter?"

"I suspect that's very likely."

"Why haven't the police told me this before?"

"They didn't connect your daughter's case with the Jogger. In fact, according to a report I read this afternoon, they didn't do much about that investigation. Your daughter wasn't cooperative. Refused to answer their questions."

"She was in shock for two days, at the hospital, and after I brought her home I wouldn't let them near her."

"The report says you insisted the investigation be dropped. You wanted no publicity."

"I said that to protect Lisa. Didn't want her name in the

papers. Even so, several kids in her class, at U.S.C., did find out what happened."

"Somebody always talks. Usually a friend."

"Which is why Lisa moved to Pacific Grove. Both her doctor and a psychiatrist—he's a dear friend, not my analyst—thought it wise for her to have a change of scene."

"I agree."

"I took her up to stay with some old friends whom we used to visit every summer. They have a son, two years older than Lisa. She used to like him when they were growing up. It seemed like a good idea for her to see him again. A fine young man! Studying law! I didn't suspect they might fall in love." She set her goblet on the coffee table. "They were married last month. He doesn't know Lisa was raped. I explained everything to his parents—I had to be honest with them—and they thought it would be wise not to tell him. There's no possible way he'll ever find out up there. Lisa seems relaxed and happy now. Completely recovered, emotionally and physically. My psychiatrist friend sees no reason why the marriage won't work. He says it has a better chance than most."

"Did your daughter talk to you about what happened in Griffith Park?"

"Of course she talked to me. Constantly. We've always had a very healthy and loving relationship—more like sisters than mother-daughter."

"How long had she been jogging in Griffith Park? The police report didn't say."

"For several months. But it wasn't actually Griffith Park. She only ran up Fern Dell—that lovely stretch of grass and trees."

"I know the area."

"I'd usually be in bed—if I had an early studio call for next morning—but I would hear her leave and always listened until she came back. She was never gone more than an hour. That's why I phoned the police that night when she didn't return. Good thing, too. They found her unconscious and called me from the hospital. I dressed and drove there immediately."

"Was she conscious when you got there?"

"No. They'd given her sedation."

"And she wouldn't answer questions, next day, so the police report contains little information."

"So! Now Lisa isn't here. What do you want to know?" She reached for her goblet again. "I like cops. Especially attractive ones." Sipping the sangria as she eyed him. "I don't know what I can tell you."

"Why was she jogging at that late hour?"

"She preferred to jog late at night, after she finished studying. She said it relaxed her, helped her sleep. Started jogging last fall and kept it up, several nights a week, until the rains began. It cleared for a few days in February, got quite warm. Typical Los Angeles weather. Crazy . . ."

"I remember."

"She'd been jogging again for several nights just before she was attacked. And you think it was this Midnight Jogger?"

"Very likely he'd been following her. I suspect he picks his victims and watches them. Observes their habits. Plans what he's going to do."

"Somebody did follow her."

"When?"

"I've only just remembered. Two nights before she was raped, she came home terribly upset. There was a man in a car. He would drive ahead, then slow for her to pass."

"Did he speak to her?"

"No. She said he only watched her, but that was what frightened her. Being watched . . ."

"This was two nights before she was attacked?"

"Yes."

"What about the next night?"

"There was no sign of him. Only that one night."

"Did she mention what make car he was driving?"

"I believe she did. . . . Yes! A gray Volkswagen. She said it was an old one. Kind of beat-up . . ."

"Did she see his face when he was in the car?"

"It was too dark. There's very little light under those trees."

"What about when he attacked her? Did she get a look at him then?"

"Not clearly. Only that he seemed young. In his twenties, she thought. He jogged beside her for a while. . . ."

"He always does."

"This was under the trees. She did say his hair seemed to be dark blond."

"What about his eyes?"

"She couldn't really see them, but she thought they were blue. Pale blue, or maybe gray . . ."

"Did he talk to her?"

"Yes. As he jogged beside her. Asked if she liked snakes . . ."

"Snakes?"

"Lisa told him she hated snakes. After that he didn't have much more to say. What a warm night it was. Do you live near Griffith Park?" She studied his face for a moment. "Why have you come here tonight, three months after it happened?"

"I realized only recently that the Jogger had attacked a girl once every month starting last November, except for two months, February and April of this year. I wondered if he'd raped a girl both those months but the police reports hadn't gotten through to me. I'm supposed to get all reports on rape in Los Angeles. I sent memos to every local division, asked if there'd been rapes in February or April that might've been overlooked in their daily flood of teletypes. A polite way to tell them I thought somebody had goofed. This afternoon I received a carbon of the report on your daughter."

"Must've been a short one."

"That's why they didn't send it through in February. Not enough information to connect it with the Jogger."

A buzzer sounded in the foyer.

"There's my date! And I'm not dressed." She set her goblet down.

Lolo rose from the sofa. "You've been a big help, Mrs. Lansing. We didn't know the Jogger drove a gray Volkswagen. Or that he's interested in snakes."

"He is a snake. I've just remembered something more— although this can't be too important."

"Let me judge."

The buzzer sounded again.

"When he had Lisa on the ground he kept whispering to her, 'I love you. I love you. . . .' Over and over."

"Did he?"

"I found that rather strange. You can let my friend in, if you will, as you leave."

"I'll do that." He headed toward the foyer.

"Come in again. Any evening . . ."

8

Driving west on Hollywood Boulevard, Lolo saw those twin rays of yellow light sweeping the evening sky and realized, as he crossed Vine, that the big arc lamps were in front of the Cinerama Dome.

That new Carlo Dario film was opening tonight.

Maybe he would catch it next week if the reviews were good. He'd seen all of Carlo Dario's pictures and this was the actor's first Western. Morita might enjoy it. They both liked Westerns. Clint Eastwood was their favorite.

Hollywood Boulevard, beyond Vine, was crowded with the usual freaks and phonies. Staring at each other, going nowhere. He turned down La Brea to Wilshire and west again toward Beverly Hills, considering, as he drove, what he'd learned from Mrs. Lansing.

Tomorrow he would have an APB sent out to every division, to question any young man driving an old gray Volkswagen. He'd tell them to look for a guy who liked snakes. . . .

He'd taken this same route out Wilshire so many times he no longer glanced at the lighted windows of the expensive shops on the Miracle Mile.

Twilight was fading into night.

Finally, he slowed the Plymouth in front of Morita's building. No trouble parking; she was the only tenant.

As he strode toward the entrance, his eyes moved up the facade of the tall building until they reached the only lighted terrace. No lights on any of the thirty-odd floors, except the vertical rows of windows marking emergency exits.

A uniformed doorman touched his cap and held one of the glass entrance doors open. "Another beautiful day, Lieutenant."

"Was it?" He crossed the spacious lobby with the elaborate decorations and lighted lamps, expensive furniture, green trees touching the high ceiling—a lobby where nobody ever met their friends—and went straight to the bank of elevators.

A uniformed youth stood at the door of the only elevator that was ever used. "Evenin', Lieutenant."

"Same to you." Vic stepped into the elevator and faced front as the metal doors silently closed. "Don't you get bored, kid? Only one tenant to ride up and down."

"It's a job, sir."

"Do you have to stand here eight hours waiting for Miss Rouvray to come in or go out?"

He grinned. "Gotta chair, 'round the corner of the lobby, where I can study."

"Any new tenants?"

"No, but I hear the bank's hopin to sell the place to some rich Arabs. When they take over we'll have a solid gold lobby. With fountains splashin' oil."

"You say you're studying?"

"Memorizin' drinks from a book of beverages."

"Drinks?"

"I wanta be a bartender."

The elevator doors slid apart.

Lolo stepped out. "I'll have a Samoan Sunset when I return."

"A what, sir?" The doors closed over his puzzled face.

Lolo was laughing as he hurried toward the front of the complex. This long, windowless corridor always gave him a touch of claustrophobia. Morita's door was in the precise center, at the far end, the middle condominium overlooking Wilshire. From her terrace you could see the Pacific Ocean.

Between the elevator and her door were several heavy pieces of furniture—Morita claimed they were imitation French antiques that had been bought at auction from some bankrupt Las Vegas hotel—and his heels sounded on the marble floor as though the empty condominiums on either side were echo chambers.

Morita's door was ajar, as usual, and Yves Montand was singing one of her favorite love songs. Lolo entered the octagonal foyer, closing the door and checking that the lock caught.

The walls were covered with golden paper hung with African masks—horned animals and witch doctors carved from ebony. Two small sofas, one on each side, upholstered in ivory silk. Soft light from a translucent ivory cylinder hanging in the center of the mirrored ceiling.

He could already smell Morita's special perfume, which always reminded him of exotic flowers he'd seen in Samoa. When he asked her which flowers were used to make the perfume she had laughed. "Flowers? It's more likely brewed from chemicals. But it makes me feel like an African queen."

He pushed against the pair of inner doors which had been left partially open and started down the dim central corridor, hurrying now, eager to take her in his arms.

She never met him or permitted either of her servants—a middle-aged French couple—to greet him at the door. He suspected she opened the doors herself, after someone called from downstairs to warn her of his arrival, then darted back inside to wait for him. She would be relaxed and beautiful, posed on a sofa in the salon—which was what she called the fantastic living room—or stretched out on the chaise in her boudoir.

Tonight the salon was dark, so he continued on toward the sound of Montand's voice. The boudoir doors were wide open. He paused on the threshold, looking through the white and silver anteroom, and beyond the open doors of the bedroom, to see Morita reclining in her enormous bed, supported by a mound of gray satin pillows, reading a book.

Why would the Jogger whisper "I love you" to his

victims? Did he think what he did had anything to do with love?

"Eh bien, chéri! Don't stand there staring. You've seen it all before." She let the book slip from her fingers. "I could feel a flic's cold eyes inspecting me," she said, extending her arms in welcome, her thin white silk robe parting to reveal a glimpse of brown breasts.

Lolo closed the doors and went toward the bed slowly, feasting his eyes on her thick raven hair, long and lustrous, her body with the golden brown flesh of a Samoan. "Am I late?"

"Comme toujours! Flics are always late."

"Had to question somebody on my way here." He was aware of her tawny flesh against the gray satin sheets, which were the color found inside a Samoan oyster shell, as he sank onto the bed and kissed her.

Her arms enfolded him and her lips pressed against his mouth.

He was engulfed by perfume as he kissed both breasts, circling each nipple gently with the tip of his tongue.

"Been thinking about you all evening," she whispered. "About us."

Lolo was aware of the light fading. Morita had reached down to a small control panel hidden under the bedside table and turned all the lights down.

"Do you mind?" she had asked, their first night together. "I've always preferred love in the dark, but not so dark one has to grope. Only discreetly dim . . ."

Now he pushed himself back to look at her. "Discreetly dim?"

She laughed, remembering that first night.

"I noticed, as I drove across Vine, there's a new movie opening tonight at the Cinerama Dome." He was on his feet, removing his jacket.

"That new Western with Carlo Dario? They were talking about it earlier on television. Said it's his best film in years. He's very handsome. . . ."

"Care to see it?"

"Mais certainement . . ."

"Next Thursday night?" He continued to shed his clothes. "We could have a late supper after the show."

"That's a date. I know his wife, Adriana. . . ."

"Do you?"

"I told you, months ago. She's part of that group I have lunch with. Usually at L'Orangerie. A dozen of us. Mostly wives of actors and directors. I'm the only one not married. The only happy one."

"Oh?"

"All their husbands have lost interest. Adriana's a very unhappy lady. I suspect Carlo Dario has slept with several of the others and his wife knows about it. I don't see the group more than once a month. They depress me. I've told them about you."

"Told them my name?"

"Do you mind?"

"No . . ." Actually he was amused, proud that she had talked about him to her friends.

"I told them I love you."

"Why doesn't Mrs. Dario divorce her husband?"

"He's Catholic. And they have a small son. . . ."

As he slipped out of his slacks, he saw that the room was now almost dark. A faint suspicion of light came through the transparent violet curtains covering the walls. Everything, including Morita's body, seemed to be floating in twilight. The white carpet outlined the bed and chairs so they appeared to be suspended in space. He knew there was a big television screen behind the curtain facing the bed, but it had never been turned on when he was here. Morita must watch television at night when she couldn't sleep.

Yves Montand was singing another love song, but the volume had been lowered so that his voice was barely a whisper.

Lolo stepped out of his briefs, tossing them toward a chair as he returned to the bed. He stretched out beside her, sinking into the satin softness and taking her in his arms. Soon he felt her fingers stroking his tattooed thighs. Fingers that always brought an immediate response from his body.

For half an hour there was little conversation. Only faint sounds of pleasure. The private sounds made when two people feel genuine affection for each other. Then finally, the muted sounds of contentment.

For several moments they remained silent, side by side,

listening to the ghost of Montand's voice. Lolo stared at the mirrored ceiling in which their bodies floated in a calm violet sea.

"You're worried about something tonight," she whispered.

"What makes you think that?"

"Because your body—the muscles of your back—were so tense."

"You know I'm always tense. End of every day."

"Not like this. Still your Midnight Jogger?"

"Yes . . ."

"Nothing happening? No clues to follow? Pauvre flic . . ."

"I picked up some fresh information tonight. One of the victims saw his car. He drives an old gray Volkswagen. . . ."

"That should certainly keep him inconspicuous. And difficult to find."

"He also likes snakes."

"Does he? I rather like snakes myself. They're so beautiful! So primitive . . ."

"Tomorrow I'll start our computers humming to check every old gray Volkswagen in Los Angeles."

She faced him in the soft violet light. "Why are you so upset about this one rapist?"

"I hate all rapists. They're filth! Scum . . ."

"In this city hundreds of women are raped every night, but they seldom call it rape because they're paid to permit it."

"That is not rape."

"I think it is. I've never had sex with a man I didn't really love, although I've loved some more than others. That is inevitable. . . . You most of all!"

"Rape's when a woman doesn't want the man to touch her, when she didn't seek his attention or ask for it, and goes into shock from the experience—suffers trauma afterward. The law's even more specific."

"This case—this Midnight Jogger—has involved you more than any other investigation you've worked on since I've known you."

"Yes, I suppose it has. . . ."

"None of your murderers upset you this much."

"I've got to catch this guy before he kills. I know now that he's raped at least six times—six different young women—and I suspect there may be a seventh. None of these girls wanted him to attack her. He followed them like a jungle animal stalking a victim. . . ."

"Hollywood is a jungle. You know that."

"None of these rapes were in Hollywood. The one I learned about today was at the edge of Griffith Park, which is Los Angeles. The others were far from Hollywood. Beverly Hills and the Valley . . ."

"All jungles!" She reached out and grasped his hand. "Don't you have jungles in Samoa?"

"We call them forests."

"My mother was born in an African jungle. . . ."

"You never told me that before."

"I seldom tell anyone. We are, I think, reaching a new stage of our relationship. I want to tell you about my family. Which I seldom discuss. Maman came to Paris with a troup of Cameroon dancers, and found herself in another jungle! More dangerous than Africa . . ."

"She was a dancer?"

"Much more talented than I. A sensation when she first appeared on the Paris stage. Like Josephine Baker! Maman never returned to Africa. She become the star of Café Afrique, which Papa bought for her."

"You mother still dances?"

"Not since she married Papa. Maman never wanted to be a dancer, but she became one to escape from Africa. Papa's a very rich man—he owns a famous French vineyard—and Maman has retired. They live in a château. The Alpes-Maritimes, above the Riviera . . ."

"Why did you come to California?"

"I could ask you the same question."

"Yes. You could."

"I left our home on the Riviera and went to Paris for a career on the stage, but quickly discovered I had no talent as an actress or a singer. Only, like Maman, as a dancer. I'm a very good dancer."

"But you do sing. I've heard those tapes you made."

"I have a very small voice. Not a bad voice for a dancer. Maman was wise. She never sang at all. Just danced and kept dancing until she fell in love with Papa. She had no idea he was rich until he took her to meet his family. . . ."

"Your mother . . . Is she black?"

"Kind of a purplish brown. Much more beautiful than I." Her voice sharpened. "Does it make a difference? Her color?"

"With me? Both my parents are darker than you. Some of my ancestors must've been purplish brown. I was attracted to you, that night we met, by the color of your skin. As well as your smile. I thought you were from the islands. . . ."

She laughed and squeezed his hand. "Maman came from the world's largest island! Africa . . ."

"You still haven't told me why you left France for California."

"I thought I might like to be a movie star, that all one needed here was beauty—and intelligence. I knew I'd inherited both from my parents. My speaking voice is excellent, but I have no talent for acting."

"How do you know?"

"I got myself a top agent when I arrived here. Bought this condo and arranged a suitable background for myself. Every studio tested me. Executives flattered me as they ate my dinners and drank Papa's wines. Unfortunately, I didn't like any of them. I quickly realized there was no career for me in films—except as a producer. I've always been more interested in business than in acting. I discovered that becoming a producer could take years. So while considering many business possibilities—and I've made a decision, thanks to Papa—I've settled down with four charming men who amuse and love me. You've never met the other three, but I've told you I see them and you're not jealous."

"Should I be?" He smiled. "I'm your Thursday man."

"All three of them are married, with grown children. They know their wives are having affairs with younger men. But they still like their wives, love their children, and adore their grandchildren. Divorce would complicate everything. They're happy to be with me one night a week and I enjoy being with them. They are intelligent, handsome gentlemen. I lived this same sort of life in Paris. One of my patrons was, like you, a flic."

"Was he?"

"A top man at the Sûreté Nationale. Older than you and not so handsome. But tough. Like you . . . I've never accepted money for my love from any man and it has always been love. Maman taught me that a woman can love several men at the same time. Truly love them. I will accept a small gift, if there are no strings attached and it is offered with love and respect." She giggled. "A diamond necklace or a new Mercedes . . ."

"I've never given you anything like that!"

"You give me your love. That's quite enough. You see, mon flic, love is all I desire and need. My parents have provided me with good health and great wealth. A woman is born for love, lives for love, and requires love. But love fades. It can become boring, suddenly and unexpectedly. This is what happened to me in Paris. One glorious spring morning, when I wakened, I was no longer in love with anyone. My charming patrons had become dull, lost their charm. All of them . . .

"So I came here. And I shall never return to Paris. Except for brief visits. I adore the United States and intend to remain here forever. But not in Los Angeles! One day, very soon, I will have many important things to tell you and discuss with you. I plan to move north, to the wine country above San Francisco. I'm acting as official distributor for Papa's wines, as you know, and he is buying vineyards in the Napa Valley to establish an American branch of his company. I must return to France, perhaps next month, to arrange business matters and see my dear parents. But I will come back to California. To you, mon flic . . ." She kissed his shoulder tenderly. "I do love you. Truly love you. You know that, don't you? This is a fact I am telling you. I love Thursday more than any other day in the week. One day, very soon, I will have only one day in my week and that day will be Thursday. I shall say adieu to Monday, Tuesday, and Wednesday. . . ."

He kissed her firmly on the forehead.

"Now tell me," she whispered in his ear, "why you came to California. . . ."

"Okay. I will tell you." He hesitated, considering how to start, relaxing beside her.

"You, too, were in love? Back in Samoa . . ."

"Yes."

"And your love became dull?"

"No. I loved her more than I've ever loved anyone. Except you."

"Did you!"

"She died. . . ."

"Mon Dieu!" She snuggled her cheek against his chest.

"I haven't talked about this since I left the islands. She and I never made love. . . ."

"Never!"

"It was forbidden. Her family and mine were Christians. Our parents were strict. We were betrothed when I reached puberty. She was a virgin. . . ."

"You never touched her?"

"Only to hold her hand, Sunday mornings, when we walked to church. She was like a princess. So beautiful . . . We were to be married when I became twenty and she would be eighteen. Both of us had won prizes and scholarships. I was to study law, she wanted to be a teacher and work with small children. Teach them music. Our families had been friends for generations. They were building a house for us. . . ."

"What happened?"

"A month before our marriage she went with some friends—girls her age—to a distant lagoon where they planned to picnic. They wandered away from the beach and somehow she became separated from the others. She was raped in the forest."

"By whom?"

"She told her parents it was a young man she'd never seen before. He was tall, with yellow hair."

"You comforted her? Told her you loved her? That what had happened made no difference?"

"I never saw her again."

"Never? You are a pig!"

"Let me tell you. . . . We'd planned to go to a movie that night, but when I went to her parents' fale she hadn't returned from the beach. Her mother said they'd taken enough food for supper and would, no doubt, stay all night. So I went to the movie alone. That's where I was when the other girls—her friends—came back. They didn't tell anyone she'd slipped away into the forest. Young girls frequently did that to meet their lovers. They thought she was meeting me. She reached home after dark and told her parents what had happened. They tried to persuade her it was unimportant. Many Samoan girls are not virgins when they marry today. Her father told me he thought they had convinced her. What had happened was not her fault, she'd never seen the man before. Her mother walked her to her room and kissed her good night. They should've realized she was in shock—I know now, it's called trauma—but they didn't understand that. Next morning her bed was empty. . . ."

"Where had she gone?"

"She'd taken her father's old canoe and rowed out beyond the reef. They found the canoe next morning. She had dived into the ocean and drowned."

"Drowned? A Samoan!"

"Young people in Samoa aren't taught to swim anymore. Many of them drown. . . ." He turned to face her. "She died while I was sleeping and dreaming of the future, I suppose. Our life together . . ."

She saw a splash of violet on his cheek where the light was reflected in his tears.

"The police never found the man who raped her. They thought he was a seaman from a Danish freighter that had been anchored in the harbor, but there was no way to prove it. The freighter had sailed. That's what made me come to California. Her death . . ."

"Now I know why you always react so violently to rape. Why you're so determined to find this Jogger."

"I must find the guy."

"Perhaps you should talk to a psychiatrist. See what he can tell you about the personality and mentality of a rapist. Why he rapes. There's always a psychological reason, you know, for everything we do."

"I've already discussed the Jogger with a psychiatrist on staff at headquarters. Had two long sessions with him."

"What did you learn?"

"Nothing helpful. Lot of big words and vague generalities."

"I'm sure he may be excellent, but I was thinking about a working psychiatrist who has actually treated women after they were raped, who has questioned the rapists, as well as their victims.''

"That's a hell of a good suggestion."

"I've never known you to be so disturbed about any of your other investigations. And it's because of a girl you loved in Samoa. . . .''

"I've got to find this bastard. Put him behind bars. If I don't kill him first . . .''

"You would kill him, wouldn't you? And I don't blame you." She kissed him on the cheek. "I do love you, mon flic.''

"That's what he says."

"Who?"

"The Jogger. That creep with the bronze hair and pale blue eyes. He says that to his victims as he rapes them. 'I love you. . . .'''

9

Don peered from side to side as he drove through Hollywood. He kept to the dark side streets, pointing north from Sunset into the hills. Some ended in a dead end, others led to busy canyons that twisted up to Mulholland before dropping into the San Fernando Valley. He'd driven here before, many times, but had never seen any girls jogging.

He wanted to find a promising spot far from Brentwood. That opening of Carlo Dario's movie tonight had excited

him. The glare of lights and all those staring eyes made his
pulse throb faster and gave him the familiar urge in his groin
that made him tense and uneasy.

He couldn't forget the eyes of that redhead with Carlo
Dario, who had reminded him of Ella. She had smiled at him.
Was she the actor's wife or his girlfriend? He'd never read
anything about Dario's private life.

It had only been two weeks since he followed that girl in
Brentwood, watched her running through the moonlight in
her blue jogging suit, toward that tree where he was waiting.

He never saw her face, wouldn't recognize her if he passed
her on the street.

He never saw their faces. Avoided looking at them. Hoped
they wouldn't see his face.

None of them had been able to describe him when they
were interviewed in the newspapers. They'd only said that he
had pale blue eyes and dark blond hair. That hadn't been
much help to the cops. They would never find him, looking
for a guy with pale eyes and bronze hair. . . .

His eyes were gray or hazel. Ella always said they were
hazel. She should've known! He got his eyes from her.
Tomas had brown eyes. Dark brown . . .

Nobody out jogging in Hollywood tonight.

Low two-story houses, on both sides, behind little
gardens.

Hollywood was like a small town. People went to bed
early.

He had no idea what street this was, and didn't bother to
check signs at the corners.

No traffic.

Must be after eleven because it was past ten-thirty when he
came out of that restaurant.

He turned the Honda down a cross street and glimpsed a
jogger far ahead. It was a guy. First he'd seen tonight.
Always a good sign.

The gals jogged where the guys jogged. Most of them did
it to get picked up. Some were whores—he'd seen them
working Sunset—jogging alongside cars as they talked to the
drivers. A guy would slow down as they discussed prices,
then the girl would hop in and they would take off.

He drove past the faceless jogger, who was quickly lost in
the darkness.

Maybe he should try one of the canyons. There were lots of joggers on Outpost Drive or Nichols Canyon. Too much traffic on Laurel.

He would try Outpost first.

He'd returned to the Coop and changed his clothes, hanging the Mexican blouse on a hanger to air, under the open skylight, the rest of his costume in the cupboard. Sat at the makeup mirror to remove his long-haired black wig. Checked that the mascara on his lashes hadn't been smudged before putting on a short-haired black wig.

Glancing into the rear-view mirror to see that his wig looked okay.

Have to be careful, though, in this neighborhood. A Mexican, driving alone, might be stopped for questioning.

He had put on a dark sport shirt and clean dungarees before leaving the Coop to get dinner.

Halfway up Outpost Drive he saw a girl jogging ahead of his car, a skinny girl in a white outfit, with long blonde hair flopping down her back, held away from her eyes by a ribbon. He didn't like girls that tall.

Then he noticed the dog running beside her, next to the curb, on a leash—a mean-looking police dog that turned its head to stare at the Honda.

He'd seen other girls jogging with dogs and always avoided them.

The trees and shrubbery were thick with leaves, but there was no spot that looked right for his purpose. Too many curves. A car would shoot around them without any warning.

At the top of the hill he followed Mulholland until he found an open area where he parked and sat looking across the San Fernando Valley. At this hour it was a mass of twinkling lights with the distant hills black against the night sky. During the day this entire valley was usually invisible under a blanket of yellow smog.

That other valley, the one he saw from his father's arms in Mexico, had been much larger. . . .

As he sat staring at the view, he heard voices. Two guys jogging, side by side, coming toward him. He slumped down, out of sight, until they had passed.

Straightening again, he watched until they disappeared into deep shadow under some trees.

He doubted if any girls would jog alone up here.

They'd be stupid if they did. People got killed all the time on Mulholland, struck by kids in speeding cars or shoved off the road into a canyon by some transient punk. Bodies were thrown from cars and there'd been several murders.

Police cars cruised through here regularly, checking for trouble.

No place for him.

Easing the Honda onto the road, he continued west along Mulholland and turned down Nichols Canyon, taking the curves cautiously. These were sharper than the ones on Outpost. The looming houses seemed larger and were farther back from the road.

As he reached an open stretch with fewer turns, he slowed down. Not a bad spot for his purpose. You could see quite a distance down the road. Large properties with trees and shrubbery. More space between each house.

All the windows were dark. The people who lived here must be in bed or watching TV in a rear room. They wouldn't bother to look down from their front windows at passing traffic.

He noticed a FOR SALE sign and slowed to have a quick look at the house. Switched off his headlights and stopped the Honda.

It was a neat gray house with green shutters, perched high on a slope covered with ice plants. The windows were shuttered, so the property might be vacant. Young cypress trees edged the road, a row of low shrubbery behind them. Steep driveway, lined with more shrubbery, led to a two-car garage at the side of the house. The garage doors were closed but he could park his car in the shadow at the top of the drive. Nobody would notice his gray Volkswagen from the road.

He would take off his wig, as usual, in the car and remove his sunglasses. Leave them in the glove compartment. Come down the drive, hunched low, in the shadow. Crouch beside the road, hidden behind shrubbery, until he saw a girl jogging up the canyon.

He'd wait for her to come back and follow her down. Talk to her. Make friends. Grab her suddenly, before she realized what he was doing, and pull her behind the shrubbery. The thick leaves would hide them from passing traffic. Him and the girl . . .

What girl?

He didn't know whether girls jogged up Nichols Canyon.

He'd have to drive up here again—several times—and watch for girls jogging. Do that every other night for the next week. Nobody was apt to notice his car and, if they did, they would think he lived up here.

He switched on his headlights and let the Honda coast down the Canyon.

The lights of Hollywood trembled and glittered far ahead.

He started the engine as he reached the first turn and saw a jogger coming up the sloping road.

The guy was short. Needed to lose a little weight.

Curly red hair. Wearing spectacles.

No guy would wear fancy spectacles like that.

It was a girl!

She was in a yellow jogging outfit.

As they approached each other, he saw that she was leaning forward and puffing. Compact body. Pudgy. Almost fat.

This one must be jogging to lose weight. At least twenty pounds.

Maybe she jogged every night!

She wouldn't pay attention to another jogger following her.

The Honda passed her and continued down the canyon.

She hadn't even glanced at his car.

He had found the next girl. . . .

Three

10

Victor Lolo, following the directions given by the young attendant at the desk, hurried through a long and windowless corridor, checking the numbered doors.

No smell of disinfectant here, or white-uniformed nurses and gray-faced patients in wheelchairs. Only fresh-faced kids, talking and laughing, wearing bright colors and carrying books. A few older people, most likely professors, tanned and healthy looking.

He found the number he sought and checked the name, neatly typed, on a card underneath: DOCTOR CLEMENT CLOVIS.

He knocked, opened the door and entered a windowless, air-conditioned anteroom lined with bookshelves.

An attractive young woman seated at a desk looked up from her typewriter and smiled. "Special Investigator Lolo?"

"That's right."

"Professor Clovis is expecting you," she said, gesturing toward an inner door. "Go right in."

"Thanks." Crossing the anteroom, he hoped this psychiatrist wouldn't use as many unfamiliar phrases as that one at Parker Center. He swung the door open and went in.

A sandy-haired man working at a big desk piled with books and manuscripts looked up and grinned. "Inspector

Lolo? Had no idea you'd be so young." He rose and extended a hand.

"And I thought a clinical professor of psychology had to have a beard and smoke a pipe." They shook hands across the desk, both aware that they were studying each other.

"I don't look like a psychiatrist and you're certainly nothing like a detective. So much for preconceived concepts. Sit down."

He sank into a worn leather chair as Clovis, who was wearing a yellow T-shirt with a picture of Groucho Marx, folded his lanky frame onto a metal and plastic desk chair. In the reflected sunlight from a row of open windows Clovis didn't appear to be more than thirty-five. He had an intelligent face, gaunt and tanned, sharp but decidedly friendly blue eyes, and a thatch of curly hair.

"I was delighted when a pal from the D.A.'s office called and asked me to see you," Clovis said. "Sorry I couldn't be free until this morning. I'm always happy to work with the police and was even more intrigued when I learned it would be the famous Special Investigator Victor Lolo."

"Famous? Hardly . . ."

"I've been following your career for several years now, and have been fascinated by several of your investigations. I was hoping one day we might meet."

"I'm surprised you ever heard of me."

"I read every item in the papers concerning our local police. They've become increasingly more numerous. Los Angeles is high on every survey of crime in American cities.

"Unfortunately."

"Obviously one particular investigation has brought you to me."

"That's right."

"But first, about yourself. The newspapers, unfortunately, rarely divulge anything personal about a member of the police department. . . ."

"Unless they happen to get killed."

"Even then, it's only a brief report on how, when, and where. Along with the name of the dead man's wife and number of children."

"In my case that's no wife, no children."

"I, on the other hand, have one permanent wife, a temporary mistress, and two carefully planned monsters."

Lolo laughed. "An average American family."

"I can see we'll get along. Let's not be formal, shall we? Call me Clem and I'll call you Vic."

"By all means."

"Tell me about your name—Lolo—is that Chinese? You don't look Oriental."

"I'm not. As far as I know . . ."

"Mexican?"

"That's what most people think, but they're wrong."

"Your speech pattern seems basic American. No distinguishing accent."

"I was born in American Samoa."

"Samoa? I should never have guessed. But then I've never before encountered a Samoan."

"My full name is Victor Lolotai, but I shortened it when I came to California."

"How the devil did you land on the L.A. police force?"

"I was studying law in Pago Pago, but as a result of a personal tragedy—the death of the girl I had planned to marry—I decided to come to Los Angeles. Continued my studies here, at U.C.L.A., but left college when I learned it would be difficult to land a job with a first-class law firm."

"Because you're Polynesian? But you're an American citizen."

"There are many black American citizens who can't find jobs with law offices when they finish college."

"I'm quite aware of that."

"There was one professor who advised me to become a cop. He thought my legal training would be useful on the force. And, indeed, it has been. It made the examinations easy to pass and helped me advance more quickly."

"You've been a Special Investigator for—is it three years now?"

"Two and a half. How could you know that?"

"I've kept a file on you since I read that you'd been promoted from policeman to detective."

"Have you! Why?"

"Your name intrigued me. Aroused my curiosity. And

increasingly, you seemed to have gotten most of the more unusual cases—the kinky ones, including murder—to investigate and, of course, to solve. Which you do with an amazing degree of regularity."

"I've been lucky."

"Luck, I would suspect, has damn little to do with your success. You are extraordinarily capable at your job." He reached out to open a file folder containing a thick sheaf of clippings along with pages covered with written notes. "So you've come to me about one of your current investigations. . . ."

"Yes."

"That would have to be the most difficult of your cases," Clovis said, tapping the open folder with a forefinger. "The one the press has christened the Midnight Jogger."

"You're absolutely right."

"Which has remained unsolved for so many months because the rapist leaves no clues."

"I'm worried at the moment because I think the Jogger's preparing to attack another young woman. I'm afraid this time he may commit murder. We're approaching the end of the month and, with the exception of April, he's attacked every month since last November. His most recent victim was found in May. So you see, it's about time for him to strike again."

"I wonder why he missed the month of April?" Clovis chuckled. "Out of town perhaps. Have you checked Palm Springs?"

"I'm not sure he did miss. It's possible the local police didn't bother to notify Parker Center. I only discovered last week that there'd been a rape in February near Griffith Park."

"Indeed? That wasn't reported in the newspapers."

"The victim and her mother refused to cooperate and the police investigation was dropped. I didn't learn about it until I sent out a memo asking every division to check unreported rapes in April and February. I'm still hoping to turn up one for April."

"You think he performs the act of rape regularly, every month?"

"I do. Yes . . ."

"In a way that makes sense. The sort of unfortunate male who commits rape is such an introvert that, I suspect, it may take him a month to work up his confidence to the point where he can physically perform again. I don't mean, of course, the type who rapes during a burglary. Breaking and entering is also rape, and the actual physical rape of an occupant, on the premises, is only an extension of that burglary."

"I realize that."

"I've worked with the D.A.'s office frequently, during and prior to the trial of rapists. Interviewed them many times, as well as their victims, frequently under hypnosis. And I can tell you that they—rapist and victim—reveal certain characteristics which turn up with consistent regularity."

"I would be grateful for anything you could tell me that might help me track down the Jogger."

"Okay. Let me describe briefly what I've learned from both victims and attackers. I'll not burden you with psychoanalytical terms but will keep to basic facts."

"Is there any characteristic common to the victims?"

"The young women I've studied have all been introverts but not entirely repressed."

"I understand those terms from reading books on psychiatry."

"All of them had enjoyed normal sexual relations with men in the past. By normal, in this instance, I only mean they were not virgins and they had enjoyed the sexual act several times prior to their rape. Only one young woman had been married, but was divorced. She claimed her husband was impotent and I found no reason to doubt her. Most of these young women had steady, rather dull jobs. I observed that they were of average height, or less, with well-developed bodies. None of them were tall."

"The young women raped by the Jogger have been slightly shorter than average."

"So your Jogger must be short."

"All of them, by the way, had red hair."

"Which suggests he prefers females with red hair and seeks them out. All the young women I've interviewed have been shorter than their attackers. Consequently, they have less physical strength to fight back when attacked. Is there anything else you've noticed peculiar to your Jogger or his victims that hasn't been mentioned to the press?"

"No. I can't think of . . . Wait! There is something I do find odd. Two of his victims, including this one near Griffith Park, claim the Jogger said 'I love you' as he attacked them."

"Did he?"

"The last words they heard as they lost consciousness, apparently."

"I've never encountered that before. A rapist using the word love. Were any of the victims able to describe him?"

"Two of them said he had pale eyes."

"Pale eyes?"

"Pale blue. One girl said his hair was dark blond. Another described it as bronze."

"Pale blue eyes and bronze hair? Such a person would be rather conspicuous. You ought to have no trouble finding him"—Clovis laughed—"anywhere in Los Angeles."

"I suspect he may have light brown hair and, by daylight, his eyes might not look so pale and his hair wouldn't seem to be bronze."

"I agree. Light—or absence of light—plays tricks, and most individuals, at best, are unable to describe colors precisely. Also, the victims are in a state of shock and hysteria once they realize they're facing a rapist."

"Another thing that hasn't been in the papers—that I've learned when I questioned the victims—is that most of them were extremely fond of their fathers."

"I've discovered that myself, Vic, especially when I question them under hypnosis. They enjoyed a strong but completely normal attraction to their male parent. Nothing incestuous. That, I suspect, is why they feel an attraction for the rapist—are not frightened by him at first—because they genuinely do like men. That's a part of why they don't scream for help until it's too late."

"I've wondered why they don't cry out."

"They trust men because they trusted and respected their father. There's another curious similarity I've turned up about rapists. Each one I've questioned, under hypnosis, was unable to recall the face of his victim."

"Is that so?"

"Can't describe the color of her eyes. I suspect he doesn't look at her face."

"Why not?"

"He instinctively doesn't want to know what she looks like. Possibly, I would suggest, because he sees another face. What you tell me about your Jogger saying 'I love you' confirms my theory. Several rapists have claimed they saw the face of their first victim every time they raped again. Some say it's their mother's face they see."

"Their mother?"

"There is, certainly, an element of the incestuous about rape. Most rapists claim they had weak fathers but strong mothers who dominated the family because their husbands were alcoholics and frequently unemployed. The fathers often punished and battered their sons and, in most cases, abandoned wife and child, never to be heard from again. I've confirmed this whenever I've been able to interview the rapist's parents. This particular combination—strong mother and weak father—tends to produce homosexuals and rapists."

"You're saying rapists are homos?"

"Certainly not! None of those I interviewed were homosexual. I'm working on a book in which I develop a theory about the rapist. I'm convinced that he is a man in limbo."

"Limbo?"

"Frightened by the normal sexual act. Unable to perform it."

"What is this limbo?"

"The word comes from Latin. It means to be on the edge or on the fringe of something. In early Christian theology limbo was a region that borders on hell. A place, for instance, where unbaptized children are supposed to go after death. Limbo is also a condition of mental oblivion. An indeterminate, vague emotional state. In ancient times, by the way, limbo meant prison."

"Prison? That's interesting."

"I'm including case histories in my book of all the rapists I've interviewed."

"Does it have a title?"

"For the moment, I'm calling it *Limbo Man*. My theory,

quite simply, is that rapists exist in a permanent state of limbo. That's true of all those I've questioned under hypnosis. By rapists I mean the repeaters—not a casual who rapes once—but those who rape again and again."

"Like the Jogger . . ." Lolo glanced at the face of Groucho Marx on Clovis's T-shirt and realized that the comedian's eyes, behind his spectacles, were staring straight at him. He looked away at once. "Sorry. I was thinking about what you said."

"I'm convinced the constant rapist only comes alive, has an orgasm, when he rapes. He's unable to love, physically or emotionally, because nobody has ever loved him. He's never permitted a woman to love him. He's consumed, in fact, by unrecognized self-hatred. Afraid of any sort of affection, and constantly seeking to avoid it and escape from it. He probably experienced sex for the first time—sex, not love— by raping some girl when he was very young. The only time since then he's been able to achieve climax is when he rapes again. And he can complete the sexual act only with a faceless stranger. . . .

"He's a sad case because, without psychiatric help, he will never be able to experience normal love. Indeed, he will always be a limbo man, existing in a rootless world between the unreality of his daily life and the even greater unreality of the period when he's preparing to rape again. The only moment of reality for him is when rape is consummated." He hesitated, expectantly. "Does any of this make sense or does it sound like complete nonsense?"

"Yes. This helps me understand him more clearly."

"The limbo man is extremely difficult to pin down, both the real man you're hunting and the generic man I'm pursuing for my book. I've never been able to see his true face or hear his real voice. He has many faces and no single voice. I'm still searching, like you, listening and looking. . . ."

Lolo stared at Groucho again and saw that he seemed to be scowling. "This picture of Groucho on your chest seems to change its expression."

"You've noticed that?"

"At the moment he's frowning at me."

"He does that. Very useful to help intimidate my more

recalcitrant patients." He closed the file folder. "Has your Jogger left any clues behind that proved useful? The newspapers never mention any."

"Because I didn't tell them. He's left two clues, but they've been of no use whatever. A print of his jogging shoe in soft earth. The heel impression has an identifiable cut in the rubber that should be useful, if I ever find the matching shoe. He's left that print twice. Then, only last week, I learned that one of his victims—the February one—managed to catch a glimpse of his car. An old gray Volkswagen. There must be hundreds of those in Los Angeles. Impossible to find this one without a license number. And he asked that same victim if she liked snakes."

"How curious! I shall have to give some thought to that. None of my rapists mentioned snakes. . . . I'm afraid I've not given you much help.

"I'm very grateful for what you've told me. I want to think about it—everything you've said—especially your limbo theory. Any idea what sort of work such a man might do? He has to have a job in order to survive. Your limbo man and my Jogger . . ."

"Each of the rapists I've questioned did have a job and was, obviously, very good at it. Always professions where they would rarely be in contact with women."

"What kind of jobs?"

"Mostly truck drivers, mechanics, carpenters—that kind of thing. Since limbo man seldom has even casual contact with the opposite sex, he tends to channel his energy and time into his job. He seeks respect and admiration from his fellow workers, desperately showing them how good he is. But he's a lost soul, this limbo man, alone and confused in the center of a maze."

"I don't understand."

"There are famous gardens, mostly in England and Italy, where what appear to be seemingly endless paths—twisting and turning between high, clipped hedges—must be followed in order to find an exit. A way out."

"I understand now. . . ."

"But the limbo man contrives a maze within himself. In his brain. A maze that has no center and no exit. He can never escape."

11

D on raised his bare arm and, aiming carefully, threw the feathered dart across the Coop. He watched the sharp metal point bite into the center of Carlo Dario's forehead.

He had clipped a new picture of the actor from the Sunday paper and taped it to the white wall.

His aim was improving. In fact, he was getting damn good. He wondered if he would be as accurate with a gun.

But he didn't like guns, had never fired one and had cried whenever his father shot a rabbit.

He'd bought a box of darts from that novelty shop where he performed in the window last week, and every evening now, when he came home, he tossed them at Carlo's photograph. The actor's face was covered with small holes. Like some terrible disease.

Tonight he was going to see *Vaquero*, but that didn't stop him from being sore at Carlo for refusing to notice him at the opening. He wasn't as angry as he'd been that night, but he wasn't forgetting what happened. Not this fast.

He rose from his bed, where he'd had a late-afternoon nap, and crossed the Coop to pull out the darts from Carlo's face, leaving six more small holes. Returned the darts to a cardboard box on his bedside table where they would be waiting when he wanted them again.

Never hold a grudge against anyone, his mother always said.

This was more than a grudge.

Maybe if he threw the darts enough times, he would get rid of his anger.

Tonight he was going to drive up Nichols Canyon again. He'd been back several times and seen that girl twice. Tonight he would follow her.

He'd spent the afternoon at the beach again, resting for the night ahead, and hadn't bothered to eat any lunch or dinner.

After the movie he would have a hamburger somewhere—nothing more because he would have to be alert later, mentally as well as physically.

He would come back here around eleven and change into his jogging suit. Velma and Lori-Lou would be asleep by then and wouldn't hear his car.

Right now he would shower and—

The telephone shrilled and startled him. Probably Velma calling from the house to invite him over for dinner. Not tonight.

He sank onto his bed again, the striped cover warm under his bare flesh, and reached for the white receiver. "Yeah?"

"How ya doin', kid?"

"Harry! What's with you?" His eyes rested briefly on a torn paperback copy of *Don Quixote* on the bedside table as he listened to his agent's voice.

"Gotta fancy job for ya. Sataday afternoon. Birthday party for a buncha little kids."

"How old?"

"Don't know for sure."

"Boy or girl havin' this birthday?"

"Boy. Think the dame said he was four. They live out at Pacific Palisades. Their secretary—an English dame—called me this afternoon. I wrote the address down. . . ."

"Movie people?"

"Didn' say. Only that somebody seen ya last week at that pree-meer."

"Yeah?"

"They wancha to wear that same outfit ya was wearin' then. An' they wancha for two hours. Five to seven. By seven o'clock the little bastards should be pukin' all the ice cream they been guzzlin'.''

"How much they gonna pay me?"

"Hundred bucks an hour. Same's last week."

"That's great, Harry!"

"They already gotta clown act an' some guy with a monkey. I told her you'd be the class act of the party, an' ya like workin' with kids."

"Yeah. I do."

"Give ya the address when I see ya. Got another job for ya, next week, shoppin' center in the Valley. Drop by tomorrow, I'll give ya all the facts."

"Sure, Harry. See you then." He returned the phone to the coffee table and pushed himself up from the bed.

There was plenty of time before the movie to see Velma and Lori-Lou, but he wouldn't stay for dinner.

He was whistling softly as he headed for the shower.

When the cold water struck his flesh, he was thinking about the night ahead.

First the movie and, after that, something to eat. Then he'd come back here and change. When that girl came jogging up Nichols Canyon, he would be waiting. . . .

He toweled himself and dressed, put the contacts in his eyes, darkened the eyebrows and lashes, got out a short black wig.

Locking the Coop, he walked down the silent drive toward the house.

Velma's kitchen was lighted but empty.

He knocked on the screen door before entering.

Something was cooking in the oven. It smelled like roast beef. Pots were steaming on top of the stove.

"That you, Don?"

"Yeah, Velma."

"We're in the parlor."

As he crossed the lighted dining room, he noticed three places set for dinner. Velma must be expecting him to eat.

The news was on the TV screen in the dim living room, so it must be past seven. He would only stay two minutes, because *Vaquero* started at seven-thirty. He had checked the time in the newspaper.

Kong shot out from the living room to meet him.

"We're watchin' the news, honey."

"Can only stay a coupla minutes, Velma." He patted the sleek black head of the Doberman as the shiny face of the President appeared on the screen.

"Well! You can sit for a second. I'd rather talk anytime than listen to the news. Stinkypie, you can turn it off."

Lori-Lou jabbed the remote control and the President's face dissolved to black.

"Can't you stay for dinner?" Velma asked, hopefully.

Don perched on the arm of an old leather chair and Kong jumped up onto the seat. "Thanks. But I'm catchin' a movie."

"Which one?" Lori-Lou asked.

"*Vaquero*. Didn' see it the other night."

"Looks like a hit." Velma rearranged her muumuu as she talked. "I read the reviews. *Variety* was even better than the paper."

"When are we gonna see it, Mommy?"

"Maybe Saturday. The early show." Turning to Don again, she said, "Pete's comin' for dinner tonight. I'm cookin' roast beef, so there's plenty for you."

"Thanks, Velma. Not tonight."

"Pete always likes to see you. An' I enjoy hearin' the two of you yarn about Pike. You were his best friends."

"Yeah. Guess we were." He scratched Kong's ear as they talked.

"Mosta Pike's friends were trash. Buncha drunks."

"Pete drinks!" Lori-Lou exclaimed. "You know he does."

"Not like he used to, an' I'm workin' on him. Tonight he'll get one bottle of beer with dinner. No more."

"Pete's gotta bottle of bourbon in his car," Lori-Lou announced. "Takes a drink every time he goes outside."

"How do you know that?" Velma asked.

"I've seen him do it."

"Who told you it's bourbon?"

"It's the same kinda bottle Papa used to hide in the Coop."

"I'm goin' to start callin' you Miss Peekanpry."

"I know lots of secrets," Lori-Lou said, smiling smugly. "About everybody."

"Which you can keep to yourself, young lady, or you'll

find yourself in trouble. 'Specially any secrets you think you know about me." She turned to Don. "You work today?"

"Nope. Spent the afternoon at the beach. Harry Sneal called, said he's got a job for me Saturday. Private birthday party."

"Isn't that wonderful!"

Kong growled, low in his throat.

"There's Pete. Openin' the gate. Beats me why Kong still growls at Pete. After all these years."

"Kong doesn't like him," Lori-Lou observed. "Neither do I."

"Well! The two of ya better start likin' him 'cause he likes you. Pete was your father's best friend."

"Don was Papa's best friend."

"Don came along much later. Pete knew Pike before you were born. They must've been in fifty movies together. At first they only had one horse between 'em, but eventually Pike bought his own. Don was more like a son to Pike. You see, Missy, when you were born, your father was mighty disappointed."

"Was he?"

"He'd wanted a son but I didn' give him one. I felt guilty 'bout that for quite a spell. Then Don showed up an' it was like Pike had found his son."

Kong started barking.

"Stop that, you damn fool!" Velma ordered. "Stop it! You hear?"

The dog paid no attention.

"Where's my sweet Velma?" Pete boomed from the dining room.

"In here, honey." Velma got to her feet, muumuu billowing, poking at her blonde curls. "In the parlor."

Don saw that she was wearing her phony pink fingernails and green satin slippers, instead of her old sandals.

Kong had stopped barking but was growling now.

Pete Pottenger loomed large in a fringed Western shirt over faded Levi's tucked into expensive boots. Against the light from the dining room he looked like Pike, from the tousle of gray hair to the open space between his bowlegs. Like Pike, he'd had his legs broken so many times, he walked like a real cowhand. The two of them had said they were born in

Wyoming, but Pike came from New York City and Pete was a native of New Jersey. Both had been to college back East before working as actors in small parts on Broadway.

"Velma girl!" Pete lurched toward her and Velma engulfed him with a hug as she kissed him.

Don got to his feet and winked at Lori-Lou, who was scowling.

"Where's Miss Lori-Lou?" Pete, released from Velma's embrace, pretended to look for her daughter. "There she is!" he said, going toward the other end of the sofa, where Lori-Lou remained seated. "Pete's gotta little present for his other girl." He deposited a package tied with red ribbon on Lori-Lou's lap. "Sweets for my sweetie!"

"If that's more candy," Velma protested, sinking onto the sofa again, "I'm goin' to start sendin' you her dentist's bills."

"A little candy never hurt nobody, Velma."

"Stinkypie! You didn't say thank you."

"Thank you, Pete. . . ."

"No thanks required, sweetheart." He turned to Don, holding out his sun-wrinkled brown paw. "How are ya, boy?"

"I'm okay, Pete." He shook the paw.

"Ain't seen ya, coupla weeks."

"Don's doin' fine!" Velma was arranging her muumuu over her breasts again. "Gotta private party comin' up Saturday."

"That's just great!" Pete moved toward the sofa. "You been savin' this place for me, ladies?" He sat between them.

"How *you* doin'?" Don asked.

"Only one lousy Western shootin' an' all the stars are doin' their own ridin' in this one. Gettin' to be too mucha that. Ten years ago no self-respectin' thespian would venture near a live horse. You were wise to get outta the actin' racket, Don."

"Couldn't get in it. You know that."

"Can't you sit for a while, Don?" Velma asked. "Dinner won't be for another few minutes."

"Thanks. Gotta be goin'."

"Don's gonna see *Vaquero* tonight," Velma explained.

"Wanna see that one myself." Pete turned back to him.

"Know all the stuntmen, except them guys they hired in Mexico. Velma here said you was doin' your mechanical-man act for the pree-meer. Watched it on the news but didn' see hide nor hair of you."

"They never picked me up on camera."

"Had your dinner, Don?" Velma asked.

"Thought I'd get somethin' after the show," he said, escaping toward the dining room. "See you, Pete."

"Yeah, kid. Sure . . ."

"Have a good time, honey!" Velma called after him.

As Don went through the dining room, he wondered about that girl in Nichols Canyon. What was she doing now? . . .

Would she show up tonight?

Crossing the kitchen, he heard sandals slapping the bare floor as Kong's cold nose touched his hand. He looked around to see Lori-Lou clutching her box of candy. "What happened?"

"Velma said I should see you out."

"Did she?"

"She wants to be alone with Pete. They'll be kissin' an' smoochin' for five minutes. It's sickenin' at their age. . . ."

He held the door open for Kong to dart out, followed by Lori-Lou.

The evening air felt cool as they walked up the drive.

"Like some candy?" Lori-Lou held up the unopened box.

"Spoil my dinner. And yours." He saw the red ribbon in the fading light. "Pete likes you. Always bringing candy."

"But I don't like him."

"You're too young to know what you like."

"I'll never like Pete. Always tryin' to act like Pike. He hopes Mommy will marry him, an' I guess she will."

"Wouldn't you like Pete for your father?"

"He's a pig. Poppa was a pig, too, but a nice pig. I loved him."

"Your mother's gonna want another husband, I expect. Pete might be better than a stranger."

"I don't want another father."

"Pete's a good guy."

"Papa said that, someday, he hoped you'd be my husband."

Don turned, surprised, to look down at her troubled face. "Pike said that?"

"He sure did."

"When?"

"I guess, maybe, a coupla months before he got killed. We were in the car an' he was talkin' 'bout the future. How he wanted me to have a happy life. He said, 'Don's gonna make some girl a good husband. I'd be happy if he married a daughter of mine.'"

"You're too young to be thinkin' 'bout a husband, Cricket. Better go back and see if your dinner's ready."

"I hate you! Always treatin' me like a baby."

"You are a baby."

"Hate you!" She turned and hurried down the drive.

"Go with her, Kong. Home, boy! Home!"

The Doberman ran after her.

Don continued up the drive, toward his garage, thinking about that girl in Nichols Canyon again.

12

The dark canyon was silent except for twittering birds in the trees, disturbed by a cat or a prowling coyote. There must be snakes in these canyons. Even rattlesnakes . . .

But he wasn't afraid of snakes. They were his brothers. Tomas taught him that.

He relaxed, crouched on a flat stone he had discovered last night.

She didn't jog over the weekend, but he'd seen her twice this week.

Last night he had planned what he would do tonight.

Half an hour ago he had parked his Volkswagen on Courtney, the first street east of Nichols Canyon that turned north off Hollywood Boulevard and seemed to be a dead end but actually curved into the canyon. Parked there and waited for her to jog past his car.

Watched her pass but remained motionless for a few seconds after she'd gone, then drove after her around the curve and up the canyon.

Only one car had passed him, heading in the opposite direction.

He'd seen two guys jogging together, heading down to Hollywood Boulevard. It was impossible to see their faces in the faint spill of light from the sky, which meant they couldn't see him. The moon was hidden behind a row of eucalyptus trees and there were deep patches of shadow on both sides of the road.

At this hour on a Thursday night, most people would be in bed, resting for the weekend.

He'd left his Volkswagen at the top of the drive of that vacant house with the FOR SALE sign, facing the closed garage doors. Then he switched off his headlights and sat, for a moment, listening.

Not a sound.

Then, moving quickly, he'd pulled off his curly black wig and hid it in the glove compartment.

He'd already removed his contact lenses when he returned to the Coop after dinner and wiped the black from his eyebrows and lashes.

Leaving the car unlocked he got out and put his keys into a hip pocket. Buttoned it so they couldn't fall out.

Then he had lowered himself onto this flat stone, out of sight, behind a row of bushes. That was at least fifteen minutes ago.

The girl should be coming up the canyon at any moment. She wouldn't notice him as she passed because there were two big trees blocking all light from the sky.

The stone was hard under his butt and he could feel its chill through the jogging suit. Fortunately the air was warm.

A faint sound came from down the canyon.

He squinted, waiting and holding his breath, until the yellow jogging suit came into view.

She was bent low against the slope of the road. Mouth open. Sucking in the air. Red curls bobbing.

He couldn't see her face behind those fancy spectacles she always wore. Tonight their rims seemed to sparkle. He'd seen girls wearing glasses like that on the boulevard.

She kept going, legs pumping.

As he leaned forward, cautiously, she disappeared around the next curve.

It would take her at least fifteen minutes to reach the top, another ten to come back down. He had timed her last night and it had taken twenty-five minutes.

Tonight he hadn't worn his wristwatch. He never did when he planned to follow a girl.

He gave her a good five minutes, then started up the road. Running with even strides, conserving his strength for later, breathing easily. In less than three minutes he reached the house he'd selected last night where he would wait for her.

Stepping off the road, he slipped behind some shrubbery and stood there, in shadow again, facing a turn in the canyon where she would appear.

There was a light at the curve, high overhead, shining down on the road. There had obviously been accidents there.

He was blinded briefly when headlights flashed around the curve. After each car passed there was a moment of intense darkness before he could focus on the curve again.

That movie, tonight, had been crowded.

He'd bought his ticket and waited in the lobby.

Nobody had noticed or recognized him. The cashier, the doorman or any of the staff. He even walked past that usher who pushed his platform outside for last week's opening. He'd learned never to look at anyone and they wouldn't look at him.

There'd been a mob of people in the curved lobby, waiting for the early show to finish.

Everyone had pushed forward as the doors opened, but

were held back by a line of ushers as the departing audience came out.

He'd found an empty seat in the fifth row from the front—he liked to be near the screen—and sank into the cushioned seat.

Settled down, resting his head against the upholstered back of the seat—careful not to disturb his wig—as the curtains parted and the auditorium lights dimmed.

Blast of music from the screen. Hoofbeats as a dusty gang of bandits rode through a rocky arroyo.

Some of the audience applauded.

The title and credits flashed past as the camera followed the vaqueros on their horses.

In spite of his personal dislike at the moment for Carlo Dario, he found himself pulled into what was happening on the screen and, as usual, became involved. Carlo wasn't a bandit but was working with the Mexican government to arrest the bandit leader. He was on special assignment for President Diaz but, unfortunately, was in love with the bandit chief's daughter.

The story was silly but he enjoyed any movie about Mexico. Imagined himself in each scene. Wondered if his father had ever been in any of these villages where the exteriors were filmed. Could he be there now?

The girl in the yellow jogging suit appeared around the distant turn and was moving down the canyon.

His breath caught in his throat as he leaned forward to see the girl through the openings between the leaves.

She flashed past.

He stood there listening, straining to catch the sound of her feet hitting the road, but the rubber soles of her jogging shoes made no sound. Then, slowly, he rose from behind the bushes and moved down to the road, checking to see that there were no headlights behind him.

He started down the canyon in pursuit, taking long, even strides.

When he turned the first curve, he saw her ahead of him and quickened his pace.

She must be hearing his feet hitting the macadam, but she didn't glance back. All these girls were the same. None of them had ever been frightened when he followed them. It was as though they wanted the company of another jogger.

He could hear her breathing now, puffing from the exertion. Her hair, red and curly, was held in place by a beaded Indian band with a leather tassel swaying at the back.

She didn't look around, even when he caught up with her and started jogging beside her.

"Hi!" He kept his voice low and friendly. "Not much traffic tonight."

"I'm glad there isn't."

He resisted looking at her. Kept his eyes straight ahead. "You jog a lot?"

"Every night. 'Cept Saturday and Sunday. I usually have dates those nights." She still didn't look up at him. "You live 'round here?"

"On Mulholland. With my folks."

"Must be wonderful up there. All that sunshine and fresh air. I live in Hollywood."

"That's a long way to jog."

"It bothered me at first but then I got used to it. Been joggin' almost a year now. Trying to lose some weight."

He glanced down and saw that she was pudgy but not really fat. Her glasses had rims with white plastic daisies that sparkled.

"If only I could stop eatin' . . ." She reached into a pocket. "Like some jelly beans?"

"No, thanks."

"I eat 'em for energy when I'm joggin'." She popped some into her mouth and began chewing. "I'm a terrific cook."

"Yeah?"

"Maybe you'd like some pie and a cup of coffee?"

"Why not?"

"When we get to the bottom of the canyon. My apartment's 'round the corner on Hollywood Boulevard. I baked a pie when I came home from work. I'm an executive secretary in Beverly Hills—fancy boutique on Rodeo. My boss is gay. He's always tellin' me I gotta lose weight."

He saw the FOR SALE sign ahead. "Sure. I could use a cup of coffee."

"It's strawberry pie. Fresh strawberries."

"You share this apartment with somebody?"

"Oh, no! It's all mine. I couldn't live with another girl. A guy, maybe, but not a girl. I would never do that. . . ."

He clutched her arm with one hand and pushed her toward the drive where his Volkswagen was parked at the top.

"Hey! Whacha doin'?"

He didn't answer but thrust her hard, ahead of him, up the drive.

"Let go of me! What's the matter with you?" She stumbled and her spectacles fell off. "My glasses!"

He shoved her into the shrubbery, twisting her arm, aware of soft flesh under the sleeve.

"Whacha think you're doin'?"

He pushed her with both hands now, backward into the bushes. Threw himself on top of her. Felt her squirming and turning onto her back. Saw her open her mouth to scream. Covered it with a hand as he sank onto her body.

Her voice was muffled as she struggled to push him away.

"I'm not going to hurt you." He whispered the familiar words into her ear. "Not if you're nice to me."

She was hitting him with her fists.

He barely felt the blows. "Be nice. . . ." He smacked her across the side of her head.

She raised her shoulders from the ground, trying to get free.

He struck her again, much harder. Saw her head twist and fall back into the darkness. Heard it strike something. Felt her body go limp. "I love you," he whispered, leaning down to kiss her on the mouth. "I love you. . . ."

He thought of that woman's face, last week at the opening. The redhead with Carlo Dario. She had smiled at him. He saw her face now. . . .

13

The girl was dead. Eyes and mouth open. The round childlike face looked astonished. Her jogging suit had been ripped away from both breasts and pulled down to expose the curly red pubic hair.

Corletti, from Latent Prints, was kneeling beside her with a flashlight, studying the bruises on her throat.

Victor Lolo turned to Madison, from the coroner's office, standing beside him. "When did it happen?"

"Around midnight. You think it's the Jogger again?"

"I'm certain it is. Who found her?"

"Property owner from up the canyon. His dog slipped its leash while they were walking. Ran down here and discovered the body. The guy went back to his house and phoned Hollywood Division."

"Cause of death?"

"Can't be certain until we do an autopsy. Looks like she hit her head on this rock. Bleeding from the nose indicates brain injury and the position of her head looks like the neck's broken."

"I can see that."

Corletti stood up, his face troubled. "The guy who did this is a creep. That smear of blood across her mouth and cheek was done by his mouth."

"So I noticed." Lolo moved away from them toward the

drive where a homicide team from Hollywood Division were talking quietly. "You guys learn anything before I got here?"

"Not much." Frank Heller, the white-haired elder member of the team, pulled a note pad from his pocket. "Found some information in her wallet. Which hadn't been touched. No sign of robbery."

"What information?"

"Social Security card with her name—Deborah Kern— and address. Apartment on Hollywood Boulevard, typed list of names and addresses, including the place where she worked—Chic and Sleek Boutique on Rodeo. In case of accident, notify parents, Mr. and Mrs. Howard Kern, with an address and phone number in Brooklyn. She had twenty-six bucks and some change. Key ring with five keys and a nearly empty bag of jelly beans."

"Jelly beans?"

"Found her spectacles in the drive. One lens cracked." Anderson, the other man on the team, took over. "And it looks as though a car was parked here recently." He motioned up the drive toward a spot in front of the garage.

"Let me see." Lolo followed Anderson up the drive, with Heller at their heels.

"Unfortunately, there's been no rain lately," Anderson continued, "so there's nothing to take a print, but you can see traces of tires."

Lolo saw them. Faint shadows on the clean surface. "You won't get any prints there. Obviously the girl jogged up from Hollywood Boulevard and was on her way down again. The Jogger must've waited for her up the canyon. He probably hid behind some bushes on one of the other properties, then followed and joined her. That's what he always does. Jogs with the victims. Let's have a look for the spot where he was waiting." He walked ahead of them down to the road and up the canyon. "This sure as hell puts an end to my theory that the Jogger lives in Hollywood," Lolo said.

"What made you think that?" Anderson asked.

"Because he'd never raped a girl in Hollywood. My theory was that he hadn't because he didn't want us looking for him where he lived. I was wrong."

"This isn't Hollywood. It's Los Angeles. So he could still live in Hollywood," Heller observed. "The guy must know we don't have a real description of him. I, for one, don't believe what those other victims said, that he has pale eyes and bronze hair. The guy would be so conspicuous we'd have picked him up long ago."

Lolo sighed. "I agree, Frank." As they climbed the canyon, checking each drive, he realized Heller was puffing a little and immediately slowed his stride.

Anderson went ahead of them up the next drive and stopped to look down at something. "Here's something!"

Lolo hurried to join him, Heller following.

They saw a narrow path stretching from the drive behind a row of shrubbery planted across the front of the property. The ground was covered with ice plants and the path had been worn down, probably by the owner or his gardener going back and forth to water the densely planted slope.

Lolo nodded. "This would've been a good spot for him to wait while she jogged up the hill and came down again. He crouched here and watched for her, then followed her down the canyon. This is where he waited," he said, holding an arm out to keep the others back. "There may be prints. Tell Corletti to come up here."

"I'll get him." Anderson made his way back to the drive and down to the road.

Lolo turned to Heller. "I've been afraid for months that this guy would kill one of his victims."

"So have I."

"Been expectin' it, waitin' for it. And not a damn thing I could do to stop him." He heard a distant siren from a police ambulance coming up the canyon.

"Looks as though the guy's left no clues again."

"That's how it's been from the start, Frank. We know now he's attacked seven girls—I turned up another last week that happened in February but wasn't reported downtown—and there may be others lost in the files. When we get all the facts on Deborah Kern, there won't be a damn thing to connect her with the Jogger. He always picks strangers. So there's nothing to involve him with them, past or present, to reveal his identity."

"Like all those unsolved street murders where the killer never saw his victim before."

"Hundreds of those in the files. But I'm going to catch this guy. Deborah Kern died because I wasn't smart enough to stop the Jogger. I have to find him before he kills another girl."

They looked down the drive as Anderson returned with Corletti.

And the police siren died abruptly.

Four

14

Lolo wakened suddenly, surprised to find himself in his office. He'd been dreaming about Samoa. Hadn't done that in a long time . . .

It was four-thirty when he finished at Hollywood Division, and instead of returning to his apartment, he'd driven downtown.

His desk lamp was lighted and the notes he'd written before falling asleep were spread across his desk.

The electric clock said it was seven minutes past nine.

He blinked at the heavy smog beyond his open windows. The morning sun couldn't get through but had turned the smog a sick yellow.

He'd slept for several hours. No roosters crowing here, at dawn, to wake him. This wasn't Pago Pago.

There were no roosters in Los Angeles.

He would never get used to that.

Better go to the gym. Shave and shower. He kept a shaving kit and clean linen in his locker.

Have breakfast in the cafeteria. He needed black coffee. . . .

Go over his notes first.

He reached out and snapped off the desk lamp, then stared at the words he had scribbled. They were barely legible. He snatched up the pages and dropped them into the waste-basket.

The Jogger's latest victim was dead.

He had to catch the bastard fast. Put him in a solitary cell where he could sit until the shrinks were ready to question him. They should have a field day with this one.

All the newspapers would have to change their headlines. The Midnight Jogger was now the Midnight Murderer. . . .

He had less than a month to find him. That's if the Jogger kept to his schedule.

One lousy month . . .

He'd gone with Heller and Anderson to the large apartment complex on Hollywood Boulevard where Deborah Kern had lived. It was one of those two-story pseudo-Continental buildings with neat gardens, built after World War II, which had been second-class when they were new. Today they needed paint jobs and a lot of repairs. Their occupants, with few exceptions, were has-beens and never-would-be's. People on the fringe of nowhere. Limbo people . . .

The manager was a squat, fat woman with shifty eyes and an ugly face who spoke with an unfamiliar accent. She pretended shock when Anderson flashed his ID, although she'd known they were cops when she opened her door. Her eyes gave her away. Finally, she produced a key to the Kern girl's apartment but told them nothing.

Anderson took the key from her thick fingers and led the way upstairs.

The apartment was sparsely furnished and, except for dresses hanging in a big closet and family photographs on a bedside table, there wasn't much to show that anyone had lived here.

A large strawberry pie waited on a table in the center of the kitchen. The crust was golden brown and the strawberries were glazed.

"She must've baked this tonight," Anderson murmured.

Lolo had stared at the pie, thinking of the girl who'd been planning to jog up Nichols Canyon while she baked the crust and glazed those berries. Hoping to find a boyfriend to eat her cooking? Instead the Jogger had found her.

"How 'bout you, Vic? Piece of pie?" Anderson was opening a cupboard to look for plates.

"None for me."

"Nobody else to eat it," Heller said, his eye on the pie.

"I'm on a diet. You two guys enjoy it." He perched on a white stool and watched Anderson collect plates, forks, and a knife.

The young detective cut two large pieces, handed one plate to Heller, set the other down for himself, then gave Heller a fork before pulling up a chair and joining him.

The pie was so good that they each had seconds.

Lolo had watched them eat, his thoughts on the dead girl and the Jogger.

Heller, this morning, would call the girl's family back East, and using his most comforting voice—he'd been an actor at one time—tell them of their daughter's death, make whatever arrangements were necessary, and politely ask a few casual questions.

Anderson would pay a visit to that boutique to question her employer. But he would probably turn up nothing there on the Jogger. . . .

Lolo had a sudden urge to phone Morita and, for a moment, listen to her cheerful voice.

What would she be doing at this hour?

Still asleep?

Or relaxing on the terrace of her condominium eating breakfast?

He'd enjoyed several breakfasts on that terrace overlooking Wilshire. . . .

He reached across his desk for the phone but thought better of it and let his hand drop.

It had been hours since he'd eaten anything.

He'd taken Morita to the Bistro for supper after the Carlo Dario movie and, afterward, drove back to her condominium.

It had been midnight when he reached home and he'd barely gotten to sleep when Hollywood Division called to report it looked as though the Jogger had killed a girl in Nichols Canyon.

His office was getting noisy with the roar of morning traffic rising from the nearby streets.

Morning and not a rooster crowing . . .

15

on slept late.
    When he opened his eyes to squint at the skylight, he saw a clear blue sky. The angle of sunlight pouring into the Coop told him it must be about eleven. Squirming around in his narrow bed, he checked the electric clock and saw that his guess was close. The hands of the clock were at ten forty-seven.

Wiggling his toes under the sheet, stretching both legs, he watched the one tree branch visible through the open skylight. Green leaves moving in a light breeze.

That girl last night. The blood on her face . . . .

His stomach knotted as he remembered.

She must've struck her head against something when she fell. Maybe that rock he sat on earlier. That must've given her a nosebleed. She couldn't have been hurt bad. . . . .

He thrust the unpleasant picture from his mind.

Reaching out blindly, he found the portable radio on his bedside table and switched it on, turning the dial to KFWB for the news.

Another bomb had exploded somewhere. A place with a foreign name he'd never heard of before. Bombs were always exploding. Cars piled up in heavy fog on the Coast Highway. Young couple arrested for abusing their baby.

Abusing was a fancy word for beating. How could people do that to a baby?

He listened until the story about the bomb was repeated before he snapped off the radio.

He smiled. Nothing about the Midnight Jogger.

Stupid cops didn't know a damn thing. They would never find out he was the Jogger. Never catch him . . .

The radio and newspapers had been saying less and less. It was as though they wanted to keep the whole damn thing quiet. Some of those girls had never been reported and, when they were, nothing was said about where the attack had happened. Only the general neighborhood . . .

Maybe they wouldn't guess it was the Jogger last night. That was okay with him. . . .

He ought to do his laundry this morning. There were always dirt marks and grass stains on his jogging suit. This time there might be blood spots.

He had to see Harry Sneal. Find out about that private birthday party tomorrow . . .

He didn't feel like listening to Velma, so he wouldn't do his laundry. The washer and dryer were in a room off her kitchen and whenever he did laundry he always had to eat breakfast with her. Most days he didn't mind, but he was in no mood to listen to her blabbing this morning.

Better get breakfast before he saw Harry. It would be close to noon, but his agent never left his office for lunch. Maybe he'd take him a hamburger. That always put Harry in a good mood.

Throwing the sheet aside, he jumped out of bed and headed for the shower.

Half an hour later, showered and dressed, wearing a short-haired black wig and his contacts, he backed the Honda out from the garage.

No sign of Kong as he coasted down the drive toward the open gate.

Velma's garage door was raised and her station wagon wasn't parked inside. She must've gone to the supermarket and taken Kong with her. Left the gate open so she could drive straight in when she came home.

He turned up Poinsettia toward Hollywood Boulevard. Found a parking space on a side street and walked to one of the spots on the boulevard where he liked to have breakfast.

This one had a long counter down one side with a row of white Formica-topped tables against a big window facing the street.

The early lunch crowd wouldn't show up for another half hour, so he sat at the empty counter. Three waitresses seated at the far end of the counter were drinking coffee, gossiping and giggling, and a fry-cook was wiping one of his griddles with a greasy rag.

Don glanced at the windows reflected in a long mirror behind the counter as he watched the people on the boulevard. He was aware that one waitress had left the others and was coming toward him behind the counter.

"Hi! Breakfast or lunch?"

He saw that it was the youngest waitress, small and thin, in a skimpy white uniform, white cap perched on her dyed blonde hair. "Breakfast. Scrambled eggs, sausages, toasted English. Coffee while I wait."

"Right away." She called his order to the fry-cook as she moved toward the coffee urn.

Somebody had turned on a radio and the blare of a rock combo came from small speakers high on the walls.

Don listened to the music as the skinny waitress brought his coffee. He emptied three packets of sugar into it while she sorted out a knife, fork, and spoon at his place.

"When I leave," he said, "I'll want a hamburger to go."

"Sure."

"With a container of black coffee."

She gave the take-out order to the fry-cook as she rejoined the other waitresses.

Don sipped his hot coffee, considering the afternoon ahead. Maybe he would catch a movie. That always relaxed him. Always new ones opening on Friday.

As he ate breakfast the counter slowly began to fill with people who looked as though they worked in the neighborhood.

He had a second cup of coffee, and when the waitress set a paper bag in front of him with the hamburger for Harry Sneal, he realized that some guy on the radio was talking about unemployment in California. . . .

The place was getting crowded.

". . . *Nichols Canyon, where last night, according to the Hollywood Division of the L.A.P.D., the Midnight Jogger found another victim. This time the Jogger has murdered the young woman. . . ."*

Murdered?

Don snatched up his check and the paper bag.

The voice continued but nobody was listening.

As he paid the cashier, he remembered that he hadn't left a tip and hurried back to the counter where the waitress was clearing his place and another customer was waiting to be served.

The waitress looked up and smiled when he dropped three quarters on the counter. "Thanks. Thought for a second you forgot me."

Outside he lost himself in the crowd on the boulevard and walked back to his car in a daze.

That girl was dead. He didn't even know her name and she was dead.

Hadn't meant to hurt her . . .

Couldn't even remember her face. Hadn't really seen it. Only her red hair and those fancy spectacles she was wearing.

He'd never seen the faces of any of those other girls. Hadn't looked at them, purposely, so he wouldn't be able to remember their faces if somebody showed him a photograph or he passed one of them on the street.

That guy on the radio hadn't given the girl's name. Maybe they didn't know who she was. Could be she didn't carry a purse when she jogged. He hadn't noticed one. But then, he hadn't looked. He wasn't interested in her money. . . .

Don drove his car without any sense of direction.

He would go to a movie this afternoon and lose himself in the pictures on the big screen. He always did that when he saw a movie, as though he jumped up onto the screen and became a part of what was happening there. Like in that Woody Allen movie . . .

But first he had to see Harry Sneal.

The paper bag was propped up in the far corner of the seat, so the coffee couldn't spill.

He peered from side to side at unfamiliar streets, with no

idea where he was, until he recognized Franklin and turned right toward Vine.

His hands, grasping the wheel, were cold and his body was shivering. He had to pull himself together before seeing Harry. The agent's sharp eyes never missed anything.

Don slowed the Honda down Vine and pulled into the curb several buildings beyond Harry's, then sat there, still clutching the wheel, staring at nothing.

Reached for the paper bag and pulled out the container of coffee. Folding the bag carefully to keep the hamburger warm he set it on the seat again. Harry wouldn't miss the coffee.

He opened it and dropped the plastic top out the window, held the container to his lips with both hands, and sipped the black coffee.

Felt better, more relaxed, his hands no longer trembling.

Somewhat composed he hesitated in front of a door with RENTADDRESS painted in large red letters and HARRY SNEAL in smaller black letters underneath before entering the windowless office. Near the center of the room, a fat blonde sat at an unpainted kitchen table piled with mail, reading a paperback mystery.

She looked up but dropped her eyes to the paperback as she talked. "Hiya, handsome!"

"Harry in?"

"Harry's always in." She continued reading without looking up again. "Got no place to go but here. One of his clients the other day said Harry only goes out for funerals. Lotsa his friends been poppin' off lately. All those old actors he used to handle . . ."

Don passed the table as he crossed the room. He'd never known whether the blonde rented space from Harry or Harry rented from her. There were two inside doors along the far wall. One had HARRY SNEAL on it, but the painted letters were so faded you could hardly read his name.

He opened the door without knocking and went in.

Harry was sitting at an open window, his back to the door, peering down at the street. "Who is it?"

"It's me, Don."

"How ya doin', kid?" He swiveled around in his creaky leather armchair. "Didn't see your car."

"Parked it down the street." Don handed the paper bag to him. "Brought you a hamburger."

"Wish my other clients was as thoughtful, but none of the bastards are." He opened the bag and dug into it for the hamburger. "Pull up a chair while I eat."

Don removed several old copies of *Variety* from a battered chair and moved them to the rolltop desk, careful not to disturb the piles of faded letters. He pushed the chair closer to Harry and sat facing him as the agent chewed hamburger and sesame bun in his small trap of a mouth.

"Was thinkin' 'bout goin' out for lunch, but you saved me the trouble. An' the money," he said, spitting crumbs and sesame seeds as he spoke. "Don't like to leave the place, ya know? Get some important calls durin' the lunch hour."

Don realized that his hands were shaking again. He rested them on his knee, clutched together to control them, so Harry wouldn't notice.

"Like to walk up the boulevard, at least once a week, an' eat at Musso's. Been havin' lunch there forty years or more . . ."

Harry had talked about Musso's ever since Don had known him, but Pike Splain said he'd probably never been there. This was part of Harry's routine to impress his clients.

He saw that the hamburger and bun had vanished. They probably filled the little guy. Tiny eyes above a big nose that was too large for his face. Thin gray hair and small hands with baby fingers. He had fished the paper napkin from the bag and was cleaning his fingers while he sucked sesame seeds from between his teeth. He dropped the crumpled napkin into the bag and tossed it out the window.

"Well, now! Lunch consumed, we can transact a little business."

Don glanced down at Harry's feet in their scuffed loafers. He must buy his clothes in the children's department at Sears. The trousered legs were so short his feet didn't reach the floor. Now he was fumbling in his pockets, pulling out notes he'd scribbled on bits of torn paper, searching for the right one.

"Here we are, kid!" He held up a slip of paper as he stuffed the others back into various pockets. "This here birthday party's tomorrow aftanoon. Sataday. . . ." He studied the writing. "You're to ask for a dame named Vernon—Vikki Vernon—Vikki with two ks. She spelled it out for me. Sounded English. Said she's secretary for the people givin' this party for their kid. The kid's four years old. I'll write the address down. . . ." Fingering another pocket and pulling out a small pad with a pen. "They wancha from five to seven. Hundred bucks an hour." Writing on the pad as he talked. "Told 'em to have the cash in advance. The address is Tramonto Drive, Pacific Palisades. I'm writin' the street number down. . . ."

"You said they want me to wear that bandit costume I wore at the *Vaquero* opening last week?"

"Same outfit." He stuffed the pen back into his pocket. "Whacha got planned for this aftanoon?"

"Thought I'd see a movie."

"Movies! They gimme a livin' but I ain't seen a pitcher in ten years. No more big stars. Nobody I wanna pay six bucks to see." Harry ripped the page from his pad and handed it to Don. "I suggest you drive out there this aftanoon an' take a look at the setup. Hard to find some of them private estates, an' ya don't wanna get lost tomorrow. Know what I mean?"

"Okay. I'll drive out there," Don said, glancing at the words on the small rectangle of paper, always surprised at Harry's neat handwriting. "Vikki Vernon. Sounds like an actress."

"Maybe she was. Before she became a secretary. Easiest way to find the place is to take Sunset all the way down to the beach, then north on the Coast Highway. Stop in at any gas station an' they'll tell ya how to find Tramonto Drive."

He folded the slip of paper, pushed it into a pocket of his jeans, and brought out a folded twenty. "For that job I did Saturday."

"Thanks, kid, I got another job for ya next week. Shoppin' center in the Valley. They ain't decided which day they're havin' their sale an' we're still discussin' price. I'll set it by Monday. Call me 'round noon, if I ain't called you."

"Sure, Harry. I'll do that."

"Lotsa people seen you at that *Vaquero* pree-meer. Never had so many calls before."

"Yeah?"

" 'Nother one today. This guy's talkin' 'bout havin' you for a party he's throwin' for his wife. Asked if you had a white sailor outfit. Ya know? The kind they wore in the Navy durin' World War II? With them bell-bottom trousers . . ."

"Velma Splain will know where I can pick one up."

"Don't go to no trouble till I fix a date. Seems this guy was a sailor when he met the dame he married. Still married to her!" He smiled, something he rarely did. "Ya know, kid, you been doin' pretty good lately. An' I'm tryin' to raise your price again."

"Yeah?"

"I asked this Navy character for a hundred an' fifty, an' he didn't even quiver. That'll be three hundred for two hours. Howsat?"

"Terrific!" He realized, as he got up to leave, that his hands were no longer trembling.

16

The ragged palm tree was gone.

Some bastard had cut it down while he was away from his desk. Or it could have been done this morning when he couldn't see anything because of the heavy smog.

He'd returned from the autopsy half an hour ago, but had been checking reports and talking on the phone, facing the door, not looking toward the windows.

The empty space where the tree had been was like the hole left in a face after a front tooth had been knocked out.

He glanced down at the lot, nearer at hand, but it was deserted. That Mexican woman had probably gone home to the barrio to cook dinner for her husband and five kids.

Without them, the Mexican woman and the palm tree, there was nothing worth looking at from his windows.

This had been a bad day from the start, in the middle of the night, when they called from Hollywood Division reporting a rape in Nichols Canyon.

An overweight girl who ate jelly beans and baked strawberry pies. She would've made some guy a good wife.

He had paced the autopsy room, beyond the harsh circle of light pouring from overhead onto the gleaming metal table.

He always attended the final rites performed on any victim whose death sent him seeking their killer.

The coroner had turned from the table, peeling off his rubber gloves, to tell him what they had found. Cause of death was the result of a severe concussion or a broken neck. Either one could've killed her. She'd been unconscious from the moment her head struck that rock.

So now the Jogger was a murderer as well as a rapist, and two men from the murder squad of the Sheriff's Department task force had joined the investigation.

And he—Victor Lolo—had to find the Jogger fast. Put him behind bars or send a bullet through his head.

Except he'd never yet shot a man, even though he always carried a gun while on duty.

Most likely he would kill the guy with his fists. If he ever got his hands on him . . .

In the past hour he'd reviewed everything that was known about him. Read all the notes in his file folder, each typed report and flimsy that had come to him since the first day of his involvement with the case.

This afternoon he would send out a new memo to every division, asking them to look for a Caucasian male, approximately twenty-five, medium weight and height, with pale gray or blue eyes and dark blond hair that, in certain lights, had a burnished-copper look. Suspect could be driving an old gray or dusty black Volkswagen and he likes snakes. . . .

All these facts had gone out in separate memos but had never before been condensed into one. Maybe this time some cop would notice the car and get the license number.

He could only pray for luck now. Hope for a break of some sort . . .

That's how most cases were solved, somebody phoning in with a single small piece of information that held the answer to everything.

He wouldn't sleep tonight. His small apartment would be like a cell. He would be the prisoner, pacing in his bare feet, moving from room to room, standing at each window, hoping for a breath of fresh air.

Where was the Jogger at this moment? Still asleep, like an exhausted animal that returns to its cave after a kill?

Had he meant to kill this girl?

It could've been an accident. . . .

Maybe he didn't know that rock was there.

Was his cave in Los Angeles? Hollywood, most likely . . .

He'd suspected, since last week, that the Jogger hadn't raped a girl in Hollywood because that was where he lived, but last night's victim was found in Nichols Canyon and that was on the edge of Hollywood.

A matter of two or three blocks . . .

That psychiatrist at U.C.L.A. had talked about limbo.

The Jogger existed in limbo but with a roof, a door, and a street number.

Where was this guy's limbo?

And unless he relaxed somewhere for a few hours later today, he was going to find himself in limbo tonight.

He needed to talk to someone, not about the Jogger or any of his other investigations, but about more pleasant things.

If he stepped outside his office into the long marble corridors, he would hear nothing but cop talk. The foul language and obscene jokes of his fellow officers had never amused him, and since his last promotion he seldom took part in such conversations. Because of this he knew they called him an oddball and a loner.

And he was!

Even back home, in the islands, he'd never had more than

two or three close friends. His life had been spent with his family and the girl who was to be his wife.

What could he do this evening to relax? Maybe a quiet dinner at his favorite Mexican restaurant, the only one that reminded him of Pago Pago. They didn't have Samoan food, but there was a happy, smiling crowd enjoying good food to the sound of Mexican music.

Restaurants back home had roofs of tin or were thatched with palm fronds. Some had no walls and stood open to the Pacific breezes. All the people looked happy. Many were friends of his family.

In Los Angeles restaurants, the only people he ever recognized were fellow cops with their wives or with some broad they'd picked up for the night. He always felt alone in Los Angeles.

Except for Morita! But this was Friday. . . .

Maybe she would be free for dinner.

He snatched up the phone and dialed. Turned, as he waited, to stare at the empty space that had always held a palm tree. That old tree had been a permanent reminder of Samoa and now it was gone. . . .

"Madame Rouvray's residence."

"How are you, Georges?"

"Ah! Monsieur Victor."

"Is she there?"

"Of course, Monsieur. Un moment . . ."

He stared at the sky, barely visible between the high office buildings, until the extension was lifted.

"Mon flic! Where are you?"

"Downtown. I know it's Friday, and late to be calling, but I wondered if you'd be free for an early dinner?"

"I was expecting you to call, so I've kept the evening free."

"Did you!"

"I read in the paper about your Jogger. Knew you'd be having a bad day and hoped you might call for dinner. And since you are very tired and I always prefer a quiet restaurant, what about Trader Vic's?"

He smiled. "I was about to suggest the same place."

"I've already made a reservation for seven. That gives you time to go home. Shower and change . . ."

"I'll pick you up at six-thirty."

"Perfect. We'll take the Rolls. Then you won't have to drive. I also wanted to see you this evening for a very special reason. I have a surprise for you. A very big surprise . . ."

"I don't like surprises."

"I hope you will like this one. I've made several decisions. Big decisions, chéri. But I won't tell you what they are until after dinner. A bientôt . . ."

17

The address on Tramonto Drive was spelled out in metal numbers on a white brick wall on both sides of the impressive entrance.

As Don slowed the Honda, he saw tall grilled gates standing open and a fancy house at the end of the drive. Lots of flowers and trees. Several old cars, probably belonging to workmen or servants, were parked along the drive.

Continuing on past the entrance, he slowed to a stop and sat there at the side of the road, eyes and ears alert.

The only sound came from some birds in a row of trees lining the street in front of the next house. All these estates had walls around them and glimpses of gardens through closed gates.

He got out of the car and walked back slowly toward the open gates.

He'd had no trouble finding the address.

He wondered who lived here. Whoever they were, they'd seen him at the opening of Carlo Dario's picture last week.

He was no longer thinking about last night. He'd learned to do that, so nothing disturbed him. He could clear his mind and forget everything unpleasant. He only thought about what he wanted to remember. The good things. Like when he was with Ella and Tomas . . .

Reaching the entrance to the property, he hesitated, peering up and down Tramonto Drive.

There wasn't any traffic moving.

Why were these gates open and all the others closed? Maybe, like at Velma's, everybody had gone out and they'd left the gates open for their return.

That would be foolish. Leaving their house empty.

There must be servants. A place this big would have several.

Better be careful.

Stepping forward, cautiously, he looked up the drive toward the house. It was what, in California, they called a villa—whatever that might be—kind of low, one story, with a tiled roof and an arched entrance over closed double doors. The house seemed to be spread out, with many rooms and lots of windows. There was a wide stretch of lawn in front on both sides of the drive, with flower beds. White roses in Mexican pots on either side of the entrance.

From far away he could hear the whirr of a lawn mower. It must take several gardeners to take care of a place this big. The owner had to be rich.

There weren't any people or cars in sight. Garages would be in the rear.

He wanted to get a closer look at the house.

Moving off the drive into a narrow space between the outer wall and shrubbery, he bent low and darted toward the side of the property—a trick he'd learned in Texas, when he wanted to check some big old mansion behind a high wall.

These walls in California were much lower, the properties smaller.

He was careful not to crush any plants with his sandals, so the gardeners wouldn't notice someone had been here and report a prowler.

Nobody could see him moving behind these bushes.

He kept going until he reached the side wall and followed that until he reached a spot where he faced a terrace at the back, with patio furniture and striped parasols. No sign of family or servants, but a gardener was mowing the grass.

There were more flowers back here. Some of them, in the distance, seemed to be in a separate garden. Lots of flowers.

He saw where the drive continued on to a row of garages far in the back. All the garage doors were open and the parking spaces empty.

Maybe they would let him do his act on the back terrace.

He looked forward to this party. There would probably be some important movie people here with their kids.

Some children really believed he was a mechanical figure, although there was usually one smartass boy who suspected the truth and would kick or pinch him.

Stepping carefully, not making a sound, he edged farther toward the rear. Now he had a better view of the terrace. It was much larger than it seemed at first.

Someone was coming out from the house.

He ducked down behind a bush and cautiously peeped out. Two people. A tall woman, her black hair streaked with white, and a short woman who looked Mexican. The tall one was doing all the talking, explaining something about the terrace, maybe planning for tomorrow's party. The Mexican woman was wearing a blue uniform, so she must be a maid or the cook.

The tall woman could be the wife of the owner. She was sun-tanned and wearing a black sweater with gray slacks and leather sandals, a gold chain around her neck with a big medal of some sort hanging in front that swayed as she walked. She looked to be middle-aged, not pretty. He hadn't seen her at that opening last week.

She didn't look in his direction, and as they moved across the terrace, toward the distant flower garden, Don turned and slowly made his way back the way he had come.

Suddenly he had a terrific idea. He'd never thought of such a thing before. But then, he'd never worked at a fancy place like this. Private parties had been mostly in Hollywood apartments full of creeps. This was a big estate owned by rich people.

He would be able to get a better look around tomorrow, maybe see inside the house. Check everything. Rich people were careless about money. These people didn't lock their gates. Maybe they wouldn't lock their windows.

What if he came back next week and robbed them? Take nothing but cash. You couldn't trace money. Maybe five hundred or a thousand!

With what he had in the bank, that would get him to Mexico and keep him going until he could find a job. He wouldn't be able to do his mechanical-man act in Mexico. Not in a small village, and that's where he wanted to live. A village like the one where he had lived with Ella and Tomas.

He would never be able to find that one because he'd never known its name.

Most of all, he wanted to locate that mountain where Tomas had held him in his arms and showed him a view of the valley. He couldn't have been much more than three years old. . . .

And he would find another snake in Mexico. One exactly like Satan. His first Satan . . .

Have to think about this. Make careful plans . . .

Reaching the open gates, he hesitated but saw no sign of life in any direction. He ducked low and went out through the open gates into Tramonto Drive, then straightened and ran toward his car.

18

The elegant restaurant was quiet, as always, in spite of its crowded tables. There was muted laughter from time to time, and the faint sound of drawn corks. Conversation was low and laughter discreet.

As they ate dinner, Lolo studied Morita across the table. She was the only woman he'd ever known who looked even more beautiful when she was eating. Perhaps because she ate with such appetite. Tonight her glossy black hair was swept high on top of her head, where it was arranged in a thick coil twined with pearls, and she was wearing a plain yellow dress that made the other women look overdressed. Around her shoulders was a white scarf embroidered with a design of silver and violet.

She glanced at him provocatively, but said nothing.

He picked up the delicate wineglass in his brown fingers, uncomfortably aware of their size, and drained the last of his wine.

Driving here in the black Rolls, they'd enjoyed a glass of champagne from the built-in bar as a new Montand number played on the stereo. Riding in the silent Rolls with silver-haired Georges in his gray uniform at the wheel was like floating across a dark pool in Samoa.

Lolo looked up as the waiter refilled their wineglasses and wondered if he was Hawaiian. The youth wasn't tall enough—or heavy enough—to be Samoan.

Morita gave the waiter one of her flashing smiles and, as he departed with their empty wine bottle, turned back to her food. "These prawns are delicious. A perfect dinner . . ."

"It's Polynesian deluxe. Better than I ever ate in Samoa."

"There are several Chino-Polynesian restaurants in Paris, but none serve food as subtle as this. My favorite restaurant in Los Angeles! Our first meal together was here. At your suggestion. And I've never eaten here with anyone but you, mon flic."

He raised his glass. "To us . . ."

She snatched up her wineglass. "Toujours à nous!"

They drank, their eyes locked across the table, set the glasses down, and gave their attention to the food again.

He was grateful that she hadn't mentioned last night's murder, had asked no questions. He'd pushed the Jogger out of his thoughts, at least until tomorrow morning. He was aware that she was waiting for him to speak before starting a conversation. "You've never told me . . ."

She looked up, smiling, from her plate. "Yes?"

"How long Georges has worked for you. Where you found him."

"Georges is the perfect servant, but he isn't a servant at all. And I didn't find him. He and his wife were a gift."

"What do you mean?"

"A precious gift. I pay them an enormous salary, of course. Georges is my major-domo, my butler, chauffeur, and bodyguard. . . ."

"Bodyguard?"

"He carries a gun at all times."

"Does he?"

"For which, of course, he has a proper license. And his wife, Claire, is my proxy mother and confidante. My own dear Maman knows her and approves."

"Your mother found them for you to bring to California?"

"No. Although she was delighted. I've told you—one of my protectors in France was an official of the Sûreté."

"Your Paris flic!"

"Georges was also a flic. But, of course, not mine!"

"In Paris?"

"Starting as a young gendarme in Pigalle and promoted,

year after year, up through the ranks to Inspector. He was retiring when I was preparing to leave for the United States. My protector knew Georges was unhappy about living in the country on his pension and spending the rest of his life gardening. Knew that both of them—Claire and Georges—had always talked of living in California. He brought them to meet me and, of course, I adored them instantly. Georges is making more money than he ever earned at the Sûreté and Claire loves it here. It is a perfect arrangement and in the future will be even more perfect for all three of us."

"They're also very fortunate."

"And so am I!"

They finished the last of the wine as their dinner plates were removed.

Lolo frowned unconsciously, remembering how little he had accomplished today.

"All evening, mon flic, I have been thinking of our future. Planning for both of us! You and I . . . While you sit there scowling, worrying about your missing Jogger."

"Was I? Yes, I was. I'm sorry." He smiled. "You said on the phone you have some sort of surprise. . . ."

"I do, indeed! And I must tell you about it—in a moment—because it concerns you."

"Does it?"

"A decision must be made."

"By whom?"

"By you, chéri. I've already reached my own decision."

"Pardon, Madame. Monsieur . . ."

They looked up to see the sommelier.

"Would Madame care for a cognac?"

"I would like champagne," Morita announced solemnly.

Lolo nodded. "A bottle of Pommery. Same vintage we had last time."

"Certainly, Lieutenant." He bowed and departed.

Morita lowered her voice. "This is a very important evening in my life."

"Is it?"

"And yours."

"Every evening I spend with you is important."

"These next few moments will be a turning point in both our lives."

"I've never heard you this serious before."

"Love is the most serious thing in one's life. Not sex, but love."

"I agree."

"I'm about to make you a proposition. Two propositions."

"What do you mean?"

"First of all, I've a business proposition to offer you. . . ."

"Business?"

"And after that, a more personal proposition . . ." She glanced toward the distant bar. "Before I do this I require a glass of champagne to give me the courage to speak directly and frankly. And honestly." She was smiling again. "After you hear my two propositions—and you must agree to both— we will drink a toast to the future. Our future."

Lolo, puzzled, watched the sommelier returning from the bar with a silver tray that held a wine bucket and two champagne glasses.

He placed a glass in front of each and, after showing the label to Lolo, wrapped the bottle in a napkin to remove the foil and wire net before uncorking the champagne. Poured a swallow for Lolo and, after he tasted it and nodded, filled both glasses.

Lolo raised his glass toward Morita. "To your mysterious propositions. Both of them!"

"I will most certainly drink to them."

They touched glasses and drank, eyes on each other again.

"Maintenant! The glorious moment of truth . . ." Setting her glass down, Morita began: "For the past two years my dear father has been searching for a vineyard in Northern California. One he could buy and expand as the American branch of Château Rouvray. Six months ago I found exactly what Papa wanted in the Napa Valley, and last month, after a thorough personal inspection, he signed all the complicated legal documents. The vineyard's present name will be changed to Rouvray Vineyards. I shall make an announcement through a series of advertisements in the major American magazines next winter. . . ."

Lolo raised his glass again. "My congratulations to your father."

They drank.

"I came to the United States," Morita continued, "to sell the wines of Château Rouvray to the American people. . . ."

"Yes. I know that."

"I haven't told you that I've been completely successful."

"I'm not surprised. I've seen your ads."

"Our American sales have tripled as a result of those advertising campaigns I created."

Once again he lifted his glass.

"Quite simply, Papa wants you to take over as executive manager of his new California vineyards. That is my first proposition."

"Take over?" He set his wineglass down.

"I've written Papa dozens of letters singing your praises."

"But I know nothing about making wine! Only which wines I like to drink."

"You will not need to know a damn thing about the making of wine. The finest of Papa's staff from Château Rouvray are flying over to take charge of the new enterprise—specialists in every phase of viniculture. You'll learn quite enough from them. As I did, before I came to California. You've everything going for you, chéri. Your Polynesian mystique will charm everyone—the men as well as the ladies—and you are accustomed to dealing with people. Judging them . . ."

"Only criminals."

"There are enough criminals in the business world—involved with the marketing of our finished product—to keep you amused. Most important, you've an excellent mind. Searching for answers to every question. Above all, you are honest! The most honest man I've ever known. I'll be working with you, of course. I shall continue to supervise sales and advertising. The two of us—you and I—will run the American branch of Château Rouvray. What do you say?"

"I can't believe your father is serious."

"But he is! I will show you his letters. Dozens of them! From the start he has wanted a young American as manager. Not a stuffy businessman with preconceived ideas. Papa wants you."

"Without knowing me?"

"He trusts my judgment in everything. Especially men. I've sent him extremely flattering descriptions of your experience and your personality."

"Slightly prejudiced?"

"Completely prejudiced. Papa is particularly interested because you are a flic—and a special investigator—with the Los Angeles police. Does this idea appeal to you?"

"I've always dreamed of one day achieving success in the world of business. When I was a kid I wanted to own a fleet of fishing boats. Never thought of being a cop. Or planned to be one. That was an accident. I've told you I studied law. . . ."

"Which will certainly be useful in this setup. The staff of the new vineyards will be French and American. Even Georges will be an important part of our organization."

"Georges?"

"And his wife. Georges is to supervise security matters and shipping. He will do the hiring and handle personnel. Claire's to be in charge of the restaurant—an authentic auberge—which Papa plans to open for visitors to the vineyards. A famous chef will be flown over from France."

"How soon does all this happen?"

"At once. Papa must have your answer within the next two weeks."

"But I can't leave the police until I've caught the Jogger!"

"Damn the Jogger!" She smiled. "Perhaps nobody will ever catch him. Have you considered that?"

"Constantly."

"One thing I haven't told you. You will, of course, have an enormous salary."

"That's always nice."

"And Papa hopes that one day we will give him a golden brown grandson."

"What did you say?"

"That's my second proposition. Considerably more personal than the first. You're the only man I've ever wanted to marry."

"I'll be damned."

"What do you say to that?"

"The man's supposed to propose to the woman. Even in Samoa."

"Does it matter? Anyway, you haven't."

"I've never given any thought to marriage since I arrived in Los Angeles."

"You're still in love with that girl, but it's impossible, mon flic, for anyone to love a ghost."

"I'm aware of that."

"Papa and I must have your answers in two weeks. I phoned him this evening. Told him I was seeing you tonight and would offer you our propositions. Both of them. He was delighted. Papa wants you to manage his new vineyards and I want you to manage me. I love you, mon flic. Truly love you. As I've never loved another man."

"I must sort things out before I can give you—either of you—an answer."

"I realize that. Eh bien! You have two weeks."

He laughed. "I'd better catch that Jogger in one hell of a hurry!"

She picked up her unfinished glass of wine. "I've always gotten everything I ever wanted in my life. Now I want you."

"What about Monday, Tuesday, and Wednesday?"

"I shall never see them again, any of them. I'll send them charming notes of farewell. My week, in the future, will have but one day." She held out her wineglass.

Lolo snatched up his glass and clinked it against hers.

She laughed. "Everyday will be Thursday."

He drank but his eyes were troubled.

19

A beefy middle-aged guard in a tan uniform watched Don shoving his platform toward the open gates. "What the hell you got there? Some kinda dolly?"

"I stand on it." He slowed the platform to a stop. "You havin' a birthday party here?"

"That's right."

"I was told to ask for Vikki Vernon. I do a mechanical-man act."

"Follow this drive 'round to the right. They've put up a tent on the back terrace. You'll find the lady there. She's runnin' the whole damn party. Ask anybody. They'll know where she is."

"Thanks." He rolled his platform up the drive, through bright late-afternoon sunlight, toward the front of the villa where teenagers in red monkey jackets were lined up near the entrance, waiting to park the cars that would soon be arriving.

He'd left his Honda on Tramonto Drive, where several cars were already parked, but as yet none were lined up in here.

Turning right where the drive branched, he pushed his platform toward the side of the villa. A small brown leather suitcase—it had belonged to his mother—containing his costume rested on the platform with his sombrero, leaving both hands free to grasp the metal railing and control the direction of the silent wheels.

No gardeners working in the flower beds today, but everything looked freshly watered.

Turning again, at the corner of the villa, he continued on, past open windows, toward the rear of the property. Now he could hear voices. Lots of people, talking and laughing.

Reaching the remembered terrace at the back, he saw a long refreshment counter under a striped yellow and white canopy where three black waiters in white jackets were arranging glass dishes on serving tables near a row of big metal freezers that must hold a lot of ice cream. A white-and-red-striped canvas tent had been set up on the terrace. All the sides were raised and he could see that a wooden floor had been put down for people to dance. White plastic folding chairs circled the outside of the tent with pots of yellow and white daisies that hadn't been here yesterday. More patio chairs around tables under green parasols and, off to one side, an elaborate bar where two scarlet-coated barmen were sorting bottles and glasses.

Behind all this and beyond the edge of the terrace was a view of the distant ocean, far below, sparkling in the sunshine.

Don glanced around to find a good spot for his platform, away from the refreshment counter but not too close to the dance floor because the music would distract him. Maybe near the big windows with sections of sliding glass pushed back so people could go in and out of the villa.

He glimpsed what seemed to be a large living room inside, where people were moving about. Probably servants getting everything ready.

These people must be loaded! Spending so much money for their kid's birthday party.

He rolled his platform to a spot in front of one window but clear of the open ones. In this spot he'd be shaded by a tall sycamore tree and wouldn't have to stand in hot sunlight while he did his act.

He locked his platform in position facing the terrace. There was enough room for him to slip onto it from the back, but nobody would be able to pass behind him. He didn't like it when people did that. Especially kids.

Picking up his suitcase and sombrero, he carried them

toward a plump black maid who was wiping one of the plastic chairs with a cloth. "Where can I find Ms. Vikki Vernon?" he asked.

She straightened from her work and motioned toward the open tent. "That thin lady in black slacks. That's her."

"Thanks." He saw as he approached the tent that it was the woman he'd seen yesterday. She was middle-aged. Tall and skinny. Straight black hair with some white, cut like a man's. As he crossed the dance floor, he noticed she was wearing black slacks and a plain gray shirt today, with some kind of metal ornament hanging from a silver chain. She was telling two guys in coveralls how she wanted potted flowers placed around a low bandstand at the far side of the tent. She had an English accent.

"You understand? In a row."

"Sure thing. Brought extra pots. We'll get more from the truck."

She noticed Don as they left. "Hello! You look lost. Can I help you?"

"I'm Don Farrell. I do the mechanical-man act."

"But you're so young. I had no idea." She smiled. "I saw you last week at the premiere. I thought you were smashing."

"Thank you, ma'am." He flashed one of his special little-boy smiles.

"It was Mrs. Dario's idea to have you perform this afternoon for their son's party."

"Mrs. Dario?"

"Mrs. Carlo Dario. I'm the Darios' secretary. We both thought the children might enjoy your act and you could help keep them quiet," she said, pulling several small white envelopes from a pocket of her blouse. "I have your fee." She glanced at the envelopes. "Two hundred for two hours."

"That's right."

"Jolly good!" She handed him one of the envelopes and returned the others to her pocket. "Your agent said cash."

"Thanks." He saw MECHANICAL MAN typed on the envelope, with 200 underneath.

"You've brought that same costume you were wearing last week?"

"Yes. Where can I change?"

"The man who's doing a clown act is changing in the dressing room down by the pool. You can use the powder room." She called to the maid. "Minnie! Can I bother you for a moment?"

The maid put down her dust cloth and hurried toward them.

"You can leave your clothes in the cupboard. Nobody will bother anything in there."

"Yes, ma'am." He slipped the envelope, unopened, into a pocket of his sport shirt as the maid joined them.

"Minnie, will you show Mr. Farrell to the powder room? He's going to change in there. What's the best place for you to do your act, Mr. Farrell?"

"I work on a small platform."

"I know you do."

"I've already placed it in front of that big window."

"Oh?" She turned to look. "That's a perfect spot. Hope the little monsters won't distract you too much. They can be a nuisance."

"I'm used to working with kids."

"I'll be here somewhere if you need anything."

He followed the smiling maid through the open window and across an enormous living room where several women were talking and laughing. No sign of Carlo Dario or his wife. None of the women glanced at him as the maid led him toward a large entrance foyer. The front doors stood open and he saw the parking attendants outside, waiting for more guests to arrive.

The maid opened a door on one side of the tiled foyer.

"Is Mr. Dario goin' to be here?" he asked.

"Couldn't say. Ain't seen him all afternoon." She chuckled. "But then, days go by an' I never see him. When he's off somewhere makin' another movie. Better lock this door while you're inside."

"I'll do that." He went into the powder room, closing the door and snapping the lock. He saw that there was a mirrored makeup table with a fancy pink satin armchair in addition to a pink washbowl and toilet. Neat piles of hand towels were laid out on a low table.

He set the suitcase down, resting his sombrero on the makeup table, then opened the cupboard where shallow pink shelves held fresh bars of soap and more towels. He'd never seen so many clean towels. He would leave his suitcase in there on the floor.

Don removed his short black wig and set it on the makeup table. He opened his suitcase and brought out the long-haired black wig.

Then, slowly and automatically, he stripped and put on his costume. First the tight black cord trousers. He pushed them inside his white socks, then put on the elaborately decorated leather cowboy boots and pulled them up over his trousers. Next came the embroidered Mexican shirt with its ruffled cuffs.

Then he put on the long black wig and combed it carefully. Placed the short wig and comb in the suitcase. Snapped that shut. Left it in the cupboard and closed the door.

Next he buckled the leather gun holster around his waist, the fake revolver on his left hip.

Tonight he'd brought his snakeskin vest, which he hadn't worn for Carlo Dario's opening because it would've been too hot under all the lights. He didn't button it down the front, because it looked better hanging open. People could see his Mexican shirt.

He draped the bandolier with its wooden bullets over his right shoulder so it hung down his left side.

Carefully adjusted the sombrero over his wig and tied the leather thongs beneath his chin.

After he was finished, he stepped back to study the full effect in the large mirror hanging above a table. Not bad!

He looked like Carlo Dario, but he also looked like Tomas. His father . . .

Last of all he pulled on the gray rubber gloves, tucking them under his ruffled sleeves. Then the soft black leather gauntlets over the rubber gloves.

Now he must prepare himself to do his act. Rid his mind of disturbing thoughts.

He made his way back through the living room toward the open windows.

A larger group of women stood in front of a big stone

fireplace filled with potted flowers, talking and laughing, while several small children were tossing pillows on a white sofa that must be fifteen feet long.

He avoided looking at them and nobody glanced at him as he passed.

There were other sofas and lots of tables with big lamps. The place was like a hotel lobby. Comfortable chairs, flowers in large bowls, paintings on the wall facing the long wall of windows with their view of the patio.

Outside, moving quickly, he edged along the window and stepped onto his platform, still unnoticed. As his body began to relax, he let his eyes dart in every direction.

The bandstand was now circled with daisies in white pots, and a long-haired blond musician in a shiny silver jacket was tuning his drums. Across the terrace was a shelved aluminum cart on wheels, and a young guy dressed in white—from shoes to tall chef's hat—was pulling out metal trays with plates of fancy food and arranging them on long tables covered with red tablecloths. The black waiters were setting up racks of ice-cream cones on their refreshment counter.

Don became aware of someone standing close to him, on his right, and was surprised to face a clown in full costume and makeup. He saw at once that his own clown costume was better.

"Hi! You the mechanical man? I hear you gotta great act. My name's Clyde."

"I'm Don." He held out his gauntleted hand and watched the clown's bare hand shake it and pull away fast.

"Wow! You gotta artificial arm?"

"Trade secret."

"We all got 'em. Why don't we have a beer after we finish here?"

"Sure. Why not?"

"Okay, Don. See ya later. Watch out for these kids. They're killers."

Don looked around to see a sudden rush of small children, laughing and screaming, come running across the terrace.

The clown skipped along with them, grasping two little girls by their hands and dancing them toward the refreshment counter.

Music blasted from the bandstand unexpectedly.

He turned to see three freakish-looking guys in silver jackets playing "Over the Rainbow." A middle-aged couple wearing shorts and sunglasses was already dancing. More children, along with some older people, spilled out from the villa, hurrying toward the music.

Nobody noticed him yet.

He saw Vikki Vernon moving among the guests, conspicuous in her plain gray shirt and black slacks. They were like a uniform.

Turning to the window and peering into the big living room, he saw there were more people inside, talking like they were old friends. They must be coming in through the front entrance. More children running and playing games.

No sign of Carlo Dario.

"Hiya, Don."

The voice startled him and he looked around to see an old man dressed in what Velma called "Mischa's Eyetalian outfit" and carrying a brightly painted hand organ with a small monkey in a duplicate costume perched on top. "Mischa! How are ya?"

"Can't complain, kid. Still livin' in the Coop?"

"Sure am."

"How's Velma?"

"Same's always."

"Tell her I was askin' for her."

"I'll do that."

"See ya later. Gotta start workin'. The lady awready paid me. C'mon, Tarzan!" Patting the monkey on the head. "Doncha bite nobody today." He began to revolve the handle of his hand organ, but its wheezy tune was soon lost in the music from the combo.

Don had met Mischa soon after he came to Los Angeles. The Russian worked as an extra at all the studios and was an old friend of the Splains.

He would duck both of them—Mischa and that clown—when he finished here. Change his clothes and take off fast.

Better start his act.

He let his body slump into a pose that looked awkward but was easy to hold. Felt muscles relaxing as his mind shut out all sounds. Began to move his arms, jerking them abruptly, aware that a few people were stopping to watch him.

His hands were getting cold under the two pairs of gloves and the temperature of his body was dropping.

For another five or ten minutes he would be somewhere between reality and a state of suspended consciousness, aware of everything but slipping toward that moment when he'd be performing automatically, without seeing faces and unaware of what happened around him unless some loud noise or sudden motion caught his attention and pulled him back to reality.

He realized that a blurred flash of red and white was the clown turning somersaults.

More of the parents were dancing. They reminded him of Texas. . . .

That day Mrs. Dinwoodie made him go to dancing class. He was so shy he wouldn't dance with any of the little girls. The skinny woman who taught them pulled him from a corner across the slippery floor and ordered him to dance with one of the girls. The minute she let go of him he'd run out of the room and fled across the open field behind the school. He must've been eight or nine years old. Mrs. Dinwoodie never made him go to dancing class again. That was when everybody thought he couldn't talk. He'd fooled them. All of them . . .

He remembered another time. He was in high school—that was California and he was talking—and there was that girl who was so plain. He'd never seen such a plain girl! He'd gone to his senior class dance and noticed her across the room. Except for a few parents and teachers, they were the only ones not dancing. He'd felt so sorry for her, he circled the dance floor to where she sat on a wooden bench.

She had looked up, surprised.

He could still see her big brown eyes. That's when he made his big mistake. "Don't you like to dance?" he asked.

"I love to dance!" She was on her feet, holding out her arms.

"I—I'm sorry. I don't know how."

He remembered how her smile had faded before he turned and, without looking back, hurried outside into the night.

When he returned to his foster home Mrs. Parsons had punished him, beat him with a leather strap that had belonged to her dead husband. Because he lied. She wouldn't believe he'd been sitting alone in the stable behind the gym. She tried to make him say which girl he'd been with. "Did you touch her? Have sex with her?" He kept telling her the truth, but she only beat him harder. Told him he'd be damned in hell for lying.

He ran away again that night. Headed north . . .

A small child squealed. Loud and up close.

He forced himself back to the present and saw a small boy with reddish-blond hair, squirming in Ms. Vernon's arms.

"This is a wonderful mechanical man, sweetheart. Like a real man. A present for your birthday."

"No! No . . ." The boy shook his head violently, trying to escape.

"I saw him at your Daddy's premiere last week. He's dressed just like Daddy in the movie. Like a Mexican vaquero. Your Mommy thought you'd like to see him."

"No, Vikki! Put me down."

"All right." She set him down reluctantly and shrugged as she looked up at Don. "He'll be back later. I promise you."

Don watched her pursue the child through the crowd as his body continued performing.

He had seen Carlo Dario's son. . . .

A group of slightly older children, chasing one another, were silenced as they came upon him and stood staring. Boys in front, girls giggling behind them. All about the same age, five or six, dressed in their best for the party.

Raising his right arm suddenly, he swooped down. His gloved forefinger pointed at the nearest boy, who squealed and stumbled back.

"Teddy's a coward!" Another boy's voice. "A big coward!"

"I am not!"

The second boy came closer, acting brave, and grabbed the outstretched hand.

He saw the kid's eyes widen with surprise.

"It's a wooden hand!"

The others pushed forward and a girl reached toward his gauntleted hand.

Don jerked his arm back abruptly before she could touch him.

All the children retreated, squealing, toward the refreshment counter, where the waiters were handing out cones with double scoops of ice cream.

Rich kids had everything but didn't appreciate anything. Always throwing tantrums. Screaming and kicking . . .

Some of the parents glanced at him as they passed. He saw they were carrying birthday presents in fancy wrappings. Every size and shape. Expensive looking. They piled them on a large table off to one side near the refreshment counter.

Don saw no sign of that clown or Mischa with his monkey. They must be working the other side of the terrace.

Nobody ever gave him a birthday party when he was four years old.

He continued his act automatically as he tried to remember where he had lived when he was four.

San Antonio? Dallas? He couldn't be sure. . . .

Ella said that Tomas left them for good when they lived in El Paso. But that was when he was six.

Did he have a party that year? Not likely . . .

Ella might've baked a little cake for him with one candle stuck in the top. But he couldn't even recall that. . . .

He got only one present for his birthdays after Tomas left them. A candy bar under his pillow when he woke in the morning or beside his plate when he sat down for breakfast. Sometimes there would be a new shirt or a pair of shoes. . . .

He looked around as he heard a man's voice above all the other voices and the music. Carlo Dario! He had come out of the villa with an older man and they were heading across the terrace.

Don froze. Maybe Carlo would notice him.

They didn't glance in his direction as they passed. Carlo was greeting friends, shaking hands with the men and kissing the women.

The crowd was much larger now.

As Don observed the people, he continued to perform— arms moving, body twisting—automatically.

He looked for Carlo but the actor had disappeared.

A young security guard, in uniform like the guy at the front gate, was moving through the crowd, peering in every direction.

This party must be costing Carlo Dario a fortune. Movie stars had so much money, they didn't know what to do with it.

Two men to his left stood with their backs to him, talking. He recognized Carlo's voice but couldn't make out what he was saying. They hadn't gone far! The actor and the older man.

As more people hurried out from the villa, Carlo greeted them, moving back a little as they passed.

Don slowed the rhythms of his body as he tried to hear what they were saying. He turned his face away slightly so he wouldn't seem to be listening, but strained to catch their conversation.

The actor's voice was more distinct, deeper than the other man's. ". . . and I want no part of their lousy script."

"You've read it?"

"Even worse than the last."

"I agree, but your fans will love it."

"They would have to be morons. I'm surprised any of the critics liked *Vaquero*, but I can't believe they'll sit through this tripe."

"Unfortunately, you have no script approval."

"My contract doesn't say I have to accept every piece of trash they want me to do! At least tell them I don't like the damn script."

"I will. First thing Monday."

The guy must be Carlo's agent. Don was aware, as they talked, that the man kept looking up at him. He was surprised by what the guy said next.

"Did you like Adriana's surprise for your son's birthday?"

"What surprise?"

"Turn around. Look behind you."

Don was conscious of Carlo turning as he went into a series of motions with his arms and legs. Now Carlo had to notice him.

"What the hell's this?" Carlo asked.

"Mechanical man." The agent moved closer and Carlo followed. "Didn't you see him at the *Vaquero* opening?"

"Where?"

"At the entrance. As we went inside."

"No. I didn't. Whose idea was this?"

"Publicity boys, at the studio."

"This guy's supposed to look like me?"

"Well . . . Something like that."

"Big deal!" He turned away, the agent following, and went toward the villa. "I want you to tell them this new script's impossible. . . ."

Moving more slowly, Don watched them go inside. The actor hadn't looked at him last week and now, when he did, all the bastard could say was "big deal." Don seethed with disappointment as he continued to do his act. Nobody was noticing him now. Carlo might've at least said he was good, that his act was terrific. . . .

Conceited bastard. He hated Carlo Dario. . . .

Better forget the whole thing. At least for the moment. Empty his head of everything negative.

That's what the yogi in Frisco had always told him. Clear everything that's not positive from your mind. Think only relaxing thoughts. Think peace. . . .

He shut out the voices and the music, the shrill screams of the kids, and continued performing, no longer aware of anything. Enclosed in silence . . .

Driving up that mountain with Tomas and Ella. The old Chevy in trouble. Creeping around each sudden curve in the road . . .

His mother telling him not to look down until after they reached the top.

Tomas holding the wheel with both hands, singing old Mexican songs.

The Chevy coughing and rattling, like it was falling apart.

His father laughing a lot, more than he'd ever heard him laugh before.

He wondered if Tomas had had *Don Quixote* in his pocket that day?

Such a happy day . . .

He couldn't have been more than four.

Did he really remember what happened when they drove up that mountain, or only what Ella told him had happened?

His mother repeated the story many times.

He didn't even know where they went that day. Ella said it was Mexico, but she couldn't remember the towns they visited. Villages, across the border from El Paso. Somewhere in Chihuahua . . .

Did they have mountains in Chihuahua?

Tomas said they could see for miles when they reached the top.

Was it a mountain or only a hill? He would never know until he saw it again. That was something he had to do. Find Tomas' mountain.

When the car finally came to a stop, he couldn't see a thing. Only gray mist that covered the whole world.

Or had Ella told him that and he only imagined seeing the mist?

She had spread out a cloth on the grass and opened all the paper bags they had brought filled with food. He'd never seen so much food before and never saw that much again. . . .

Tomas had opened cans of beer from a bucket filled with ice and poured some into paper cups for him and Don. He remembered that! First beer he'd ever tasted. He could still feel the cold bite of it on his tongue, the warmth spreading through his body.

The mist had disappeared as they ate and a pale yellow sun sent golden rays across the endless green valley.

Tomas had held him up, balanced on one hand. "Look at that, niño! You may never see such a sight again!"

He had looked down into the deep valley and hadn't been afraid, but Ella had screamed, afraid Tomas would drop him.

Some day soon he would drive back to Mexico. Follow his father's map. Find that mountain again . . .

They had spent the night with a Mexican family in some village, all of them crowded into one room. The people had seemed to be old friends of Ella and Tomas. The woman cooked dinner over an open fire and there was dancing and singing and nobody had slept. Don finally did and woke the next morning against something warm and soft. Discovered it was a goat. When he kissed his mother, she had laughed but Tomas shouted: "My son stinks like a goat!"

He wondered if that was where his father went when he left

them, back to that village where he had friends. Back to his mountain . . .

Tomas' map would take him there. He would find his father or someone who would know where he was. . . .

He became aware of children's voices again, looked down and saw Carlo's son with a little girl.

They were staring at him, wide-eyed and solemn. Studying him.

"It's not a real man," the boy was saying.

The girl giggled. "Big toy!"

"You 'fraid of it?"

"No. Are you?"

Don dived toward them suddenly, gloved finger pointing. They jumped back, squealing, and turned to escape through the crowd.

Don drew back and thought of the only real birthday party he'd ever had.

Mrs. Harper . . .

She was the kindest of his foster parents. Some had been jailers but she was kind. The only one who reminded him of Ella. Mrs. Harper was a widow, her children grown up and moved away, so she raised other people's children the court turned over to her. One at a time. Said she didn't have the energy to be a mother to more than one.

He was talking then—that was Bakersfield—and told her his name was Jerry Farrell, but he didn't know what year he was born or which month. And he had no idea where he was born.

Mrs. Harper followed astrology charts in the newspapers and bought magazines that told her about how the stars influenced your life. She was always working out her chart, telling him what was going to happen. Good and bad. She was an Aries and said that, unfortunately, anyone who had that sign was sort of flighty. He'd been with her several months when she said she was convinced he was a Virgo. She could tell by the way he acted, things he said and did. His birth date was probably September, near the middle of the month, but she picked September thirteenth. She said thirteen was a lucky number. His mother had always said the same thing.

He felt a slight chill move through his flesh and saw that the sun had dropped behind some eucalyptus trees.

The dance floor was crowded, mostly with adults. The children had gathered in a mass of frantic activity on the far side, beyond the tent, and were lined up at the refreshment counter.

Standing there, motionless for a moment, Don became furious again at Carlo Dario. Not noticing him at the opening of his movie. Saying, tonight, he hadn't seen him. *"This guy's supposed to look like me?"* Arrogant bastard . . .

"Would you care for some ice cream?"

He looked down at a dish of ice cream held by a young woman with red hair. It was the redhead who'd been with Carlo Dario at the opening.

"I'm Mrs. Dario."

"Thanks. I never eat anything while I'm working."

"I understand." She smiled again.

He realized her eyes didn't turn away as he stared at her. He'd stopped doing his act and was gripping the railing of his platform with both gloved hands. A necklace around her neck sparkled with diamonds.

"I asked Vikki to see if she could get you to perform here today. We both thought the children would enjoy seeing you. Are you an actor?"

"No, ma'am. I just do this."

"Well, you're very good."

"Thanks."

"Your agent told Vikki that you also perform at private parties for adults. Not only for children."

"Yes, ma'am. I do."

"Well! Next time we give an evening party, I'll have Vikki call you again. See if you're free."

"That would be great."

"I suppose your act is different for adults."

"Oh, yes."

"That should be interesting. This ice cream's starting to melt, and I must get back to our guests. If you want ice cream later, there's lots more." She hesitated, looking up at him and smiling again, then turned and carried the dish toward the refreshment counter.

A nice lady. She talked to him. Not like her lousy husband. And she had smiled at him, like at the opening.

Her smile and red hair still reminded him of Ella. About the same height. His mother hadn't been much older. That night they took her to the hospital . . .

He wondered if she was happy with her husband. Did she love him? The way Ella loved Tomas . . .

Don turned and looked through the big glass window into the living room. Women were sitting on all the sofas, talking and having drinks. He'd never seen such a big room, except in a movie.

He faced the terrace again. There were more people now, and the children were running and shouting. The combo was playing louder to make itself heard.

Nobody looking at him.

Standing there, holding onto the railing of his platform, he had an idea. A way to have enough money to get to Mexico and find that village and Tomas' mountain. Find Tomas . . .

He would come back here at night, and he would take the money from Carlo Dario. Or take something he could turn into money.

He needed five hundred bucks. Maybe a thousand.

What about those diamonds Carlo's wife was wearing? They had to be diamonds. He could sell them easily once he got to Mexico.

They were her diamonds, but Carlo had paid for them. And they would be insured, so they wouldn't lose anything.

He began to study the terrace more carefully as he resumed his act, checking each window.

So many windows that some of them were sure to be left open at night.

He would come back one night next week.

Five

20

Don watched the two Mexican kids as they ran toward a distant corner of the new shopping mall, still tossing that floppy plastic bag they had passed back and forth while they were watching him. The older boy had it hanging over his shoulder as they turned the corner. They were up to something. Maybe collecting yesterday's vegetables from trash cans behind the supermarket.

This was probably the last job he'd be doing for a while. Maybe for a long time.

He told Harry Sneal when he paid him his commission for Saturday's birthday party that he was going up to Frisco for a while and wouldn't be free for any more jobs, including the private party where that guy wanted him to wear a sailor outfit for his wife.

If he got enough loot from Carlo Dario's house, he would never come back to L.A. again.

He was going to follow Tomas' trail on that map. Across northern Mexico.

Tijuana, Mexicali, Nogales . . . All the way to Ciudad Juárez!

It was too hot today for the clown costume and rubber mask, so he'd worn his spaceman outfit: everything white, from helmet to boots, with white gauntlets over his rubber gloves. The white jumpsuit was cool and he wasn't wearing a mask.

157

His platform was protected from the sun by the roof of the arcade facing a central plaza.

This morning he was working in front of a big linen store that was having a summer sale.

Lots of young mothers shopping with children.

Don didn't like the Valley because it was always several degrees warmer than Hollywood, but he'd worked this spot last month and it stayed pretty cool, even on a warm day like this.

His body was moving automatically and he was paying no attention to the row of people in front of him.

After he saw Harry Sneal, he'd withdrawn most of his money from that bank on Hollywood Boulevard. Now the cash was locked in the Coop—almost seven hundred in twenty-dollar bills, including the money from Saturday's job—so he had it ready to leave tonight. Only he wouldn't be going to Frisco. . . .

His thoughts were interrupted by unexpected laughter.

Several women with shopping bags were facing his platform. Some clutched small children by the hand or had them in collapsible baby carriages. They were laughing as they watched something behind him.

He didn't like it when this happened because he knew someone would be standing there who was either taking poses and imitating him or was about to prod him in the back with something.

His body tensed with anticipation.

He continued to move his arms and legs but didn't turn to see what was causing their laughter.

Something fell across his right shoulder. Heavy but kind of soft. Like a piece of rubber hose. Something alive? Moving across his chest, sliding down the left sleeve of his jumpsuit.

A snake!

The women were screaming.

With a quick movement of his right arm, he reached up and snatched the snake from his left shoulder, holding it up where he could see the twisting body.

A king snake. Maybe three feet long.

"Satan . . ." he whispered. "My friend."

The two Mexican kids appeared from behind him. Their eyes were wide as they watched him handle their snake, the

empty plastic bag still dangling from the older boy's hand.
Lifting the snake higher, he tossed it toward them.

The women moved out of the way as it glided into the sun
with the Mexican boys in pursuit.

Don resumed his pose and slipped back into his routine as
the women moved away with their brats. Some of the kids
were crying, frightened by the snake.

Satan! The first snake he ever owned.

That was something Ella had told him later. . . .

He'd been crying and Tomas called him a baby. "Soon
you'll be a man. Can't be afraid of things, niño. Always
crying when you scratch a finger. Can't have no son of mine
acting like a baby."

His father had thrust a big snake into his hand.

He didn't realize, until much later, that it must've been a
little one.

"Always hold a snake behind the head." Tomas had pulled
the snake by its tail until only the eyes looked out from
between his clenched hand. "That's the way, niño! That's my
brave little man."

Ella was furious. "I don't want him to have no snake."

"He'll keep it for his pet. Its name is Satan. All snakes are
named Satan."

Every snake he owned after that—and there had been
dozens—had been named Satan.

His mother wouldn't let the first one in the house and he
had put it in a cardboard box behind their shack for the night.

Next morning, the box was open and Satan was gone.

One night later on, when he was being punished, Ella had
locked him in a cupboard. He sat there on the floor, crying
softly, until he heard his father's voice. Tomas had come
home for dinner and was arguing with Ella. He had stopped
crying at once and listened. Heard them talking about him,
about why he was being punished.

Tomas had gone out again but returned right away.

The cupboard door had been unlocked and flung open.
Tomas loomed against the candlelight. "So my son's been
bad again! Here's company for him." Something thumped on
the floor beside him, then his father slammed the door and
locked it again.

He sat there in the dark, aware of Ella crying, as something moved across the floor. Reached out and touched the cold scales of a snake. Pulled his hand back and sat there, not making a sound, aware of the snake a few inches away.

After a long time he felt it move across his bare knees. From its weight, sliding over his lap, he knew it was a big one. Then, after what seemed hours, he carefully felt along the coils until he found its head. He stroked the hard skull as his father had taught him and sensed the snake settling down. It was resting its head in his open palm.

Ella said they were sleeping together, he and the big snake, when Tomas unlocked the cupboard door next morning.

That Satan stayed with him longer than any of the others. It followed him like a dog during the day and slept in his crib, coiled beside him, every night.

Since then he always had a snake. Until he came to Los Angeles . . .

He continued his act until the owner of the shop came out to pay him, then went inside into the office and changed into his sport shirt, Levi's and sandals. Ate a hamburger at one of the counters in the shopping mall before driving back to Hollywood.

The gates stood open when he reached Poinsettia Place and he heard voices from the television set as he drove past the open side windows. Velma would be watching one of her soap operas with Kong asleep, beside her. Lori-Lou would be in school.

He left the Honda in the drive while he went into the Coop.

After putting his spaceman outfit away, he unlocked the cabinet, removed the contact lenses, and cleaned his eyebrows and lashes with cold cream, but didn't take off the short black wig.

In less than an hour he was at the beach stretched out on a beach towel, sunglasses hiding his eyes.

If anyone noticed him, they would think he was asleep.

Instead he had a lot to think about. A careful plan to work out . . .

He'd removed his short black wig in the parked car, when no traffic was approaching on the Coast Highway, and locked it in the glove compartment.

Lots of people were sunbathing on the hot sand. Children

played farther down the beach. Some macho types were tossing a big rubber ball.

He had to work out an exact plan for tonight.

How he would get into Carlo Dario's house in Pacific Palisades.

That wasn't far from here. Tramonto Drive overlooked the beach. He wondered if they could see this spot from up there. . . .

He hadn't pulled a job like this—robbed a house—in more than ten years. That was before he came to Los Angeles. . . .

And he had to plan his escape to Mexico. . . .

He wanted to stop off at Snake City. See the owner, Chief Naja, and spend tonight in his motel. See his friends, all those snakes, because he would never come back again.

Then take off for Tijuana tomorrow morning.

21

Victor Lolo parked his Plymouth in the open space that a guard at the entrance had told him to take. He picked up the manila envelope from the hot leather seat and walked back to the row of one-story fake Spanish adobe buildings which the guard said still contained the executive offices.

He'd been here years ago on an investigation involving missing cans of film. The place hadn't changed. It only looked more rundown and shabby.

In the days of silent films some big stars had worked at this studio. Now they shot television shows with actors who would never be stars.

He noticed CONROY PRODUCTIONS on a faded sign above the open entrance to the center building and went inside, out of the smoggy sunlight, into a dim lobby with no air conditioning. The air tasted as though it had been dead for a long time.

He was in a rotten mood this afternoon. Must be careful how he talked to this girl. Although it was several weeks ago, she would still be recovering from her experience. Today, with a new picture of the Jogger, he had an excuse to see her again.

A blonde in a tight dress designed to advertise her boobs looked up from a copy of *Variety*.

"I'd like to see Miss Casparian."

"You an actor?"

"No. I'm not." He snapped the words at her.

"There's a casting call this afternoon for some TV pilot and Zena's handling it. The director's using Mr. Conroy's private office. Didn't see Zena go out for lunch, so she may be in there now."

"Where would that be?"

"Fourth door on the right. You'll see a sign says Harrison Conroy. Go right in."

"Thanks." He crossed the lobby toward an inner archway leading to a long hall with small overhead lights.

"You're handsome enough to be an actor," she called after him.

"God forbid!" He strode toward the fourth door.

This was the first time he'd left his office today, except for lunch in the cafeteria. He'd been sitting at his desk, staring at the empty space where that palm tree had been, waiting for something to happen, hoping the phone would ring, but the only calls concerned routine police matters on several of his other investigations.

Since last Friday night, his mind had been occupied with three completely different problems. The Midnight Jogger, above all else, then the idea of leaving the police to manage a vineyard, and, finally, the idea of marriage.

He paused at the fourth door and saw a small sign with HARRISON CONROY in golden letters on black.

Beyond the reception area, an inner door stood ajar but he couldn't see the private office beyond.

"Anybody here?"

"If you've come to audition, you're early." After a moment the door opened farther and a young woman came out, her face in shadow. "The call's for two o'clock. You can wait if you wish. . . ."

"Ms. Casparian?"

"Yes . . ."

"I'd like a few words with you."

She stepped forward, into the light from the overhead fixture, frowning.

The light made her dyed red hair an ugly color.

He heard her small gasp of surprise. "You remember me?"

"I hoped never to see you again. Why have you come here?"

"It's been a month since we talked at your apartment. Should've gotten back to you before this. I've got another picture I'd like to show you."

"I only returned to work last week." She shrugged. "Okay. We can talk inside." Turning back into the dim inner office. "My boss is in Palm Springs today. All the shooting stages are busy, so they're using this suite for casting." She sank onto a white leather sofa and motioned for him to take the armchair facing her.

The leather chair was deep and cold from the air conditioning. He saw that the only light came from a shaded lamp on the desk which, like most of the other furniture in Conroy's private office, was Hollywood antique-Spanish. Heavy curtains covered the windows as though daylight and the real world weren't allowed in.

"You've caught him?" she asked. "The Midnight Jogger . . ."

"Not yet."

"I hate him. Hate him . . ."

"Every victim says that."

"You know all of them?" The thought seemed to surprise her. "You've talked to them?"

"I've seen four of the others."

"Only four?"

"One girl moved away. Got married."

"I'll never marry now. Not ever . . . Of course you couldn't talk to his latest victim. The one after me. He killed her."

"Yes."

"I'd like to kill him. He deserves to die."

"All his victims feel that way. At first, each of them felt revulsion. Then anger."

"I was furious. Still am."

"And, finally, they want revenge. Like you."

"If I knew who he was—where I could find him—I would buy a gun and kill him."

"That would be a great mistake. The police are the ones to find him. Not his victims."

"But you haven't found him, have you? And if you ever do, you'll only turn him over to some stupid judge who'll set him free. Let him out to rape and kill again. I've been reading in the papers how the courts set rapists free or give them short sentences."

Lolo carefully avoided any comment on the judicial system. "Have you remembered anything more, Ms. Casparian, about that night? Some small detail about the Jogger you haven't told me before?"

"I've remembered nothing. And don't want to. Can't you understand? I don't want to remember him! I'm trying to forget him."

"Would you look at a picture I've brought?" He opened the manila envelope.

"You showed me that when you came to my apartment."

"Not this one. That was a composite made by a police artist. An amateur. This is a portrait I've had done. I collected the Jogger's description from the testimony of every victim and combined them into one list, then I gave that to a professional artist." Slipping a Xerox copy of the drawing from an envelope. "I want you to study this, if you will. Take your time." He held out the picture and observed her expression, hopefully, as she stared at it and saw that she was frowning. "Is this more like him?"

"It looks nothing like him. Nothing at all."

"You're certain?"

"I remember his horrible pale eyes. These are much too dark."

"Okay, Ms. Casparian. Sorry I've bothered you." He took the drawing from her trembling fingers and slid it back into the envelope. "I hope next time I can show you his face in a police lineup." He rose from the cold chair. "And you can point him out to me."

"I won't have to do that, will I?"

"I'm afraid all his victims will be asked to do that. When we finally catch him."

"I could never face him."

"At the moment it looks as though we may never find him. Good morning, Ms. Casparian." He turned toward the door, manila envelope in hand, and left the office without glancing back.

One young actor sat in the center of the row of red folding chairs in the reception room. He looked up, hopefully, and got to his feet.

Lolo saw that he also had a manila envelope in his hand.

"My agent sent me for the audition. Looks like I'm the first. . . ."

"Good luck, kid. Hope you have better luck than I just had."

Outside, hurrying toward the parking area, he dropped his manila envelope into a trash receptacle.

Another hunch that hadn't worked.

He would go back to his office and worry about those same three problems for the rest of the afternoon.

Catching the Jogger, managing a vineyard, and getting married . . .

22

The afternoon seemed much warmer. His flesh burned in spite of the lotion he'd rubbed into his body.

He'd been lying here, pretending to be asleep, but his eyes were open behind the sunglasses and he was still going over what he had to do. Working out a plan that couldn't fail.

He would drive down to Pacific Palisades after eleven o'clock, with nothing in the car. Pack everything but leave his backpack and one suitcase in the Coop. Go back and get them after he finished the job and was in the clear. Then head for Orange County and stop off to see Chief Naja at Snake City.

The old man would be asleep, but that didn't matter. He owned the motel, so he was probably used to being wakened in the middle of the night.

Stay there tonight and start off again in the morning.

After he'd seen the snakes . . .

Then, in another hour, he would be in Mexico.

There would be no trouble at the border. With his dark blond hair, they wouldn't think he was Mexican. He'd tell them he was spending the day in Ensenada and driving back to Long Beach tonight. . . .

After tonight he would never see Velma again. Or Lori-Lou . . .

Velma was one of the nicest women he'd ever known. He didn't like leaving without telling her he wasn't coming back.

His rent was paid to the first and she could sell his Volkswagen and everything he left in the Coop. That should give her a few bucks for her kindness, not that she needed the money.

He would miss them. Velma and Lori-Lou . . .

There'd been other women as kind to him as Velma. He'd been forced to leave all of them like this. Suddenly and in the night . . .

Without explanations.

He'd stayed with some of them a lot longer than he'd been with Velma.

That nice Mrs. Clark in Texas, who thought he was a mute. He didn't say a word while he lived with her. And that woman in Porterville—he was talking then—who ran a home for kids with no family. She wasn't as nice as Mrs. Hawkins in Visalia, but he'd known a lot worse. Much worse! All those foster homes from Texas to California. He'd lost count. . . .

He moved his head slowly and looked up and down the beach. The sun had brought more people out today, but most of them stayed south of Malibu.

This was kind of a private beach, but nobody ever chased you off.

Children building sand castles, with two young women wearing floppy straw hats watching them from under a bright red parasol. Probably their mothers.

Not many teenagers. Most of them had jobs during the day and only came to the beach on weekends.

Closing his eyes, he went over his plan once more.

When he got to Tijuana he would sell the Honda and buy another secondhand car. Maybe work out a deal. Trade his car for another with fifty bucks thrown in.

He would tell them he'd stolen the Honda. That way they'd hide it or some chop shop would take it apart. Nobody could ever trace it back to him.

Good thing he spoke pretty good Spanish. But then, he was practically a native. He'd never known whether he was born in Mexico or Texas. Ella never told him. . . .

Maybe he should get rid of the Honda in San Diego or even

before he drove that far, so he'd have a different car when he crossed the border. The police might be looking for the Honda. If not right away, they would be later. . . .

Why hadn't he thought of that before?

With a different car and his Social Security card he would have no trouble getting across the border.

He was damn lucky to have that card.

Once he was safe in Mexico, he would call himself Ed Hannaway again. Been several years since he'd done that.

He'd had no proof of his birth or any other identification when he left home. For years he had nothing but Tomas' name written on that piece of map. Which, of course, didn't prove he was Tomas' son . . .

The torn map Tomas always carried in his old leather wallet.

He'd been eighteen when he found that Social Security card.

After that he kept on using phony names when he came to Hollywood and got his first job as a stuntman.

He'd been using the names Rick Geraldo and Don Farrell and had told them at the casting offices that he'd taken those names to work in the movies but that his real name was Ed Hannaway and showed them the Social Security card. His driver's license was also in Edward Hannaway's name.

Edward Hannaway would never know he was using his card.

He'd been hitching north to Bakersfield, on his way to Frisco for the first time, and had spent the night in his old sleeping bag hidden by weeds at the edge of an orange grove.

Voices wakened him at dawn. Mexicans, laughing and talking.

He pushed himself up far enough to see them working among the orange trees.

After crawling out of the sleeping bag, he had rolled it up, stuffed it into his nearly empty backpack, and strapped that onto his shoulders.

Standing low so the Mexicans wouldn't notice him, he had crept toward the highway through the high weeds. There was a deep culvert he'd fallen into the night before when he was looking for a spot to sleep.

He saw, by daylight, that it was too wide to jump.

Maybe he'd better scramble down the culvert and climb the other side. He could break a leg if he tried to jump it and fell again.

He kept going along the edge of the culvert, checking the position of the sun to be sure he was still heading north.

Tomas had taught him how to do that.

He slid down the dry earth, body thrust back to break his descent, and reached the bottom without twisting an ankle. Pushed through the weeds growing in the culvert, searching for a low spot to climb up on the other side—stepping carefully, since he knew there would be rats and snakes and he didn't want to step on a sleeping rattler.

Finally, he reached a spot where some of the weeds had been broken and crushed, as though a large animal had fallen there.

He moved more slowly, peering from side to side. The culvert was deep because it had to hold water in the rainy season.

He pushed the weeds apart and looked down at the ground.

Somebody was sleeping there.

A kid with long yellow hair bleached by the sun. Looked to be in his teens. Wearing a torn T-shirt and faded dungarees. Must've been cold last night, without any cover. He leaned closer and saw that his eyes were open, staring at the morning sky.

Moving closer, stepping cautiously, he reached down and touched his hand. The flesh was cold. The kid wasn't asleep. He was dead.

His eyes were blue and his skin was dark from months in the sun.

He pushed more of the weeds aside and saw there was dried blood on his T-shirt and dungarees.

Something had killed the kid. Maybe a car had hit him and he crawled down here to die.

There should be money in his pockets. Working quickly, out of sight from the highway, he felt in each pocket but found nothing.

As he straightened to leave, he remembered where he always kept his own money.

He removed the kid's shoes quickly. Old and badly worn gym shoes. Saw that he had no socks and his feet were filthy.

Folded between an inner sole and his foot were a birth certificate, Social Security card, and two ten-dollar bills. When he separated the money he found a note printed in pencil.

> My name is Edward Hannaway.
> In case anything happens to me please notify
> my mother, Mrs. William Hannaway. She
> lives at 806 Adams Street, Wilmington,
> Delaware.
> Thanks for your kindness.

The note was signed Eddie Hannaway.

Don discovered that he was crying as he folded the note with the twenty bucks and stuffed them with the Social Security card and birth certificate into his hip pocket. That money bought his breakfast and paid for food until he reached Frisco.

Somewhere, on his way north, he'd torn the note into little pieces and scattered them into another culvert.

Mrs. William Hannaway probably never found out what happened to her son, which maybe saved her from a lot of sadness.

The Social Security card and birth certificate would help him in Mexico, along with his driver's license. He'd be Ed Hannaway, at least in the beginning, but later he would go back to his own name—the name Tomas and Ella had given him—Geraldo O'Farrill.

He'd used lots of names but never that one before. His own name. Geraldo O'Farrill . . .

He realized his stomach was growling. Maybe he would have an early dinner, somewhere in Hollywood. Go to a movie after that and get to the Coop around eight.

He would spend the evening packing what he needed to take with him tonight. Everything he could fit into his backpack and his mother's suitcase.

Many things had to be left behind. His clothes and all his mechanical man costumes. He would never do the act again.

Must travel light, especially if he was going to sell the Honda. Might have to walk for a while before he found another car . . .

He remembered that night he'd left home the first time, after that neighborhood woman told him Ella was dead and people would be coming to take him somewhere.

Remembered how frightened he'd been.

He'd packed the few clothes he had and his good pair of shoes, along with the torn paperback copy of *Don Quixote* with Tomas' map folded inside.

They were his only possessions. Two things that belonged to Tomas. Nothing of his mother's.

He had coiled Satan on top of an old sweater and snapped the suitcase shut.

He remembered how frightened he'd been as he left the shack where Ella's dresses still hung in the cupboard and started up the empty highway his mother said led north. No idea where he was going in the dark, only that he had to get away before those people came to take him.

He'd cried, knowing nobody would hear him. Afraid in the darkness. Startled by the smallest noise. Diving off the highway whenever he saw approaching headlights.

When he got too tired to walk anymore, he found a spot under a tree where he opened the suitcase and took Satan out. Coiled him around his warm arm before he stretched out with his head on the old leather suitcase and slept.

In the night Satan had slipped away.

That was the first time he'd been completely alone. . . .

He would go to a movie tonight after he ate dinner. That would relax him before he went back to the Coop and started packing.

Couldn't remember when or where he saw his first movie. Was it Mexico or Texas?

He only remembered that Ella sat next to him holding his hand because the giant cowboys galloping on the screen frightened him. The first picture he saw was a Western and the star could've been Gary Cooper, but he wasn't even sure of that.

He'd been going to movies ever since.

At first, while he was living in foster homes, it was only once a week and only if his foster mother gave him a quarter for the work he'd done. Or if he could snitch one from her purse.

Since coming to Hollywood he'd seen a movie most

weeknights. Never over the weekend, because you had to wait in line to get in and he didn't like people crowding against him.

His favorite movie star was Jimmy Dean.

He wasn't born when Jimmy died, but he'd seen all his pictures. Again and again. Whenever they showed them on Hollywood Boulevard or on television.

While he was living near Pasa Robles, he learned that the spot where Jimmy was killed in his brand new foreign car was only a short distance away. He walked there with his best friend from high school, who showed him the spot, across from a filling station. The exact spot where Jimmy had died . . .

Standing there, across from that filling station, he had wept for Jimmy.

After that he went there many times. Always alone.

He wondered what kind of movie theaters they would have in Mexico today. Probably only little ones in the small towns, showing old pictures he'd already seen . . .

Mexican films were terrific!

He liked to drive downtown to the Million Dollar Theater on South Broadway and see the new ones.

Always searching the actors' faces. Looking for Tomas. Wondering if his father still worked in crowd scenes.

He knew he would recognize him.

Tomas would be forty-seven now, but would probably look younger.

His mother said Tomas worked in lots of Mexican movies.

He had to find Tomas. . . .

That's why he'd always wanted to go back to Mexico. And to see the village where he was born.

Locate that mountain where Tomas held him up in his hand to look down at the green valley . . .

He had to see that valley again.

He'd never had enough money to go back, but he would have it tonight.

Carlo Dario was rich. He wouldn't miss it. . . .

Tonight he would be on his way.

And one day, very soon, he would find Tomas. . . .

Six

23

Don parked his Honda on Tramonto Drive, pulled the ignition key out, and slipped his keys into a hip pocket, buttoning it so the keys couldn't fall out or jingle when he walked.

He sat there in the darkness, senses alert, hunched down out of sight but listening for every sound. No lights were visible in distant houses and no traffic in either direction. The only sound was a blur of music from somebody's television set, but that was very faint and seemed to come from a big house he could see outlined against the night sky on the other side of the street.

He'd driven past Carlo Dario's property but saw no lights in any of the distant windows. He was parked several houses away, inconspicuous between two old cars that must belong to servants, since all the fancy cars would be locked in garages at the rear of each property.

His backpack and Ella's suitcase were in the trunk, filled with his belongings, all he'd been able to cram into them. He would buy new clothes in Mexico. Wouldn't need much at first.

He'd changed his mind as he packed them and decided not to return to the Coop. When he left here he would head for Orange County, spend the night with Chief Naja and be off again in the morning.

This way he wouldn't waste any time. . . .

He wasn't wearing a wig tonight. All three wigs were rolled up carefully with his clothing. He'd wear the short ones in Mexico to make him look like a native.

The trunk was locked, but he wouldn't lock the car in case he had to leave here fast.

He got out and closed the door silently, then, moving casually as though he had every right to be here, stepped onto the sidewalk and started down the street.

The only light came from a street lamp and, because of the trees, it didn't give much light. He recognized the white-painted brick wall around the Dario property before he saw the metal numbers. No light was hitting them, so they looked black against the white bricks.

The gates were open.

Did that mean the Darios had gone out? Maybe there was nobody there but a couple of sleeping servants. Or did they always leave their gates open?

He slipped inside and, crouching low, moved along a row of bushes he hadn't noticed before, creeping toward the house.

No lights shone in any of the shuttered front windows.

The front doors were sure to be locked.

He took the right drive, jogging silently, his rubber soles making no sound, and followed it around to the rear where he hesitated at the corner.

The patio looked different tonight. Much larger. The big tent and all the other signs of the party were gone.

There were several lights in the distance. Two of them were near the swimming pool, which he had only glimpsed Saturday, and another was above the five-car garage. All the doors were closed.

He eased along the rear of the house toward the big windows in front of which he'd placed his platform.

Slowed his steps as he approached the wall of glass and saw that two sliding panes were open.

He stopped and stared at the dark opening. No lights inside.

Had Carlo gone out with his wife and left those windows open for their return? So they could put their car in the garage and be able to get into the house without a key?

He stood for a moment, frozen, listening for sounds from inside.

A dog barked far away, but didn't bark again.

There had been no dogs here last Saturday.

He edged closer to the open window.

Still no sound from inside the villa.

He reached into a hip pocket and pulled out the small flashlight he'd picked up at a Thrifty this afternoon. Held it ready as he stepped into the dark living room and moved to one side, so he couldn't be seen against the open windows.

Where would they keep their money here? In table drawers or in a desk?

He aimed the flashlight until he found a table. It had a flat top, no drawer. And he couldn't remember seeing a desk.

More likely, money would be kept in a safe—a wall safe—or in a dressing-table drawer in the bedroom.

He hadn't thought about that. Where the money would be kept.

If it was in a safe, he wouldn't have a chance. Only a professional could open a safe.

And he didn't know where the bedrooms were.

Maybe there would be something valuable in this room that he could sell in Mexico.

The beam of light moved on as he considered what to do.

He could take some small but expensive object.

Maybe a picture. A painting! They were supposed to be valuable.

He raised the flashlight higher and let it move across a wall. There were no pictures. Redirected it toward the big white sofa he remembered seeing. There had been a coffee table with all kinds of valuable-looking objects.

Somebody was seated on the sofa.

Don froze.

"I knew you'd come back."

He snapped off the flashlight, realizing his flesh was cold with shock. It had been a woman's voice.

"In fact I've been expecting you. Waiting for you."

Should he turn and run? Through that open window. Back to his car.

"I thought you might return Sunday night. And last

night . . ." She didn't sound frightened, seeing him here. "I've been sitting here each night."

It was Carlo Dario's wife. What did she mean? Waiting for him . . .

"I've wanted to see you again ever since our eyes met in front of that theater. I had our secretary call your agent and arrange for you to be here for my son's party. I took you ice cream as an excuse to talk to you, hoping you would sense my feelings. Knew you would come back. And here you are. . . ."

He still didn't say anything. Afraid to speak.

"I'm glad you came back. I've been thinking about you. Constantly . . ."

His finger, as though he no longer controlled it, pressed the small button and the ray of light reappeared on the tiled floor at his feet.

He hadn't realized that he'd lowered his arm.

Now the arm raised itself until the light was on her face.

She was smiling, wearing some kind of thin yellow robe through which he could see her pink flesh, arms and legs. Her golden red hair was the same color Ella's had been.

"You've not said a word. You aren't afraid, are you?"

"Why should I be?" The chill had left his body.

"Wouldn't want you to be afraid of me. And you don't have to worry about the others. My son's in a separate wing. His room's between our secretary's room and the cook's. They both look out for him. You met our secretary—Vikki Vernon—the English lady. . . ."

"Yes."

"She's been with us since my son was born. They can't hear any sounds from this part of the house. You and I are completely private here."

"Your husband?"

"I've no idea where he is." She laughed. "That's not quite true. I've a pretty good idea where he is. One of several places. He's never home at this hour. Rarely eats dinner here. And he seldom returns until after midnight. Some nights not until dawn. You don't need to worry about Carlo. We have separate suites. Haven't slept together since I became pregnant. Ours is a typical Hollywood marriage. I've adjusted, but only because of my son. As soon as he's old enough to understand—when my psychiatrist says it will be all right—I plan to get a divorce." She reached out and turned on a large table lamp. "You look different tonight. I'm glad that long black hair was a wig."

He snapped off the flashlight and thrust it into a pocket.

"And your eyes are blue. I thought they were brown."

"Contact lenses."

"And your hair's an odd dark blond. Has anyone told you lately you're a very handsome young man?"

"No, ma'am."

"You look even younger tonight. How old are you?"

"Twenty-seven."

"You look more like seventeen. You've had lots of girlfriends?"

"Yes, ma'am."

"I'm not surprised. With your looks." She rose from the sofa suddenly.

As her thin robe swayed open, he saw that she wasn't wearing anything underneath.

She held out a hand to him.

He saw a flash of diamonds.

"We go this way." She started across the silent room but turned back, her hand still reaching toward him. "I won't bite you. At least not too much."

He took the outstretched hand and followed her, aware that she was slightly shorter. Glanced down and saw her bare feet between the folds of her robe.

She led him across the immense room and, pausing at an open archway, touched a wall switch that turned off the lamp.

He saw that she was taking him through a long unlighted corridor with open windows on both sides. There was enough light from the sky for him to see curtains hanging at the sides of the tall windows.

"Here we are," she whispered. "My own private suite." She went ahead, still holding his hand, through an open door. "My husband had the architect do that when he designed the house. Everything separate." She touched another silent wall switch and lights came alive in another large room. "This is my boudoir. . . ."

It was like no room he had ever seen.

"I never had a boudoir until I came to California." She led

him across the gold and white room toward another open door. "In New York our whole apartment was smaller than this. And we were happier there. Both of us. Working in separate Broadway shows. I'll never be that happy again."

She stepped through the door into a dark room and fingered another wall switch. Lights came on in a large bathroom, visible through an open door, and faintly revealed a bedroom with an enormous bed. Like bedrooms he'd seen in movies . . .

She touched another wall switch and the lights went off in the boudoir.

"Sure your husband's out?"

"Even if he were home, he would still be far away. His suite's on the other side of the villa. We have our own lives, both of us. I don't care how many babes he takes to bed and he doesn't give a damn what I do. You can toss your clothes on that chair."

He began to undress as she stepped out of her yellow robe.

"Not that there've been all that many. In my bed. I'm always very careful." As she talked she heard the low hum of the Mercedes. Carlo was back.

Don heard the motor. "That your husband?"

"One of the servants coming home from a movie. I have to really like someone—be genuinely attracted to them—before I invite them to my bed."

Her red hair and firm, plump body reminded him of Ella. Tomas had pinched his mother's flesh, laughing as she squealed, slapped her on the bottom before they collapsed into bed.

She held out her arms. "As I welcome you now . . ."

He sank slowly onto the cool sheet beside her, trying to see her face more clearly, as they embraced, stretching his legs out when her arms slipped around his body.

"You're very handsome," she whispered. "I love you. . . ."

"Nobody ever told me that before."

"No one! Not ever?"

"Not ever."

"I can't believe that. . . ."

He placed his lips against hers, felt her tongue dart, like a small snake, into his mouth.

She was aware of tears on his cheeks. Was he crying? She felt his body start to move, tentatively, across her thighs.

As his muscles obeyed he was unable to stop the tears that flooded from his eyes.

24

Lolo was singing as he showered.

This day had been a total loss.

Nothing had turned up on the Jogger or on any of his other investigations, and there was no new case of any importance that required his attention.

Not a single new lead in the Jogger case. The extra men from Homicide were grumbling because there was nothing for them to do.

He didn't feel like singing, but Samoans always sang in the shower.

At the moment it was an old song he'd heard his father sing many times when they were fishing or working together. He knew the melody but had forgotten the words.

Pray God he would sleep tonight.

Last night he'd tossed for hours. Thinking about the Jogger . . .

Did the Jogger sleep well?

Or did he lie awake, half the night, planning where he would look for his next victim?

Lolo toweled quickly, checking his elaborate tattoo marks in the full-length mirror behind the bathroom door. Tattoos on both thighs, red and blue against his brown skin. They had been needled into his flesh when he was on a boring leave in Honolulu. The tattoo artist swore the designs were authentic Samoan, but when he returned home, after his hitch in the Marines, his father had laughed and said they were Tahitian. He was the only Samoan with a Tahitian rear end.

Moving around his small apartment, he tied a lavalava around his hips, one that his mother had made and sent him last year. The design was of black leaves and white blossoms. Like no flower he'd ever seen in Samoa.

He suspected the material had come from Korea.

Pausing at the low chest holding his record player, he snapped a lever and watched the needle arm descend.

He turned off the lights, except for a shaded lamp on his bedside table, as the pulsing throb of Samoan voices filled his bedroom with a whisper of drums stroked by bare hands. Their sweet murmuring sound nearly always helped put him to sleep.

It was warm again tonight, so he yanked the cover off his bed and pulled the thin blanket and white top sheet down to the foot. Then he stretched out on the bottom sheet, resting his head on a pillow.

He thought about the Jogger immediately as he settled down.

The Midnight Jogger case was the toughest he'd ever worked on, as well as the longest. And he was no closer to catching the bastard than he'd been the first day he was assigned to the investigation.

There would be a phone call from the Chief, any day now, asking questions.

He wondered what would have happened if he'd been on it earlier. There'd been three rapes before the *L.A. Times* called him the Midnight Jogger. He'd read that article but wasn't ordered on the case for several more weeks, not until he'd finished a murder investigation and the two killers were behind bars.

He was always complaining because he didn't get onto a case sooner, but the Chief didn't like to move him in until the local division—where the crime took place—asked for help. When they did, it always meant they were in trouble.

By then evidence would have disappeared and clues been overlooked or, many times, forgotten.

He snapped the lamp off.

No reading tonight.

Turning his back to the row of open windows, he knew this was going to be another bad night.

Lucky if he got three hours sleep.

In the faint light from the distant street seeping through the thin window curtains, he could make out the dark shape of a tapa cloth hanging on the wall facing the foot of his bed, and saw a reflection of a curtained window in the glass covering a framed Gauguin reproduction.

His two most prized possessions.

He'd found that tapa cloth in a secondhand shop downtown, and bought the Gauguin in Westwood when he was studying law at U.C.L.A. and working nights as a waiter in an East Indian restaurant. The woman in the picture reminded him of his mother. That's why he'd bought it. That peaceful, half-asleep, smiling face.

Would he ever see his family again? Not likely. He had no desire to go back to Pago Pago and the stink from all those fish canneries because he was afraid he wouldn't be able to escape a second time.

A comfortable apartment like this didn't exist in the islands at a price he could afford.

He would miss all the conveniences he'd found in California. While the only thing Samoan that was lacking here was the sound of cocks crowing . . .

If he ever moved to an apartment with a garden, he would buy himself a rooster, with several hens to keep him happy.

Maybe one day he could send his parents enough money to fly to Los Angeles.

Would they come?

Did he want them living here?

His mother would be after him constantly to get married. Even worse than in her letters.

The thought of marriage brought him back to Morita and those vineyards in northern California.

If he took that job, he could easily afford to bring his parents from Samoa, set them up in a nice house on a hill above the vineyards, not far from where he and Morita would be living. . . .

Would Morita approve of his bringing his family from Samoa?

Morita!

Did he want to marry Morita?

He wasn't certain. . . .

Did he, for that matter, want to marry any woman just now?

His life was complete without marriage.

Would he be happy managing vineyards?

He didn't know a damn thing about growing grapes. . . .

The Midnight Jogger!

Where was the Jogger tonight? This minute.

Prowling the city, looking for his next victim? His gray Volkswagen nosing through the dark streets . . .

He realized that he was falling asleep. . . .

25

Don wondered if she was asleep.

It had been several minutes since he'd pulled himself away from her and rolled onto his back, his legs thrust out, staring at the invisible ceiling. He didn't know when she turned off the lights.

Not a sound in the villa, no whisper of distant traffic.

He heard her breathing faintly in the dark.

Wondered what he should do now. Get up and try to find his clothes.

He was wide awake, mind alert.

Hadn't expected anything like this to happen.

He'd come here to steal enough money to get him to Mexico, to pay his expenses for a couple of months until he found Tomas or got himself a job.

He wondered if there was any money in this room. . . .

She must have a purse here. A dame like this would have a lot of cash hidden away. . . .

"What are you thinking?" she whispered.

The unexpected question startled him. "Nothing. Not a thing . . ."

"My name's Adriana. . . ."

"Adriana?"

"Adriana Austin . . . That's the name I used when I was on the stage in New York. Actually, I'm Mrs. Carlo Dario. But neither of those names seem real to me. Because my husband's name isn't really Carlo Dario. We both worked on the stage in New York, but I've never worked out here. Not in the movies . . . What's your name?"

"Don . . ."

"Don what?"

"Don Farrell. F–a–r–r–e–l–l . . ."

"That's your real name?"

He hesitated. "No . . . My real name's Geraldo O'Farrill. Spelled F–a–r–r–i–l–l . . ."

"Irish?"

"My mother was. She had red hair, like you. My father's half Irish, half Mexican. . . ."

Her fingers found his hand in the dark and held it as they talked. "There was something about you, standing on your platform at the opening, that attracted me suddenly. Touched my heart. Nothing like this has ever happened to me before and I can't explain it. Even to myself. The whole time I watched Carlo's lousy movie, my mind was on you. But when we came out from the theater, you weren't there."

"I always leave when everyone goes inside."

"But you got my signal. When I smiled at you."

"I saw you smile."

"And you smiled back. I thought the birthday party would give us another chance to look at each other. You would see where I lived and maybe come back." She squeezed his hand. "And here we are. We've made love and now we can talk and make plans. I've wanted to find a lover. I'm only twenty-nine—two years older than you—so there's not much difference in our ages. My husband's thirty-four. . . ."

"Don't you love him?"

"Not anymore. How can I! He doesn't love me. Sleeps with every available actress under twenty. And there must be hundreds of them. He won't agree to a divorce and I plan to go along with that until our son's fifteen. Then I'll get myself a lawyer. Meanwhile . . . I hope we'll be able to see a lot of each other. We'll have to be careful. I don't want him ever to find out. You understand? We must get a place where we can meet and nobody will ever know. Maybe your apartment . . ."

"I'm sorry. I can't see you again."

"Why not?"

He felt her hand tighten around his.

"Don't you like me?"

"I like you a lot."

"I love you, Don. Truly love you . . ."

"I'm leaving Los Angeles tonight."

"What do you mean, leaving? For good?"

"I'm going to Mexico. To look for my father . . ."

"Your father?"

"I haven't seen him since I was a kid. I've got to find him."

"Leaving for Mexico tonight? Why did you come here?"

"Well . . ."

"Wasn't it to see me?"

"I came here to get money."

"Money?" She released his hand.

"I was going to steal it. Enough to keep me going for a few months in Mexico."

"Steal it?" A sob escaped from her throat.

"When I saw this place last week, I knew your husband was rich. Like all movie stars . . ."

"He's in debt. Like most movie stars."

"I thought the house would be dark tonight. That you and your husband would be out."

"Then you didn't come back to see me."

"No, ma'am."

"What a fool I've been."

Lights came alive in several shaded lamps.

He sat up, startled, embarrassed by his exposed flesh.

She reached up and grasped his arm, pulled him down beside her. "I still love you. Even if I never do see you again. I will never forget tonight. Not as long as I live." She kissed his bare chest, brushing his flesh with her lips. "You can't say, ever again, that nobody has told you they love you."

"There was one other person."

"Who?"

"My mother."

"Mothers don't count. Where is your mother?"

"She died. When I was eight . . ."

"You poor kid. What did you do?"

"Started out on my own."

"Where was your father?"

"He left my mother years before. I'm going to Mexico to look for him. If he's still alive . . ."

"How old would he be?"

"In his forties. I think . . ."

"That isn't old."

"I have to find him. Ask him a lot of things. Mostly about my mother . . ."

"You'll find him." She leaned over and kissed him on the lips. "I know you will."

He took her in his arms and quickly touched his lips to her cheek, her forehead, her throat, and the tip of her nose, remembering how he had done this to Ella. "My mother called these butterfly kisses." He pulled back and looked at her. "You're the first woman I've ever slept with."

"I can't believe that!"

"It's true."

She realized, from the sound of his voice, he was telling the truth. "You never loved another woman?"

"Not this way. Not like tonight."

"I do love you, Don. . . ."

"Not Don. I've never liked 'Don.' I told you, my real name's Geraldo. My mother always called me Jerry."

"Jerry . . . Isn't there some way, after you find your father, you could come back here?"

"That might not be for years."

"I don't care how long it is! Meanwhile, you could write me. My husband never sees my mail. I'll have Vikki watch for your letters. You'll do that, won't you? Write me! Every week . . ."

"You really want me to?"

"You've got this address. You will write, won't you?"

"Okay. I'll write."

"Is there some place where I could write you?"

"I don't know where I'll be staying."

"Doesn't matter. You write me. No later than next week. So I'll know you're all right."

"I've never written a letter to anybody. . . ."

"Where did you live after your mother died?"

"Foster homes, mostly. Sometimes, when I was running away, I slept in the fields, until I was picked up and put in another home. I never told anyone my real name or where I came from. . . ."

"You have a car?"

"Yes."

"How much money?"

"Coupla hundred bucks I've saved and the money I got for your party last week. Enough to get by for a few weeks."

"I'll give you some more." She rose from the bed and reached for her robe."

"No. I won't take it." He got up and stood watching her. "I couldn't do that."

"But I insist." She pulled on her robe as she went toward a door. "I would worry if I thought you didn't have enough for food and a place to sleep."

He watched as she opened the door and saw it was a closet filled with dresses. The bathroom door stood open and there were two other doors, but he had no idea which one led to the room she had called her boudoir. He saw that she was lifting a small leather case down from a shelf and resting it on a chair.

"This makeup case has a trick lock. No key, but a combination."

He picked up his shorts and began to get dressed.

"Nobody knows the combination but me." She was clicking some kind of mechanism in a metal panel beside the lock. "That does it!"

He saw the lock open.

She lifted the leather lid and began to feel along the edge of a padded lining.

He watched her pull a zipper open as he continued to dress.

She pulled out a plastic envelope. "No one, not even Vikki, knows I hide money here. It's my own money. Interest from investments my husband doesn't suspect I have. A girl has to think of the future, even if she is married." She took out a neat bundle of bills held by a large rubber band and brought them across the room. "Here's five hundred in twenties."

"Five hundred?"

She thrust the money into his hand. "No strings attached. You owe me nothing. Only a letter next week to let me know you're all right. And one day soon you'll be coming back."

He looked down at the bundle of new twenty-dollar bills. With what he already had, there would be enough for him to survive several months. By that time he would find some trace of Tomas. . . .

"Take it. No argument."

"Okay." He thrust the money into a pocket of his dungarees. "But I'll pay you back. I swear."

She moved close to him, her eyes searching his. "Promise you'll come back. Soon as you can."

"I promise." He put his arms around her and kissed her on the mouth.

"Don't you have any friends in Los Angeles?"

"I've never made friends. Real friends . . ."

"Neither have I." As she talked, she closed and locked her makeup case and returned it to the closet. "All those people you saw here last week were Carlo's friends. Not mine. I've not found a true friend—except, I suppose, Vikki—since we came out from New York." She shut the closet door and turned back to him. "Vikki's a good friend. She protects me. Defends me. Even from my husband. If you ever need me, call here and ask for Vikki. In fact, she usually answers the phone. You can talk to her. I'll explain everything to Vikki tomorrow. She'll understand about us. In fact, she'll be delighted."

"I've never known anyone in Los Angeles I felt I could trust. I like snakes better than I like people."

"Snakes? You're joking."

"Always had a pet snake when I was a kid." He hesitated. "I'd better go."

"You're heading for Mexico tonight?"

"I'll stay with a friend tonight in Orange County. He's got lots of snakes."

She moved into his arms again and they kissed. Quickly and finally. "Come. I'll show you the way out of this prison." She walked ahead toward one of the other doors, flung it open and led him through the dark boudoir. He followed, as she switched lights on in the corridor, back to the living room.

"I won't put any lights on in here. You can see the open windows."

"Yes." He walked beside her, past the long white sofa, toward the windows. "Don't you lock these at night?"

"I unlocked them tonight—and every night since the party—because I expected you."

She held up her face again, closing her eyes.

Don kissed her, lightly this time. "Thank you. For everything." He stepped out onto the terrace.

"Write me next week!" She watched him turn toward the drive and realized there were tears in her own eyes now. Moving slowly, she stepped outside and stood there, listening.

And suddenly she knew what she was going to do.

She had a brilliant plan of her own. . . .

A wonderful plan!

She would get back at Carlo for all the cruel things he had done. Change their marriage. Their positions in this house. Their personal relations . . .

That would keep everything in her control until Jerry returned.

Then one happy day, in the future, she would become Mrs. Geraldo O'Farrill.

They would still be young. Both of them.

She heard the muffled sound of his car.

Waited, motionless, until the sound faded into the night.

Then, moving with purpose, she turned and, leaving the windows open, hurried through the villa toward her husband's suite. Forced herself to cry as she ran down the corridor to the central atrium—she'd learned to cry on cue when she worked on Broadway—and continued on to the open doors leading to another corridor.

Tears were flowing down her cheeks.

"Carlo!" She called his name, knowing he would be asleep.

There was no sound from his suite as she reached the open doors.

"Carlo! Carlo!" She snapped a wall switch and hurried across the handsome masculine sitting room.

"Carlo! Wake up!" The door to his bedroom stood open, but as usual, he was sleeping soundly. "Carlo!" She screamed his name and saw the light from the bed lamp as she entered.

"Adriana! What is it?" He pushed himself up in his big antique bed.

She began to sob. This had to be done just right.

"What's happened?" He threw back the sheet and got out of bed, buttoning his pajama jacket.

"I've been raped!"

"What?"

"Raped! It was horrible! He must've gotten in through an open window."

"My God!" He took her in his arms.

She smiled as she hid her face against his shoulder.

"I'll have to call the police."

"No!" She hadn't thought of that.

He released her and turned to the telephone on the bed table.

"No, Carlo! No! You mustn't. . . ."

But he was picking up the phone.

Seven

26

Don was keeping to the slow lanes of the Santa Ana Freeway, avoiding the big trucks. He didn't want to risk an accident that would involve him with the Highway Patrol.

The drivers in the fast lanes wouldn't notice him or his car.

There was a haze of fog in the air, or was that only exhaust fumes from those trucks?

He was leaving home once more. Hopefully for the last time.

It wasn't likely he'd ever see the Coop again. Or Velma and Lori-Lou.

The first time he left home, that night Ella died, there hadn't been this much traffic.

Whenever he heard a car behind him or saw headlights, he'd ducked off the highway and hidden in the weeds until they passed.

When they were out of sight he'd picked up his suitcase again, Satan inside, and continued on his way, with no idea where he was going, only that he wanted to get far away from the place his mother had died.

He had walked until he was too tired to go any farther and slept with Satan coiled around his arm, resting his head on the suitcase, so nobody could swipe it while he was asleep.

That's when Satan slipped away in the night, leaving him without a friend. He'd searched for a while, in the cold light of dawn, but realized the snake was gone and, finally, continued on his way.

All the way to California! But that had taken several years. . . .

Now he was on his way again.

Back to Mexico this time, where he would look for Tomas . . .

Tonight he had money, more money than he'd ever owned in his whole life.

He would stop off at Snake City and see Chief Naja. The old man would be asleep, but he'd be glad to see him. He would ask questions about Velma and Lori-Lou and recall the last time they all were there, when Pike was alive. Velma had taken Lori-Lou to Disneyland but Don had stayed at the motel with Pike and listened to Chief Naja tell stories about when he worked in the movies. That was how Pike first met him. The Indian had worked in Westerns for years and eventually saved enough money to open Snake City with its Western-style motel. That was when land was cheap. Long before Disneyland.

It would be good to see Chief Naja again.

Another hour would go by before he turned off the highway and up that side road to Snake City.

He would have a warm bed tonight.

He thought of the cold nights he'd shivered in fields when he didn't even have a sleeping bag.

It was months before that first lady had taken him in. He'd long ago forgotten her name.

She had fed him and given him a place to sleep—the room belonged to her son who was missing in some war—but had turned him over to the police next morning after she'd cooked his breakfast.

He told those cops he didn't know his name, or where he came from.

They put him in his first foster home.

Tomorrow he would be Ed Hannaway when he crossed the border at Tijuana, but once he was in Mexico, he would use his real name.

Geraldo O'Farrill . . .

That's the name Tomas would remember.

He would tell everybody he was Tomas O'Farrill's son.

He'd used Jerry Farrell for a while, when he lived in Frisco. He'd wanted a new name when he came down to L.A., and when somebody asked his name, unexpectedly, he'd remembered Tomas' favorite book and blurted out Don Farrell. . . .

Always spelling it *Farrell* when he had to write it out.

When he opened his first bank account, he said he was Edward Hannaway and showed them Hannaway's Social Security card and birth certificate. Had used Edward Hannaway whenever he took a job. Explained to Pike and Velma that he called himself Don Farrell when he came to Los Angeles. They understood because Pike's real name was Harry Splain. He called himself Pike because it sounded more like a cowboy's name.

The air felt damp against his face and he saw the fog was getting heavier.

Another half hour and he should reach Snake City.

He realized that he was whistling.

On his way again . . .

27

He was swimming under water surrounded by some incredible fish.

Bright-colored fish. Red, yellow, and even purple. Big ones he'd never seen before.

This had to be Samoa.

But how did he get back here?

He kicked his feet but was unable to rise to the surface.

Peering overhead, he could see bright sunlight on the lagoon but nobody was swimming.

That was strange. Usually you swam with a friend. Not alone . . .

A bell ringing? Seemed to be close. Under the water.

That was impossible. No telephones down here . . .

Telephone?

He came awake with a start.

The phone was ringing on his bed table.

He checked the illuminated dial of the clock beside the phone.

Ten to one?

Damn! He'd slept less than an hour.

The phone continued to ring.

He reached out and lifted it to his ear as he turned on the bedside lamp. "Lolo speaking."

"Did I wake you, Vic?"

"No problem. Only got to bed half an hour ago. Who's this?"

"Johnny Gurlink. Malibu Sheriff's Station."

"What's up, Johnny?"

"Got something interesting. I think it's your Jogger."

Lolo sat up in bed, wide awake. "But it hasn't been a month since he killed that girl. Is it murder again?"

"No. A rape. And it's not his usual victim. He's raped a married woman in her bed.

"Then it couldn't be the Jogger."

"Hold on, Vic. I remembered that memo you sent out. Saying the guy likes snakes."

"That's right."

"This guy likes snakes."

"Maybe all rapists do."

"Something more. This dame got a good look at him. Saw his face as they moved from living room to bedroom. Her description of the guy matches your Jogger. Pale blue eyes, dark blond hair. And he looked to be in his twenties."

"That's the Jogger."

"There's something odd about this dame. I've a strong feeling she knew the guy, from the way she reacted when I questioned her—as though she's protecting him. I got a feeling she'd seen him before. . . ."

"Where are you now?"

"At the scene of the rape. One of the other guys is questioning the victim again. In her bedroom. I've come to the living room—it's half a block away—to call you."

"Where's her husband?"

"He's in what they call a boudoir—next to the wife's bedroom."

"Maybe I should drive down there."

"I think that might be a good idea. We're getting nowhere. And I've a feeling the dame's hiding something. Maybe with your good looks you can get it outta her."

"What's the victim's name?"

"Adriana Dario."

"Dario?"

"They tell me her husband's a big movie star. Carlo Dario. Far's I'm concerned the last big star was Spencer Tracy."

"I saw Carlo Dario's new picture last week."

"Then you know who he is."

"Where'd this rape take place?"

"Their residence. Tramonto Drive, Pacific Palisades. Good-sized property with a big house."

"Was Dario there when his wife was raped?"

"Claims he was asleep. They occupy separate suites. Typical Hollywood marriage."

"Anyone else on the premises?"

"Three people. Their small son, age four, a Mexican cook, and an English secretary. Female. All were asleep. You're always beefing because you're not in at the beginning. Here's the start of one for you, Vic. Be my guest."

"Thanks, Johnny."

"This could be a big one. Although Dario's doing everything to keep it quiet. Says he doesn't want publicity and I've promised to see what we can do."

"Any reporters on the scene?"

"None. Nobody's notified the press. We'd like to put an end to this one fast. Residents of Pacific Palisades like their privacy."

"Give me the address." He snatched up a pencil and wrote on a pad beside the phone. "I'll be there in half an hour."

"See you."

Lolo put the phone down and stared at the address.

Was it possible?

The Jogger had raped Carlo Dario's wife. . . .

28

The headlights swept across a series of small, neatly painted signs on posts along the Freeway.

SNAKE CITY

Don smiled and slowed the Honda to read the directions. Two miles and turn right . . .

He continued on and more signs flashed past.

Last time he came here Pike Splain had been driving. He'd sat in front with Velma between him and Pike, Lori-Lou and Kong in the back.

He had passed the lights of Disneyland, on his right, fifteen minutes ago.

Not so much traffic now.

He wondered if Adriana was asleep. . . .

This was the first time he'd ever made love to a real woman. He felt relaxed and happy. Maybe that's why he'd been whistling. . . .

It had never been like this before. Of course those others were young girls. They had fought him.

This sure had been different.

He'd gone there to rob Carlo Dario, take something from his home, something valuable he could sell when he reached Mexico. Instead he had gotten cash. And he didn't have to steal it! That money was a gift. She had said so. Insisted he take it. Her money . . .

Carlo would never find out what his wife gave him. She wouldn't tell him.

He'd never had so much money at one time in his whole life. Maybe he wouldn't look for a job right away, but would continue across northern Mexico until he located Tomas.

And he would find him. He was certain of that now!

The headlights hit a larger SNAKE CITY sign and he turned off the highway onto a side road sloping up a hill covered on both sides with tall trees.

Another sign: SNAKE CITY MOTEL. This one was red neon and had a smaller blue-neon VACANCY blinking underneath.

He swerved the Honda off the road and slowed to a stop parallel to the office. None of the motel windows, under a long arched arcade, were lighted. Only four cars parked. One of them would belong to the Chief.

There was a flicker of colored lights in the office. Chief Naja was watching television.

The place hadn't changed, except for a big banner, hanging across the distant entrance to the snake houses at the rear, suspended from a wooden archway:

WELCOME TO SNAKE CITY
Chief Naja, Prop.

The words were painted in red on the white canvas banner.

He left his backpack in the Honda and, leaving the door open, headed for the office.

As he stepped onto the flagstone walk that ran through the arcade, past all the rooms, the office door opened and a tall figure in an Indian bathrobe came out.

Don hesitated, waiting for the old man to speak first.

The hooded black eyes studied his face from their pouches

of brown flesh. Straight white hair hung down, covering his ears, onto both shoulders.

"You come late."

"Remember me, Chief? I was here before. Several times."

"I remember all faces. You come with Pike Splain and his family. He say you were friend."

"That's right."

"Why you come back without Pike?"

"Pike's dead."

"I did not know. He was good man."

"I'm on my way to Mexico. For a vacation. I wanted to see your snakes again."

"You are welcome. How long you stay?"

"Just tonight."

"I get key for you." He turned slowly and went back to his office.

Don watched him through the open door taking a key from a wall hook. He pulled out his wallet. Mustn't let the Chief see how much cash he had. Although most of it was in the backpack.

The old man came toward him, holding out a key with a dangling tag.

"I give you number seven."

He took the key from the wrinkled brown hand. "How much?"

"Pay tomorrow. When you go."

"Don't I have to sign something?"

"Friends never sign anything."

"Thanks." He shoved the wallet back into his hip pocket.

The Indian grunted and headed back to his television set.

Don parked the Honda facing the arcade, where he could see the number seven gleaming in metal on a closed door.

The room was large and air-conditioned. There were twin beds. All the furniture looked Mexican and a glow of light from two shaded lamps revealed several framed pictures of Indians on horseback.

He rested his backpack on a chair and went outside again.

As he passed the closed doors and curtained windows, he glanced across the parking area toward a similar arcade on the other side. No cars parked in front of those rooms.

The old man had a good thing here. Twenty rooms to rent and all those snakes in the back. You had to buy a ticket to see them, but most people would want to do that.

The fog was much heavier up here in the hills.

He disturbed wisps of gray mist as he walked along a high wire fence. The side of the first snake cage.

He could smell them. No other smell like it . . . A musty scent—a moldy underground smell—like when you turned over a shovel of rich black earth.

If you ever kept a snake for a pet, you knew that smell and got to like it.

His mother complained when Tomas gave him his first snake. She objected to the smell in their shanty, but his father persuaded her to keep the snake.

This smell was getting stronger. There were a lot of snakes here. He remembered from his other visits.

The cages were made of heavy chicken wire above metal sheathing buried deep in the ground. A single small bulb glowed above the center of each cage.

He peered through the pattern of wires and saw the bare earth floor. No snakes in sight.

Reaching the corner of the cage, he glimpsed the opposite cage. There was a broad cement walk between them, separating the two rows of cages.

The wooden box office, like a little house, was in the middle of the entrance walk.

He started down the wide center walk between the rows of silent cages, pausing to read the sign on each door.

The first was KING SNAKE, then COBRA, followed by RATTLESNAKE and COPPERHEAD.

As he expected, all the doors were locked.

Continuing on, toward the rear, he realized the cages were larger than he'd remembered. Maybe the Chief had enlarged them.

They were partially protected, overhead, by sheets of cast iron covered with vines placed to give shaded areas to the snakes during the day.

The cement walk divided and continued on, out of sight, on both sides.

He turned back toward the box office along the opposite row of cages. PYTHON, BOA CONSTRICTOR, and BLACKSNAKE.

Peering through the chicken wire, he glimpsed an adobe wall at the rear of each cage with rows of arched holes along the bottom. Some were small but there were three big holes in the PYTHON cage. These were entrances to the snake houses.

All the snakes would be inside at this hour.

A faint sound made him turn and he saw a pinpoint of red coming toward him. He realized it was a lighted cigarette as the robed figure of the Indian loomed out of the fog.

"Heard someone walking in the dark." He didn't remove the cigarette from his mouth and it moved up and down as he talked. "Knew it was you."

"You have sharp ears."

"Indian is like coyote. I hear everything that moves in the night. My ancestors were chiefs in New Mexico. *Naja* is ancient name of serpents."

"My father was half Mexican."

"I, too, have Mexican blood. Tonight your hair is not black, like last time."

"I had it dyed. For a movie job."

"When I was in movies—with Pike Splain—they made me wear long black wigs. You like snakes. I remember from other visits. . . ."

"Snakes are my friends."

"Most people are afraid of them."

"You must have a good business. Lots of tourists."

"Pretty good in summer. And I sell venom to hospital in Tijuana. Milk my snakes for them to make serum. Cure people much sickness." Pulling a key from a sagging pocket of his robe. "I will open door for you. Blacksnakes. No poison."

"I know."

"They are asleep, but if you go in their cage, they will wake up and come out to see you." He unlocked the door.

"Maybe in the morning. Right now I think I'd better get some sleep myself."

The old man shrugged. "I leave door unlocked, you change your mind."

They walked side by side, in silence, under the arcade.

When they reached room seven, Chief Naja raised a hand in parting and continued on toward the office.

Don unlocked his door and stepped inside. Closed it and checked, automatically, that it locked. He was too tired to open his backpack for his pajamas and stretched out on the bed nearest the door without turning the cover down.

Suddenly he realized he'd left something behind in the Coop. His father's paperback copy of *Don Quixote*!

He'd put it on the foot of his bed where he'd be sure to see it as he left, but he hadn't noticed it in his hurry to get away.

And inside that paperback was Tomas' map, a corner torn from a map of Mexico, with a list of the places his father had visited on a piece of paper—they were marked in red on the map—along with a printed card for Snake City he had picked up on one of his visits here with Pike and Velma.

His father's map . . .

He could remember the name of every town and village: Tijuana, Ensenada, Nogales, Agua Priéta, Guzman, Ciudad Juárez. . . .

Those were the names that would take him to Tomas.

Someday he would go back to L.A. and get them.

His father's book and his map . . .

Velma wouldn't throw them out.

Those were the only things he ever had that belonged to Tomas.

He'd always meant to read *Don Quixote* but never had the time. Such a long book . . .

He heard the muffled hum of a car passing on the road. Not much traffic coming up from the freeway.

Nobody knew where he was, except for that old Indian. His friend.

He'd sure as hell gotten back at Carlo Dario for his rudeness at the birthday party and, before that, at the *Vaquero* opening.

Made love to his wife.

Hadn't planned that. Only wanted to take something valuable from Carlo's home. Something small he could sell for cash. He got Carlo's money instead. Even though his wife said it was her money!

What a joke to play on Carlo Dario!

He didn't feel angry at Carlo anymore.

He'd get up early tomorrow and cross the border into Mexico before it got crowded with tourists.

He had no idea how far Ensenada was from Tijuana. He'd never been to Ensenada. . . .

Ensenada!

"Tell me, Señor, do you know a Señor Tomas O'Farrill? I'm his son."

He began to go over his plan again. . . .

And fell asleep.

29

Tamonto Drive was poorly lighted, but Lolo saw two police cars parked near the entrance to a walled estate, and as he slowed the Plymouth, a young officer got out of one car. The other car was empty.

"Lieutenant Lolo?"

"Right."

"Lieutenant Gurlink said for you to pull inside. Park near the house."

"Thanks." He swerved his car through the open gates and continued at a crawl toward the house. It was a big place with elaborate gardening. He saw lights through open doors straight ahead and slowed to a stop.

As he got out and strode toward the entrance, he noticed cars from the Malibu Sheriff's office parked on both sides.

Gurlink was waiting in a brightly lighted foyer. "Heard your car, Vic." They shook hands. "Been more than a year."

Lolo walked beside him, into an immense living room with

a lot of expensive furniture and a glare of lighted lamps. The first person he saw was the actor. Carlo Dario, sitting on a big white sofa, was wearing a striped robe and smoking a cigarette. A thin middle-aged woman in a tailored gray robe, hunched down in a big chair, was also smoking. She had straight black hair, cut short, streaked with white. Two young detectives he didn't recognize stood near an open window, in a wall of glass, facing a dark patio. The window stretched the length of the big room.

Gurlink paused as they reached the center. "Mr. Dario, this is Lieutenant Victor Lolo. He's a Special Investigator from downtown. I want him to talk to your wife."

Dario nodded.

Lolo hesitated. No point in saying he'd seen Dario's new picture last week. "Were you on the premises, sir? When this incident happened . . ."

"Guess I was. I'd been out all evening. Returned home maybe an hour before my wife came screaming through the house. I'd only just fallen asleep."

"Were you in the house when the attack took place?"

"I've no idea. When I came home there was no light in my wife's suite. I noticed as I drove past her windows to put my car in the garage."

"You heard no sound from her bedroom?"

"Nothing. Too far away. I came in through an open window to my own suite, which is on the other side of the house."

"Do you always leave your windows open?"

"Afraid we do. Not much crime in Pacific Palisades."

"I may want to talk to to you after I've seen your wife."

"And this is Ms. Vernon. . . ." Gurlink motioned toward the seated woman. "Personal secretary to Mr. Dario and his wife."

"I was asleep, Lieutenant." She crushed her cigarette in a crystal ashtray. "And I'm rather a sound sleeper. This house is enormous. Four separate wings. I'm in the one with the nursery, where young Aldino sleeps."

"Thank you, ma'am." He turned to Gurlink.

"Mrs. Dario is waiting in her suite." He motioned toward an archway leading to a long corridor.

"I think my wife should let me call her doctor, but she refuses to see him." Dario rose from the sofa as though to detain them. "Perhaps you can persuade her, Lieutenant."

"I will certainly try."

"Lieutenant Lolo has had more experience with rape victims than I," Gurlink explained. "As I told you, sir, your wife seems calm. If Lieutenant Lolo thinks she requires medical attention, we will send for a police doctor."

Dario shrugged. "Do what you think's necessary."

As Lolo walked beside Gurlink through the silent villa, he considered the husband's cool attitude. The self-assurance of an actor? Carlo Dario, in person, was better looking than on the screen. Seemed slightly older without makeup, but then most actors did.

"Here we are." Gurlink slowed his steps as they approached a closed door. "There's only one servant, a Mexican woman. She knew nothing, so I sent her back to bed before she became hysterical. Detective Steiner's been talking to Mrs. Dario ever since I called you. Now it's your turn." He opened the door into a softly lighted sitting room. "Mrs. Dario calls this her boudoir. She's in the bedroom."

An inner door stood open into a brightly lighted room.

As he walked toward it, beside Gurlink, Lolo saw the woman seated on a white satin chaise. Redheaded and pretty, younger than her husband, she was wearing a robe made of some pale yellow material, hands folded in her lap.

"One thing I should tell you," Gurlink murmured. "We found two hairs on the pillow—dark blond—left by the attacker. Sent them downtown for tests. No prints anywhere."

Mrs. Dario looked up as they entered.

Steiner noticed her looking toward the door and rose from his chair facing the chaise. He raised his eyebrows, indicating he'd learned nothing.

Gurlink approached the chaise. "Mrs. Dario, this is Lieutenant Lolo. He's from headquarters downtown, and he'd like to talk to you. He's a specialist in rape cases."

"Why not?" Her eyes hadn't left Lolo's face. "Although I'll tell him what I've told you."

He was aware that Gurlink was leaving the room with

Steiner. "I'll try to make this as fast as possible, Mrs. Dario." He heard the door close. "You will have answered some of my questions when the other officers asked them. I would like to hear your answers because I've no idea what you said." He pulled the chair closer to her and sat down.

"Well . . . My husband was out and I was alone in the living room. I'd turned the lights off and was smoking a cigarette, sitting in the dark. I frequently do that. Look out, through the open windows, at the terrace and the garden. It's the most peaceful time of day. And I saw a dark figure coming toward the window. I put my cigarette out so he wouldn't notice me. I watched him—it was a young man—coming through the window. At first he just stood there, looking around, then he took out a flashlight and snapped it on. Held it up and aimed it across the room, from side to side. That's when he saw me."

"Did you scream?"

"Nobody could've heard me." She hesitated, frowning. "I know who you are. I've seen your picture in the papers. Many times. Read about you. You're the detective who's been hunting for that Midnight Jogger."

"That's right. And I'm here because certain things you've told the other detectives made them think your attacker is the Jogger."

"He couldn't be! That's impossible."

"Why is it impossible?"

"Well, I—I don't know. . . ."

He saw that his question had confused her. For a moment, he would remain silent. Force her to continue.

She looked away from him, toward a wall of curtained windows, frowning slightly. "He couldn't be the Midnight Jogger. I can't believe that." She faced him again. "What did I tell them that makes you think he is?"

"You said he had dark blond hair."

"He did."

"The Jogger has dark blond hair. One of his victims described it as bronze, the color of his suntanned skin."

"That's quite true. It was. . . ."

"You said this man has light blue eyes."

"Yes . . ."

"And he likes snakes."

"He told me he did."

"What exactly did he say to you about snakes?"

"Let me think. . . . He said he'd never known anyone—never anyone in Los Angeles—he could really trust. He liked snakes more than people. Had a pet snake when he was a kid."

"He's told another young woman he liked snakes. It's the Jogger, all right."

"No! He can't be!"

"Why not?"

"Because . . ." She hesitated, fingers picking at the edge of her robe. "Is what I'm saying off the record?"

"If you wish."

"Absolutely confidential?"

"Yes." Now the truth would come spilling out.

"I believe we have a mutal friend, Lieutenant. . . ."

"Oh?" Now she was going to say she'd met the Chief at some party.

"I believe you know Morita Rouvray. . . ."

"I do." He'd forgotten what Morita had said.

"Such an incredible young woman! So beautiful, yet obviously a very successful businesswoman as well. We lunch together, a group of us, at least once a month and she's taught us which wines to drink. Morita frequently talks about you."

"Does she? I had no idea. . . ." Damn Morita.

"Don't suppose you have a twin brother?"

"I have one brother, but he's not my twin. He's in Samoa. Married, with five kids."

"What a pity. . . . You won't repeat a word of what I tell you to my husband?"

"You can trust me, Mrs. Dario. What you're saying isn't being taped or transcribed by a police stenographer. You can deny everything you tell me and I'll have no proof you said it."

"This young man couldn't be the Midnight Jogger because he didn't rape me. I swear he didn't."

"What do you mean?"

"I brought him here, to my bedroom. Invited him into my

bed. I wanted him to make love to me. There's no crime in that, is there? We were adults. Breaking no law . . ."

"No, ma'am. Making love is not a crime. Not yet."

"I told my husband it was rape, but I had no idea he would call the police. I wanted him to think it was rape. Nobody else . . ."

"Rape or not, this man still may be the Jogger. He's raped several young women. We can't be sure how many. And he's killed at least one."

"I don't believe this young man would kill anybody!"

"The Jogger's a psychopath. I've got to find him, Mrs. Dario, before another girl dies. You were lucky. For some reason, apparently, he didn't harm you. He could've just as easily murdered you."

"I refuse to believe that." She shuddered and suddenly buried her face in her hands. "He told me he loved me."

"That's what he tells every girl he rapes."

"He didn't rape me. I willingly enjoyed sex with him."

"But you have a husband! A child . . ."

"I used to have a husband. Carlo changed after we came to Hollywood. I lost him when my son was born. I've no idea why. . . . That's when he, quite openly, began to sleep with other women. Carlo likes a new face every night. He told me if I wouldn't go along with that, he would divorce me, but he preferred to continue as we were. I agreed, for the sake of our son. Since then I've had several brief affairs. Nothing serious or permanent. A woman my age needs love—sex—as much as a man. I was attracted to Don immediately. . . ."

Lolo straightened on the chair. "You know his name?"

"He told me it was Don. . . ."

"His last name?"

"Farrell. Don Farrell." She wouldn't give him Don's real name.

"Don Farrell . . . Did he say where he lived?"

"No. Nothing like that."

"When did you first see him? Obviously, it wasn't tonight." He hesitated. "I've a feeling you invited him to come here."

"I didn't. Not really . . ."

"What then?" He held his voice down, in case anyone was listening outside the door. "Where did you first see him?"

"The night my husband's new picture opened. There was a big premiere at the Cinerama Dome."

He saw that her fingers were no longer picking at the robe. This was the truth she was telling him now. "Farrell was at that opening?"

"He was paid to be there. He does a mechanical-man act standing on a platform outside the theater."

"Your husband saw him?"

"Carlo walked past without noticing him. My husband, as usual, was talking to his agent. But I saw him and was attracted to him. Even with his long black wig. He was supposed to look like Carlo in the picture. Maybe that's what attracted me to him. He did look like Carlo when he was younger. I stood there staring at him. He does this mechanical-man act like a robot, but he noticed me. Looked directly at me. Our eyes met and I smiled. Then I went into the theater with our friends. . . ."

"Did you see him again? After that?"

"I saw him last Saturday."

"Where?"

"Here. We gave a birthday party for our son. I'd been thinking about him, I suppose, about Don, although I didn't know his name then, because I suggested to Vikki—our secretary, Vikki Vernon—that she get him to appear at my son's party. We'd already hired a clown and a man with a monkey. I thought a mechanical man would amuse the children."

"How'd you find him?"

"Vikki did that. I think she located his agent and—"

"Just a minute." He got to his feet and headed for the door.

"You're not going to tell any of this to my husband! You promised. . . ."

"No, Mrs. Dario. I won't tell your husband." He glanced back. "Won't tell him a damn thing. I believe everything you're telling me, but I've got to find this man." He opened the door and saw Gurlink, looking uncomfortable, sitting in the boudoir. "Johnny . . ."

The detective was on his feet.

"Get that secretary. The Vernon woman. I want to talk to her."

"Right away, Vic." He headed for the corridor.

Lolo closed the door and walked back toward Mrs. Dario but didn't sit down. "What happened when Farrell performed at the party? Did you talk to him?"

"Only for a moment. I offered him some ice cream—it was a warm afternoon—but he said he never ate anything when he was working. I told him I was Mrs. Dario, that I'd seen him at the theater and thought the children would enjoy his act. He seemed pleasant. . . ."

"Did your husband notice him at the party?"

"I've no idea."

"Did your husband know you arranged for Farrell to appear at the party?"

"No. He isn't interested in anything like that."

There was a brisk tapping.

"Come in!" Lolo called.

The secretary entered, closing the door. "You wanted me?"

"Mrs. Dario tells me you arranged for a young man—Don Farrell—to perform at her son's birthday party."

"That's correct."

"How'd you locate him?"

"Through his agent. I got the agent's name from the studio publicity department."

"You have this agent's number?"

"Yes."

"Call him."

"At this hour? His office will be closed."

"Get him at home. I want Farrell's address. His agent will have it."

"Well, I suppose he would. . . ."

"Don't tell him it's a police matter."

"I understand."

"I want that address and I want it in a hurry."

"I'll have to go to my suite to get the agent's number. I'll call him from there."

"Tell me, Ms. Vernon. Did you notice anything about this young man—Farrell—anything eccentric or unusual?"

"Not really. Only that he was extremely polite. Which is most unusual in this town. He seemed rather shy. There was one thing I thought rather odd. The snakeskins."

"Snakeskins?"

"He wore a Mexican vaquero costume for his act. I didn't notice when I saw him at the theater, only as I observed him, more carefully, during the party. There was a snakeskin band around his sombrero and he was wearing a handsome snakeskin vest over an embroidered shirt."

"I didn't notice them!" Mrs. Dario exclaimed.

"I've just remembered something more," the secretary added. "There was a snake painted on each side of his platform. He does his act on a low portable platform. I saw the painted snakes as he wheeled his platform toward the drive when he was leaving. He came to thank me, and said he hoped we would use him again. I watched him leave, thinking what a horrible way to make one's living." She went toward the open door. "I'll have that address for you in a jiff, if I reach his agent."

Lolo turned back to the chaise. "What was Farrell wearing tonight?"

"I don't really know. . . . I think some kind of sport shirt and dungarees. But I couldn't swear to it."

"Did you make arrangements to see him again?"

"Unfortunately, that wasn't possible."

"Why not?"

"He was leaving Los Angeles tonight. Driving to Mexico."

"Mexico!"

"To look for his father."

"Did he say where his father was in Mexico?"

"I don't believe he knew. He implied he was going to search for him."

"Damn! He'll be over the border to Tijuana."

"Not until tomorrow."

"What?"

"He's staying with a friend tonight."

"Where?"

"Didn't say. Only that his friend had lots of snakes."

"Lots of . . . I'll be right back." He turned and headed toward the open door.

Gurlink came to meet him. "Any luck?"

"You were right. It's the Jogger. He's heading for Mexico.

Contact the San Diego police and U.S. Customs. Tell them he's driving in their direction. Could be arriving at the border tonight or tomorrow morning. Give them the Jogger's description. Tell them he calls himself Don Farrell. He may have phony papers. Get an APB on the computers in a hurry."

Gurlink nodded and hurried to find a phone.

Lolo returned to the bedroom, where Mrs. Dario hadn't moved from the chaise.

"You won't tell any of this to my husband?"

"No, Mrs. Dario. If this young man is the Jogger, you've done me a great service. There's no reason to tell anyone what I've learned from you. We never reveal sources when we're given information that leads to the apprehension of a criminal. There'll be no official record of what happened here tonight. I'll see to that."

"Thank God!"

"Nothing in the papers." He turned away from her and paced the silent room until he saw the secretary crossing the boudoir with a slip of paper in her hand.

"I have Mr. Farrell's address!"

"You reached the agent?"

"Through his answering service." She gave him the slip of paper.

Lolo stared at the address. "Poinsettia Place? That's in Hollywood." He thrust the slip of paper into his pocket as he went toward the door without glancing back at Mrs. Dario.

30

Don wakened suddenly.

He had no idea where he was. . . .

A door stood open into a lighted bathroom he'd never seen before.

It wasn't his bathroom!

Turning his head cautiously, he saw another bed in the dim light from the bath. His backpack rested on the spread.

Snake City! Chief Naja's motel.

He relaxed immediately. . . .

Held up his arm and squinted at his wristwatch. He'd slept barely an hour.

Tomorrow morning, early, he would take off for Mexico. With enough money to live on for several months.

He would find some sort of job as soon as he decided where he would live. The first town where somebody remembered Tomas . . .

Would he ever write that dame? Carlo Dario's wife? Tell her where he was?

Not a chance.

He shouldn't have said he was going to Mexico. At least he hadn't told her where. Which town.

He must never write anyone from Mexico. Letters could be traced.

She said she wouldn't tell her husband, or anyone else, about him. His making love to her.

That had been terrific. Nothing like the sex he'd had with any of those others . . .

She told him she loved him. He smiled as he remembered. He had loved her too. At least while he was with her.

Maybe in Mexico he would meet a nice girl. One with red hair . . . They would get married and have kids.

He hadn't robbed Carlo Dario's house, so the police wouldn't be after him. She offered him that money. Gave it to him. Insisted he take it.

What was her name? Her first name . . . She had told him but he couldn't remember. Maybe that was a good thing.

He was glad the old Indian hadn't forgotten him.

In the morning, before he left, he would visit the snakes.

He hadn't unpacked before he stretched out here. Only took his hairbrush from the small suitcase and discovered he'd left his comb behind. On the shelf under the bathroom mirror. He'd buy a new comb tomorrow.

Closing his eyes again, he willed himself to sleep. That yogi in Frisco had taught him how to do that. . . .

Velma wouldn't realize right away that he was gone.

Lori-Lou might be the first to suspect.

After a couple of days, maybe, Velma might call a locksmith to open the door of the Coop.

What if she reported he was missing to the police?

There was nothing they could do. They would be looking for Don Farrell when his real name was Geraldo O'Farrill. Even that name wouldn't help them.

He'd be in Mexico and he would be Ed Hannaway. With a birth certificate and Social Security card. No way anybody could prove Hannaway wasn't his name. That's the name he would use if he ever returned to Los Angeles, which wasn't likely. He never wanted to see L.A. again.

He had no idea how many different names he'd taken since the night Ella died. A new one for every town. He'd never kept track of them.

He opened his eyes and noticed a triangle of light stretching across the ceiling from the bathroom bulb.

It looked like he wasn't going to sleep for a while.

Too excited.

Going to Mexico. Finding Tomas . . .

He pushed himself up from the bed and went to the door. Opening it silently, he saw the fog was getting heavier. Maybe he should see if any of those snakes had come out of their houses.

He picked up the tagged key from the chest of drawers and checked that the door locked as he went out.

His rubber-soled shoes made no sound as he walked past the curtained windows to the end of the arcade. He continued on through the fog until he saw the box office under the painted banner.

Heard the distant sound of a car on the road.

Tomorrow night at this hour he would be asleep in Mexicali. On his way to Nogales . . .

He'd never checked distances on the map, but they couldn't be far apart.

Not likely he would find any trace of Tomas in Mexicali.

Be several days, maybe weeks, before he would contact anybody who knew him. He would be following his father's trail and eventually would come to that valley beyond the mountain. Tomas' mountain . . .

He was walking through open pockets in the fog.

Passing the first cage on his left, he smelled the snakes.

He crossed the central walk through a patch of pale moonlight to the unlocked cage and checked the sign on the closed door.

BLACKSNAKE

Tried the heavy steel and wire door. It opened without a sound and he stepped inside.

Felt the soft earth under his feet as he shut the door and walked to the center of the big cage.

Saw the row of dark openings along the base of the small house.

The sweet smell of snakes filled his nostrils. He shivered with anticipation and wondered if they were asleep. Would they sense him here?

The overhead bulb made a faint circle of light on the earth.

He looked up through an opening in the fog and saw the moon. Maybe three-quarters full . . .

Heard a whisper of sound.

A large blacksnake was gliding toward him through the moonlight, coming straight to him, like a messenger sent by his father. The thought made him smile.

"I'm here, Papa," he whispered. "I'm here. On my way to find you . . ."

Another snake thrust its head from one of the holes and was peering from side to side, tongue darting, tasting the air. Now it was following the other one.

The first snake had come to a stop near his feet, raising its head to inspect him.

A third and fourth snake were coming out from the holes.

Something bumped against his ankle.

He saw that the first snake was prodding him with its snout. Letting him know he was welcome.

Don felt a curious sense of happiness, such as he'd never known in his life. As though this blacksnake was giving him a message. Telling him he would meet Tomas soon . . .

That had been his dream for so long.

Standing there, erect in the moonlight, he realized there were tears in his eyes.

Good thing his father couldn't see him.

The earth around his feet was black with snakes and more were pouring out through the holes. None of these came close but formed a circle like villagers inspecting a stranger.

He looked down at the snake coiled beside him, head raised, peering up at him, but no longer prodding his leg.

Don leaned down and stroked the black head, felt it swaying under his fingers. This one was larger than the others.

He picked the snake up carefully, felt the scaly coils circle his arm. "Satan, I've come back. You will sleep beside me tonight, as you always did. Until dawn . . ."

31

The small one-story house on Poinsettia Place was dark, a steel mesh gate at the side closed and padlocked.

Lolo ran up the steps to a shallow front porch, followed by Detective Gimple from Hollywood Division, and jabbed the bell button. He heard a chime respond as a dog barked and kept barking as it came close to the door. It sounded like a big dog.

"What's up, Vic?" Gimple asked, his voice low.

"It's the Jogger."

"I got that much on the phone from Malibu."

"I've reason to believe he lives here." He fingered the button again and glanced back toward the street where three other men from Hollywood Division waited: Gimple's partner, Perski, with Judson, a latent-print man, and Quong, from Robbery Special, an expert in breaking and entering. He'd worked with each of them before.

Lights came on in the hall, visible through curtained vertical windows on either side of the door, as the dog continued to bark.

Lolo looked beyond the silent detectives at two stripped-down police cars across the street—they had been waiting for him—and his old Plymouth parked in the drive, its front fender nudging the locked gate.

"Who is it?" A woman's voice from inside.

He faced the door again. "Police. Official business."

"Just a minute. Let me shut the dog up."

He heard her talking to the dog as a door opened and closed.

"Gotta lot of robberies in this part of Hollywood," Gimple muttered. "People keep everything locked."

The door was opened by a middle-aged woman in a quilted pink robe, her blonde hair in curlers under a plastic cap. "If you're really cops, let's see some proof."

Lolo held up his laminated card.

She squinted at it through the screen door. "Never unlock this screen door to anybody I don't know. Day or night." She glanced from face to face. "What official business brings you here?"

"You know a man named Farrell?" He slipped the ID back into his wallet. "Don Farrell . . ."

"Of course I know him. He's my tenant."

"Is he on the premises at the moment?"

"I couldn't say. . . ."

"What is it, Mommy?"

Lolo saw a young girl, in a blue robe and slippers, hesitating near the stairs at the end of the hall.

The woman glanced over her shoulder. "Go back to bed, Miss! This is no concern of yours." Facing the detective again, she asked, "Why do you wanta see Don? What's he done?"

"I can't tell you that, at the moment," Lolo answered. "Your name, ma'am?"

"Mrs. Velma Splain. I own this property. My husband left it to me when he passed on. He was in pictures—a stuntman. That's how he met Don. Don was a stuntman for a while, before he went to work on his own. Now he does a mechanical-man act for a living."

"He's the man we're looking for. May we come in?"

She unlocked the screen door and pushed it open. "Don lives in the back. . . ." She led them down a narrow hall toward the rear. "You can come through the house and I won't have to unlock that gate."

Lolo motioned for the others to follow as he trailed her past the closed door where the dog was growling and the girl still lurking at the foot of the steps.

"Lori-Lou, lock that door after these gentlemen and then go straight upstairs. You hear me?"

"Yes, Mommy . . ." She ran past them toward the front.

"Has Farrell been in trouble before?" Lolo asked.

"Never to my knowledge. He's a fine young man. I've known him four or five years."

"Does he rent a room from you?"

"Don lives in the back. Used to be a chicken house and we still call it the Coop. My husband used it for a kind of studio, but after his passing I let Don turn it into a little apartment." She guided them across a dark kitchen. "We have to go outside and through the yard." She unlocked the kitchen door, pushed another screen door open, and led them down steps to the drive.

The procession of detectives followed silently toward the rear.

"This is the Coop, gentlemen." She turned down a narrow cement walk between some shrubbery and a low building hidden by vines. "Better ring the bell and see if Don's home. I never know whether he's in or not."

Lolo moved ahead of her and located a button between the vine leaves. Pushed it hard. A buzzer sounded faintly inside. "Is there another entrance?"

"Only this one."

"How long since you saw Farrell?"

"Probably yesterday, I think. . . ."

"You didn't see him today?"

"Seems to me the last time was yesterday afternoon, and I didn't see him then. Heard his car come in."

"What time was this?"

"Maybe six o'clock. My daughter and I hadn't finished dinner."

"Did you hear him go out again?"

"Afraid I didn't . . ." She tried to see his face in the darkness. "This sounds kinda important."

"Very important, ma'am." He saw there were two locks on the door.

"I don't always hear Don. Sometimes I'm watchin' TV, and at night I sleep on the other side of the house."

"Doesn't your dog bark when Farrell goes in and out?"

"Kong never barks at Don. They're good friends."

"You have keys to these locks?"

"Afraid I don't. Don put new locks on when he moved in and I never asked for duplicates. Suppose I should've, but I didn't. . . ."

"We'll have to open the door without them." He motioned for Quong to move in.

The young Chinese smiled and opened his oblong leather satchel, resting it beside the door, as one of the other detectives aimed a flashlight on the locks. Quong studied them briefly, then selected a small tool from his satchel and went to work.

Lolo turned to Velma. "You can tell me, ma'am, while we're waiting—"

"Anything I can!"

"—what Farrell looks like."

"I'd guess Don's in his middle twenties. Never asked, and he never really said. Average height, but muscular. Keeps himself in good shape. Like my late husband."

"Color hair?"

"Black."

"Oh?"

"Kinda curly. Wears it short."

"Eyes?"

"Dark brown, I guess. Or black. Dependin' on the light. He's always tanned from the sun. From standin' in fronta some movie or in a shopping center when he does his mechanical-man act . . ."

Lolo watched the door opening.

"Okay, Vic." Quong moved aside as he returned the tool to his satchel.

Lolo stepped across the threshold into darkness.

"There's a wall switch," Velma called. "Near the door."

"You stay outside, ma'am, while I have a look in here." He felt along the wall until he located a switch and snapped it. Lights came on. A small shaded lamp on a table at the far end of a studio bed, and a shaded bulb hanging from the ceiling above a Formica-topped table.

Gimple and Perski followed him inside but remained near the door.

Lolo's eyes darted around, missing nothing. A paperback on the foot of the bed, near the door. Skylight overhead, covered with a bamboo blind. White telephone on a coffee table. Glossy photographs of movie stars tacked to white-painted plywood walls. Several of James Dean.

Moving closer he saw a photograph of Carlo Dario, pocked with tiny holes. Somebody had been tossing darts at the actor's face. No holes in any of the other pictures.

So Don Farrell hadn't liked Carlo Dario.

He checked a carved cabinet and the door to a cupboard. Both were locked. "You can come in, Mrs. Splain," he called.

She appeared, peering around as she entered.

"Sit on the bed if you will. Don't touch anything."

"Never been in here, since Don moved in." She sunk onto the bed, avoiding the paperback at the foot. "Don's fixed it up real nice."

Lolo glanced at Judson. "See if you can lift any prints anywhere."

The print specialist nodded, brought out a pair of rubber gloves from a pocket, and pulled them over his hands. Gimple was opening the door to a large cupboard filled with clothes and Perski was inspecting the small bathroom.

Lolo turned back to the plump woman sitting on the narrow bed. "Does Farrell have many visitors here, Mrs. Splain?"

"None. Far's I know."

"He must've had friends."

"Don's kinda shy."

"Girlfriends?"

"He talked about one, but I never saw her. Told me she lived in the Valley. Never came to Hollywood."

"There's a smart girl."

"Mommy, can I come in?"

Lolo looked around and saw the girl, hesitating in the doorway.

"I told you, Lori-Lou! Back to bed."

"But, Mommy . . ."

"Let her come in, ma'am. I'd like to talk to Lori-Lou."

She ran past him and sat beside her mother on the bed.

Velma placed a protective arm around her. "I'd rather you didn't question my daughter. She loves Don."

"What's happened to Don?" Lori-Lou asked, frowning.

"Nothin', honey. Not a thing."

"Do you love Don?" Lolo asked casually.

Lori-Lou nodded, her face solemn. "Yes, I do."

"Love!" her mother exclaimed. "What does an eleven-year-old know about love?"

"I do, Mommy! I've told Don I love him."

"You did what?"

"Told him when I grow up I'm gonna marry him."

"My God! Don's old enough to be your father."

"He is not!"

"Vic . . ." Judson interrupted. "This place is covered with prints. And they all belong to one person."

"Good!" He saw that Gimple was pawing through what looked like some theatrical costumes in the cupboard. He asked his next question carefully. "Did Don hold your hand, Lori-Lou?"

"Sometimes. When we walked up the drive . . ."

"Kiss you?"

"Only once . . ."

"And when was that, young lady?" her mother asked.

"Last Christmas Eve."

"That didn't mean a thing. Everybody was kissin' everybody."

Lolo pulled a chair around and sat facing them as he continued his questions. "Describe Don for me, Lori-Lou. Remember, I've never seen him. What's Don look like?"

"He's very handsome."

Velma sighed dramatically. "You never know! What a child is thinkin' . . ."

"What color is Don's hair?" Lolo asked.

Lori-Lou scowled. "You mean his real hair?"

"That's what I mean."

"It's kinda dark blond. Sorta shiny. He puts oil on it."

"His hair's black!" her mother exclaimed. "Curly and cut short."

"No, Mommy. You never knew. I've seen Don at night, when he took his wig off."

"Don doesn't wear a wig. Except that long one for his act."

"He does! All the time."

"Where'd you see him take his wig off?" Lolo asked.

"Sittin' on that chair." She pointed toward a leather Mexican chair near the cabinet. "Don keeps both his wigs in there."

"Quong!" Lolo turned toward the detective. "Open this cabinet."

The smiling Chinese carried his leather satchel behind Lolo to the cabinet.

"Tell me, young lady"—Velma was holding her daughter's wrist as though afraid she might escape—"how did you see Don take off a wig? You were told never to come in here."

"I was on the roof. Watchin' him through that skylight."

Lolo looked up at the skylight covered by the bamboo shade.

"I often did that. Nights when you were asleep, Mommy. I would hear Don's car come up the drive and I would creep downstairs with Kong, but I wouldn't let him out."

"I should hope not!"

"And I would come up here and go round back where there's a place I can climb from the top of the trash can onto that little shed, then up to the roof."

"You could've broken your neck!"

"I never did. Don heard me sometimes, but he thought I was one of the cats."

"You've done this many times?" Lolo asked.

"Oh, sure."

"Did you ever see Don," her mother asked, "when he was undressed?"

"I've seen people undressed before."

"Where?"

"Papa always walked around with no clothes on. And so do you."

"Never mind about that."

"Okay, Vic." Quong straightened from the cupboard.

Lolo got to his feet. "You can open it."

Quong reached out both rubber-gloved hands and pushed the carved wooden doors apart.

Everyone was watching.

As Lolo joined Quong, he saw three empty wig blocks in front of a trio of hinged mirrors. "He's taken the wigs with him." Turning back to Lori-Lou, he asked, "What color were his eyes?"

"Dark brown or black," Velma answered. "I was never sure which."

"No, Mommy! Don wore contact lenses. They changed the color of his eyes."

"How could you know that?" her mother asked.

"I've seen him take 'em out. There's a little drawer under those mirrors. He kept his lenses in there."

Quong pulled out the drawer with a gloved hand. "Nothing here now."

Lolo turned back to Lori-Lou. "Did you ever see the real color of his eyes?"

"Oh, yes! Several times when he forgot to wear his contacts."

"What color were they?"

"Blue. Pale blue."

Lolo smiled. "You've been very helpful, young lady."

"I've seen the color of Don's eyes when he held his snake up in the air."

"Snake!" Velma screamed. "What snake?"

"He'd let it sit on his stomach when he was stretched out here on the bed. Held it up and talked to it."

"Where'd he keep this snake?" Lolo asked.

"In the cupboard." Lori-Lou pointed to a door in the corner near the entrance. "It's a big snake."

Her mother gasped. "A snake! On my property?"

"I think it's a rattlesnake."

"Oh, my God!" Velma got to her feet, preparing to leave.

"Quong, open that cupboard," Lolo ordered. "I tried the door as we came in. It's locked."

Quong carried his satchel to the corner and rested it on the floor. He studied the lock briefly, then went to work. "This one's easy," he said, inserting a small steel device into the lock and snapping it. "There you are!"

"Open it and step back fast." Lolo pulled his gun from its holster under his left shoulder.

All eyes focused on the door.

Velma placed her arm around Lori-Lou.

Quong flung the door open and stepped back.

A large rattlesnake was coiled on the floor, head raised, eyes reflecting the lights.

Velma screamed.

"It's not moving," Quong whispered.

Gimple leaned forward to peer at it. "I think it's stuffed."

Lolo circled the coffee table, revolver aimed at the snake. "If it was alive, it would come out fast."

Perski reached down and snatched up the snake in one hand. "It's stuffed, all right." He carried it to the coffee table. Lolo thrust his gun back into its holster.

Velma turned to her daughter. "Why didn't you tell me about this? You knew Don had a rattlesnake and never said a word!"

Lolo glanced around the small room again. He had found the Jogger. This was where he lived—in a state of limbo—between victims. Hidden, all these months, in the heart of Hollywood . . .

He scowled. Something was missing here. One more piece of evidence to prove Farrell was the Jogger.

He remembered at that instant he'd forgotten to phone Morita. This was Thursday night. His night. And he'd forgotten. . . .

Damn!

Then he realized what was missing. The Jogger's car.

He saw that everyone was staring at him, waiting for him to speak. "Sorry. I was working something out. Tell me, Mrs. Splain, what make car does Farrell drive?"

"He has two cars," Lori-Lou answered.

Velma nodded. "One's a gray Volkswagen. An old one . . ."

There it was!

". . . and a black Honda," Lori-Lou added.

"Where does he keep them?"

"Don has his own garage in the back," Velma responded. "I'll show you." She led the way outside, one arm still around Lori-Lou.

As Lolo followed, ahead of the other detectives, he noticed

the paperback again, on the foot of the bed. A battered copy of *Don Quixote*.

"Don bought his Volkswagen from me," Velma explained. "It belonged to my late husband. I'd gotten a new station wagon. . . ."

"Where'd he get the Honda?"

"He had that when we first knew him."

They had reached the end of the walk.

Velma turned up the drive toward the rear, with Lori-Lou, and the others following.

"I never see him drivin' the Volkswagen anymore," Velma continued, "and it's a better car than the Honda. Durin' the day he's always in the Honda. . . ."

"He only drives the Volkswagen at night!" Lori-Lou exclaimed, pulling away from her mother and dancing up the drive. "When he goes out late."

Lolo smiled again.

Lori-Lou came to a stop in front of a two-car garage. Both doors were closed and padlocked.

"Quong! Open these."

"Right, Vic." Still wearing his rubber gloves, he set his satchel down again and examined the first lock. The others remained silent, watching him, stepping back as the lock fell open and Quong raised the door.

The garage was empty.

"Open that other one," Lolo ordered.

Quong moved up the drive to the second door. The others followed.

When he lifted the second door, a dark gray Volkswagen was revealed.

Lolo sighed. "So he's driving the Honda." He turned to the nearest detective. "Gimple! Put out an APB on a blond man with light blue eyes driving a black Honda. Somewhere between L.A. and Tijuana."

"Right away, Vic. I'll do it from my car."

"His name's Don Farrell and he's wanted for murder." Velma screamed.

Gimple headed down the drive toward the house.

"I'd like to talk to you alone, Mrs. Splain."

"Anything I can tell you . . ."

"If you'll come inside again."

"Of course."

"You wait here, Lori-Lou," Lolo ordered. "With these detectives."

"Must I?"

"Yes, you must, young lady." Her mother walked beside Lolo down the drive, turning onto the walk toward the light coming from the open door of the Coop.

"First of all, Mrs. Splain, does Don have any family?"

"His mother is dead but his father is supposed to be alive. In Mexico."

"And that's where he's going."

"He's the Jogger, isn't he?"

"I think so. Yes."

"I guessed from what you said earlier. But I still can't believe it! A nice boy like that . . ."

"Did he ever say where his father is in Mexico?"

"Told me he didn't know. Showed me a map once that belonged to his father."

"Map of Mexico?"

"Northern Mexico." She went into the lighted Coop and sank onto the bed again. "He also had a list of places where his father had lived. Wanted to visit them to look for him, or for anybody who could tell him where his father was living."

Lolo looked down at the copy of *Don Quixote* as she talked, picked it up and saw the faded pages.

Velma watched him. "Don must've forgotten to take that book. It was his favorite possession. Belonged to his father. He probably put it on the bed to pick up as he went out, then he forgot. . . ."

Lolo opened the book and saw a name written inside. He read it aloud. "Tomas O'Farrill . . ."

"That's his father."

He turned a page and found two small pieces of faded paper. A corner torn from a map. Northern Mexico. A list of towns. From Tijuana to Ciudad Juárez . . . And a printed business card. SNAKE CITY, with an Orange County address and a phone nunber.

"Tell me, Mrs. Splain . . ."

"Yes?"

"You ever hear of a place in Orange County called Snake City?"

"I know it well. It's owned by an Indian—calls himself Chief Naja—don't know his real name. Used to work in Westerns with my husband. He retired years ago and opened Snake City. It's not far from Disneyland."

"Has Don been there?"

"Oh, yes! We took him with us several times when we went to visit the Chief. Don was very excited. He'd liked snakes, ever since he was a kid. . . ."

Lolo handed the card to her. "Call this number, Mrs. Splain."

"Chief Naja's an old man. He'll be asleep."

"Wake him up. Ask him if Don's there."

She picked up the phone and, checking the card, began to dial.

"Tell him you were worried about Don and wanted to know if he's all right. But he mustn't tell him you called. And don't mention the police."

"I understand." She looked up. "Phone's ringing."

"All you want to know—is he there? And did he say when he's leaving? . . ."

Velma moved closer to the mouthpiece. "That you, Chief? It's Velma Splain—Pike's wife. . . . Remember? . . . I'm callin' because I was worried about Don. You remember the young man—Don Farrell—he was with us when we drove down to visit you? . . . You do remember! Have you seen him?"

Lolo leaned forward as if to hear what was being said on the other end of the line.

"He is!"

Lolo reached down and picked up the business card from the table.

"Came in tonight? Did he say where he's goin'? . . . Mexico! That's what I thought. Did he mention when he'd be leavin'? . . . First thing in the morning. That's fine. Don't say a word about my callin'. I just wanted to be sure he was okay."

Lolo folded the piece of map, and list of names, and the business card, slipped them into a pocket, and dropped the book on the bed.

"Sorry I woke you, Chief. I'll be drivin' down to see you one of these days. Remember! Don't tell Don I called. Good night . . ." She set the phone down. "You heard? Don's there."

"I'm very grateful, Mrs. Splain. You've been a big help."

"I certainly hope so."

"Don't touch anything here. The others will take care of everything." He turned toward the open door. "One man from Hollywood Division will stay on the premises all night. On the chance, which is unlikely, Don comes back."

Velma got to her feet. "You're goin' to Snake City, aren't you?"

"That's right, ma'am." He saw the other detectives waiting on the drive as he started down the cement walk. "Gimple! Perski! We've got him. . . ."

Eight

32

Don read the note he'd written on a sheet from the phone pad.

> Chief Naja:
> Couldn't sleep so decided to drive on. May
> never come this way again. Good luck.
>
> Don

Sixty bucks should cover everything.

He left the note on the bed where the Chief would see it right away, and put three twenties on top of it.

Snapped off the bathroom light and left the room key with the money.

Carried backpack and suitcase to the door, set them down, then snapped off all the lights before opening the door.

Stood in the doorway looking across the parking lot.

Still dark.

The fog was so heavy he couldn't see the fence on the far side of the property.

Not a sound. Only a dog barking, far away.

Same cars parked.

He carried his backpack and suitcase out to the car, put them down, and, careful not to make any noise, unlocked the door.

Lifted backpack and suitcase into the front. Backpack on the seat, suitcase on the floor.

Closed the car door and went back to shut the door to his room.

Hesitated on the walk, staring at the fog, listening.

Checked his wristwatch.

Not quite five o'clock.

Another half hour before dawn.

Lots of time.

Stop off at the first roadside restaurant that looked clean and have breakfast.

Would take an hour, maybe an hour and a half, to reach the border.

He was in no hurry.

No cars moving past on the road.

The Chief might hear him pulling out, but he wouldn't know which car was leaving.

Maybe he ought to ditch the Honda, sell it before he reached the border, and walk the rest of the way. Hitch a ride if anybody offered to pick him up.

He stepped down from the walk and went back to his car. Opened the door on the other side, silently, and eased down onto the driver's seat, closing it without a sound.

The motor was quiet as he backed out and turned the Honda toward the road.

Glancing back, he saw that none of the motel windows were lighted. Fog was drifting under the arcade and he could barely make out the row of closed doors.

Slowing at the entrance, he peered up and down the road.

Nothing in sight.

Switched on his headlights as he turned right toward the freeway.

He wouldn't stay in Tijuana but would drive across Baja until he reached Nogales. Then he would be in Mexico.

Had no idea how long that would take. Maybe a couple of hours.

He wondered if Carlo's wife was asleep in that big bed.

He'd never seen such a fancy bedroom.

Carlo in his own suite on the other side of the villa.

And he was in the clear!

Nobody knew where he was. . . .

So no one could follow him.

Must remember to get that map out of his suitcase when he reached Nogales. Tomas' map with the route his father took back and forth across Mexico.

Damn!

The map was between the pages of *Don Quixote*, along with that list of towns and villages. Also a card from Snake City that he had kept since his first visit there with the Splains.

He drove through swirling fog, down the sloping road, toward the freeway.

The freeway was almost invisible in the fog.

Lolo kept the Plymouth to a crawl, cursing under his breath at the delay. He had thought he would reach Snake City in an hour, but he'd already been driving more than an hour and hadn't passed Disneyland.

Mrs. Splain had followed him through the house to the front door, explaining that, once he passed Disneyland, there would be signs along the road telling how to find Snake City.

He knew the route to Disneyland because he'd been there several times. Two or three times alone, when he went there to relax. Enjoying the rides and the excitement. Always picking up a pretty girl and persuading her to join him for the evening. Each of them had been with several other girls, all of whom went off with young men. His girl explained they did this once a week during the summer, found a guy to pay for their evening. They met again, all of them, near the entrance gates at eleven o'clock and said goodbye to their friends of the evening.

That suited him. He had only wanted a pleasant companion to sit beside him on the rides, let him kiss her and comfort her when she was frightened, and have dinner with him in one of the restaurants. He'd never seen any of them a second time when he was enjoying Disneyland with another girl.

The last time he went to Disneyland had been with Morita.

She'd never been there before and he was afraid she'd be bored, but she enjoyed it as much as those other girls. Except she had been curious about how much each ride and restaurant was grossing, what profit the concessions were making.

Beautiful Morita!

He still had to reach a decision about her propositions.

Did he want to manage a vineyard? The thought of all the details he would have to look after—the new people he'd be working with, as well as the knowledge he'd have to pick up about raising grapes and making wine—made him scowl.

Could he succeed in such a profession?

He was happy with what he was doing, pleased with the promotions he'd gotten and looking forward to several more.

Though managing a vineyard would, of course, be less dangerous. No rapists, murderers, or other criminals.

But he liked criminals! Enjoyed the excitement of tracking them down and putting them behind bars.

Although he didn't approve of judges who, too frequently, set them free.

That wasn't his problem. What happened in the courts was no concern of his. . . .

Did he want to get married at the moment?

Marry Morita and work for her father?

He would certainly get more money than he could ever make with the L.A.P.D. in the future.

Except money had never been his goal. Not big money.

He'd never dreamed of being rich when he was a teenager in Samoa. . . .

He was happy with what he was doing, enjoyed his work. He was proud of being able to solve so many difficult and important cases. Proud, most of all, when he became a Special Investigator and was assigned to the most important investigations when local Divisions were in trouble.

He enjoyed stepping in after others had failed.

Like this latest one that he'd been able to solve!

The Midnight Jogger who had turned into the Midnight Murderer whose name was Don Farrell . . .

Was he asleep, at this moment, at this place called Snake City?

A murderer who liked snakes!

That was something the newspapers would play up when the story broke.

The guy had to be psychotic. Liking snakes . . .

A crazy who kept a stuffed rattlesnake in a cupboard!

He wondered if he'd used many different names. In other California cities, before he turned up in Los Angeles . . .

At least now they knew his name and had his prints.

He would ask Morita tomorrow what she knew about Carlo Dario's wife. She had told him the other evening that Mrs. Dario was a very unhappy lady. . . .

Most actors' wives were.

She acknowledged that Farrell hadn't raped her. She'd enticed him into her bed. . . .

He should've called Morita today. Told her he wouldn't be free tonight. He'd been free but he was putting off seeing her.

He'd phone her tomorrow—it was already tomorrow—and explain that he'd been busy with the Jogger investigation.

He could call her from Tijuana after Farrell was behind bars or on his way back to Los Angeles.

But he would never say that her friend, Carlo Dario's wife, was involved.

He'd told Gurlink to put his report on the incident at Carlo Dario's residence in a confidential file.

He would explain everything to the Chief tomorrow and an order would go to the Malibu Sheriff's office to destroy all reports. Carlo Dario wanted no publicity and his wife refused to cooperate, claimed there had been no rape.

He'd tell Morita he had caught the Jogger.

That would be sufficient reason for his not phoning yesterday.

When he talked to her he would say he wouldn't be free until next week. Wrapping up the investigation. She knew that took several days of interviewing people—including the criminal—and filling out reports.

When he pulled into Snake City he would talk to this Indian who owned the place—Chief Naja—get him to open the door to the room where Farrell was sleeping.

He wondered if the Jogger had a gun.

Not likely. Rapists never did.

Through a break in the fog, to his left, there was a faint horizontal streak of light.

That must be the sun coming up. Soon it would be dawn.

He'd decided that he would get rid of the Honda before he reached Tijuana. Before he crossed the border . . .

It would be less suspicious if he was walking. Wearing his backpack.

He would stop somewhere for breakfast and take everything from the suitcase and transfer it to the backpack. Get rid of the suitcase.

Ella's suitcase! No matter.

Better for him to travel light. Look like he was heading into Baja for a vacation. Must be lots of guys who did that every day.

The fog seemed to be lifting. Maybe the sun would burn it off.

He hadn't switched off his headlights and their twin beams seemed to push the fog aside.

He'd been on the freeway less than an hour.

Creeping in a slow lane, paying no attention to signs or towns he was passing.

A few big trucks in the fast lanes. Moving like giant shadows. Heading for Tijuana and, in the other direction, toward Los Angeles.

Maybe when he got rid of his suitcase he should junk the three wigs and his contact lenses. He would never need them in Mexico.

If the inspectors at the border searched his backpack and found three wigs, they might get suspicious.

Do that after he stopped for breakfast.

Must remember to remove the small labels from the wigs. Easy to rip them out. Then the wigs couldn't be traced.

After he sold the Honda, he would walk the rest of the way to the border.

Somebody was sure to give him a lift.

Riding in somebody else's car might make it easier to get through customs. He'd keep his backpack on the floor, out of sight, and they wouldn't think he was a hitchhiker.

That's what he would do! Sell the Honda, for whatever price he could get, and ride across the border in a stranger's car.

He would buy a secondhand car in Tijuana—he had enough money—and start off to find Tomas.

Follow the route his father took on that map he'd left behind in the Coop.

He remembered every name that was marked. Ciudad Juárez, Guzman, Agua Priéta, Nogales, Mexicali, Tijuana . . .

Of course he would be starting at the other end. Tijuana, Mexicali, Nogales, Agua Priéta, Guzman, Ciudad Juárez . . .

He'd no idea whether they were towns or villages. . . . Maybe small towns. He would see the first ones today. Tijuana and Mexicali . . .

Tijuana was a small city.

Maybe, right away, he would find somebody who knew his father!

He'd quickly learned, after he left home, that distances were too great for him to walk to Mexico.

That was years ago.

Now he was finally going to make it. Follow Tomas' trail . . .

There had to be somebody who remembered his father.

Would he recognize him?

Tomas was forty-seven now.

If he was alive . . .

He had to be alive! Forty-seven was young. Only twenty years older than he was.

He noticed the lights of a small restaurant on a road parallel to the freeway and turned right onto a side road.

The fog was lifting.

Pulling into the parking area he couldn't see any customers inside the restaurant. Only one car was parked outside, an old battered Chevy.

He locked the Honda and started past the Chevy toward the entrance of the restaurant. The old car had an Iowa license, and a lot of bags were tied on top and sticking out from the trunk. Inside the car were a young man and a girl in front, three kids in the back. He thought they were asleep, but as he passed the closed windows he saw that the young man was watching him and one of the kids was crying.

He sat on a stool at the counter as a skinny middle-aged man, wearing a spattered apron over a blue denim shirt and dungarees, pushed through a door from the kitchen. "Mornin', sir. What's your pleasure?"

"I could use some breakfast."

"We got the best."

"Scrambled eggs with sausages. Toasted muffin and coffee."

"Right away." He picked up a glass pot of coffee and filled a white mug.

"Noticed people asleep in that Chevy outside. Looked like a whole family."

"They're a sad case." He set a steaming mug in front of him. "From Ioway, on their way to San Diego an' run outta two things at the same time: money an' gas. I'll have your breakfast right away," he said, heading toward the kitchen.

Don glanced through the steamed windows at the parked Chevy as he sipped his hot black coffee. The young husband seemed to be hunched down behind the wheel.

How could they drive all the way from Iowa without enough money to get them where they wanted to go? What would they do now?

As he continued to sip the coffee, he remembered how broke he'd been that night he left home.

The skinny cook returned and set a plate of food in front of him. "I'll bring you more coffee."

"Thanks." He ate with appetite as the cook refilled his cup.

"You asked about them people asleep in that car. Young fella drove all the way from Ioway to find a job. Claims he has a cousin in San Diego. Car broke down on the highway an' with the help of his whole damn family, he managed to push it in here. Just after dark last night. I seen 'em sittin in it an', when I wasn't busy, went out an' inquired what was wrong. They told me they're on their way to San Diego where they've got a cousin. Seems this fella lost his job in Ioway an' his cousin told him he could find one out here. So he packed his whole damn family in that old car an' started out. Broke down two days ago. Cost him most of his dough to have it fixed. They stopped off at Disneyland yesterday an' that took the rest of it. Thought they'd get to San Diego last night, but they ran outta gas in front of my place."

"That's tough luck."

"I gave em' dinner las' night an' let the guy have a coin to dial Information. He had his cousin's address, but Information told him the phone was disconnected. My guess is the cousin was too broke to pay his phone bill or, for some reason, he's skipped. Whichever's the reason, these folks are in trouble. . . . More coffee?"

"No more. Thanks." He took his time over breakfast, and when he went outside, he saw the sun was up.

The fog had blown away and a breeze was shaking a row of eucalyptus trees beyond the restaurant. There was a clear blue sky overhead.

He saw that the distant highway was empty. The morning traffic hadn't started.

Walking back to his Honda, he glanced into the Chevy. The family seemed to be asleep, but then he realized the young husband's eyes were open and watching him.

Nothing he could do for them.

He unlocked the Honda and got in.

Didn't look at the Chevy as he eased out and started back toward the highway, but felt guilty for not giving them a few bucks.

He had enough to do that.

Too late now.

A yellow glow of light was spreading over everything from the rising sun.

Another hour and he would be in Mexico.

The sun had risen and put an end to the fog.

Signs along the road, as Mrs. Splain had said, guided him to Snake City.

Lolo turned the Plymouth off the sloping road into the parking lot where only one car was parked. It wasn't the Honda. He slowed to a stop in front of the office and got out.

The office door opened and a tall old man came out. His long white hair, held by a beaded band, made him look like an Indian in a Western movie. His fringed leather costume and moccasins completed the picture. "Chief Naja?"

"I am Naja."

"Special Investigator Victor Lolo, Los Angeles Police Department."

"I knew you were cop when you got out of car."

"Mrs. Splain called you."

"Yes."

"I was with her when she talked to you. She asked you about her friend Don. . . ."

"That's right."

"You told her he was here."

"I did."

"We believe he's a criminal."

"What's he done?"

"Raped several young women. Murdered one. I've come to arrest him. Take him back to Los Angeles. If you'll show me which room he's in . . ."

"He's gone."

"What!"

"I knocked on his door when I seen his car wasn't parked here. No answer, so I unlock the door. He left a note for me with money for room."

"You have that note?"

Chief Naja produced a slip of paper from his pocket.

Lolo took it from him and read what was written. "I'll keep this. Have you any idea what time he left?" He folded the slip of paper and put it in a pocket. "How long's he been gone?"

"I didn' hear car pull out."

"Did he tell you last night where he was going?"

"Mexico."

"Where in Mexico?"

"He not tell me. Say he want to see my snakes again."

"In the middle of the night?"

"Snakes are his friends. You like to see my snakes?"

"Some other time. What make car was he driving?"

"Black Honda. Not new . . ."

"What color was his hair?"

"Light brown."

"Maybe brownish blond?"

"Could be. When I seen him before, his hair was black."

"And his eyes?"

"Always before his eyes were brown, but last night they were kinda pale gray."

"Anything else you noticed about him?"

"No, sir. Nothin' I recall."

"I'm going after him." He started back to his car.

"Good luck, Officer. If that boy's done wrong, I hope you catch up with him."

"Thanks." He got into the Plymouth, made a wide turn in the parking lot and turned right, onto the sloping road, back toward the highway.

He wondered how far Farrell had already gone on his way to the border.

Maybe they would stop him for questioning.

Surely they would recognize him.

If they didn't, the guy might already be in Mexico.

And he would never find him.

Don pulled off the highway onto a side road and slowed to a stop.

He had made a decision.

That family from Iowa sitting in their old Chevy, with three hungry kids, and no one to help them.

How many times had he needed help and there was nobody. . . .

He snatched up the small suitcase and opened it, took out the three wigs, and ripped the faded labels from each. Stuffed the wigs back in the suitcase and tossed the labels out the window. Sorted through the other things he had packed. Found his missing comb and slipped it into a pocket. Nothing else he wanted to keep. Mostly shirts, underwear, and socks. He would buy what he needed in Mexico. No laundry marks in anything. He'd always done his own.

He closed the suitcase and set it on the floor again, then turned the Honda around and headed back to the highway, where he took one of the northern lanes back the way he had come.

He slowed to a stop when he noticed a deep culvert.

Tossed his suitcase into the tall weeds where it sank out of sight.

Continued north until he saw the restaurant on the other side where he had eaten breakfast.

The Chevy was still parked there.

He turned off the highway and followed an underpass that took him to the roadside restaurant.

Saw that two of the teenage children were tossing a ball near the Chevy. They were older than he had thought.

He slowed past the parked car and came to a stop.

Got out, aware of the young father pulling himself erect, behind the wheel, watching him come toward the Chevy.

The young man reached toward the handle but didn't open the door. At the same time nudging his wife.

She opened her eyes and looked around.

Don motioned for the young man to open his window. He rolled it down. "Yeah?"

"You need a car. Don't you?"

"Sure do. This one come to a stop last night an' I doubt it'll ever start again. Even if I fill her up with gas."

"You can have my car."

The young man's eyes widened with surprise. "What did you say, mister?"

"I've been plannin' for some time to get another car. You can have this one and I'll hitch a ride."

The wife squealed. "Hank! You hear what the man said?"

"I heard, honey, but I don't believe it." He opened the door and got out. "You on the level, mister? This ain't some sorta trick?"

"No trick."

"It ain't stolen?"

"Nothin' like that. I own it. The papers are in the glove compartment. Pink slip. Everything . . ."

"My name's Johnson." He held out his hand. "Hank Johnson."

Don shook his hand. "I'm Ed Hannaway."

"This here's my wife. Josie."

She smiled, timidly. "Howdy, mister."

Don turned back to the Honda. "My car's in pretty good shape. I've always taken good care of it."

Johnson followed him. "I can see that. Ain't had the money to take care of mine. Been out of a job six months. I'm a carpenter. Gotta cousin in San Diego says he'll help me find work. Only his phone's outta order. Tried to call him last night. I'll locate him when we get there."

"I'd planned to buy another car in San Diego. Now I may wait till I reach Tijuana."

"Why can't we give you a lift?"

"I'm kinda in a hurry. Goin' to meet my father in Mexico. I'll make better time hitchin' than waitin' for you."

"Yeah. It'll take us half an hour to move our things from the other car."

Don lifted out his backpack and, as they talked, strapped it onto his shoulders. "You folks had breakfast?"

"No money for that," Johnson answered. "Guy in this restaurant was kind enough to feed us last night. Told us we could park here but he'll be glad to see us leave, I expect. . . ."

"You'd better have some breakfast before you go." He pulled money from one of his pockets and peeled off two twenties. "This should pay for breakfast and get you to San Diego." He handed the money to Johnson and folded the rest into his pocket again.

"We sure are grateful, Mr. Hannaway."

"That's okay."

Johnson folded the money into his shirt pocket. "Hope that guy won't complain 'bout me leavin our old car here."

"He'll know somebody who'll give him a little money for it." As he turned back to the Honda, he noticed the man in the restaurant watching them through the window. He grinned and waved.

The man nodded.

Don took his ring of keys from the ignition, removed the car keys, and gave them to Johnson.

"Thank you, sir."

He slipped the ring of keys into a hip pocket. Wouldn't need any of those keys again. Keys to the Coop, the locked cupboards, and keys to his Volkswagen.

"The kids are hungry, so we'll have breakfast before we move our belongin's. Can't thank you enough, Mr. Hannaway."

He put out his hand. "Gotta be on my way. Meetin' my father. Can't keep him waitin' . . ."

Johnson pumped his hand up and down. "Guess you've

saved us from a lotta trouble. Don' know what we'd have done if you hadn't come back . . ."

"Forget it."

"We all thank you, Mr. Hannaway!" Mrs. Johnson called.

"That's okay, ma'am." He adjusted the backpack across his shoulder as he headed for the highway.

Lolo had kept to the fast lanes since leaving Snake City, knowing Farrell was at least an hour ahead of him.

He would certainly have lost another half hour by stopping somewhere for breakfast.

There was no Honda parked outside any of the roadside cafes and hamburger stands he passed.

Would be a waste of time to stop, even briefly, and give them the Jogger's description.

If Farrell crossed the border, he would follow him into Mexico and worry about the legality of it later.

Maybe use the phone in the office of the American customs inspectors. Call L.A. and have them arrange the necessary documents for him to follow Farrell wherever he went.

They could pull strings at the Mexican Consulate.

The fog had lifted and the air was fresh.

He breathed deep, filling his lungs.

Bright sunlight. Not a cloud in the sky.

He hoped today would bring an end to his search for the Jogger. This had been the longest case he'd ever worked on.

His inability to find the Jogger had angered and frustrated him.

He'd heard of detectives who worked on cases for years.

Like Jigsaw John—the oldest member of the L.A. police department—who held badge Number One and had worked on cases for years.

That would drive him nuts.

He liked difficult investigations that nobody had been able to crack but he could solve in three or four weeks.

Don Farrell had gotten away with his rapes for more than nine months. And at least one murder.

He might never have learned the Jogger's identity if he hadn't stupidly changed his pattern. Instead of raping another girl, he had gone to bed with a married woman, who claimed it wasn't rape because she had invited him into her bed and afterward gave him five hundred bucks so he could go to Mexico and look for his father.

And he had a strong feeling that Carlo Dario's wife was telling the truth. Probably getting back at her promiscuous husband.

Women did the damnedest things.

Only a psychiatrist could explain their motives. . . .

Mostly trucks on the road at this hour. Monsters spouting diesel smoke. A few smaller trucks.

Not a single Honda.

He wondered briefly if he would get another promotion if he caught the Jogger.

Certainly it would be played up in the newspapers. Headlines on every front page.

He didn't like personal publicity but long ago had decided it was a part of his job and unavoidable.

The Chief wanted you to be recognized when you did a good job. Said his men got too much bad publicity.

He had liked the Chief, each time they'd met. A cold man, but he was obviously honorable and decent. And he did a terrific job running the department.

Morita would be asleep at this hour. In that big bed where he had stretched out beside her so many times. Thursday nights . . .

He wondered if she would move that comfortable bed to northern California when she went up there to live. . . .

He'd reached no decision as yet, as to Morita's two propositions.

Did he want to get married, just yet, to anybody?

And if so, did he want to marry Morita?

He had never, in the past, considered marrying her. Had told her so. Several times.

She had agreed, but now she wanted to marry him.

Probably something to do with their jointly running those new vineyards. Maybe it would be better legally if they were married.

What if after a year she became bored—which could happen—and turned the vineyards back to her father? Probably, at the same time, she'd want a divorce.

He had another week to think about those two propositions.

Except Morita would be getting impatient . . .

Did he want to end his career as a detective?

Would he be happy managing a chain of vineyards and wineries?

He saw a black Honda ahead of him, moving at a crawl in the slow lane, and slowed the Plymouth as he came closer.

It was packed with belongings! Boxes and suitcases sticking out from the trunk, everything secured with ropes.

Was Farrell taking a load of possessions with him to Mexico?

Three children in the back and a young couple in the front. Looked like country people. The young man who was driving had blond hair bleached from the sun. Looked Scandinavian and so did his wife.

They turned to look at him as the Plymouth slowed beside them.

He motioned for them to pull over to the side. The young man seemed surprised but nodded and turned the Honda onto a grassy strip at the edge of the highway.

Lolo slowed to a stop behind them and got out, leaving the door of the Plymouth open.

The door of the Honda opened and the driver stepped out. Lolo saw that he was short and muscular.

"Something wrong?"

"How long have you folks owned this Honda?"

"Funny you should ask, mister. We've had it maybe half an hour."

"What!"

"Fella give it to us. Our old car broke down."

"What did this generous guy look like?"

"Pleasant fella. Medium height."

"Brownish blond hair? Pale blue eyes?"

"You know him, do you?"

"Such a nice young man," his wife joined in. "Gave us enough money for breakfast and to get us as far as San Diego."

"We're from Ioway," her husband added. "I'm out here lookin' for work."

"Did this guy tell you his name?"

"Ed Hannaway. It's on his papers in the glove compartment. Edward Hannaway . . ."

So Farrell was using another name. Maybe his real name this time. "He say where he was going?"

"Sure did. He's headin' for Mexico. Lookin' for his father."

Lolo turned and hurried back to the Plymouth.

"Are you a cop, sir?"

Lolo paused and looked back. "What's your name?"

"Henry Johnson."

"Where will you be staying when you get to San Diego?"

"Don't rightly know. We'd thought we might—"

"To hell with it." Lolo got into his car, slammed the door, and took off.

Don had covered several miles, but he wasn't tiring. He kept going at a steady pace, only half aware of the traffic passing him or the changing scenery.

It was a fine morning for walking. A few white clouds, coming in from the ocean, were moving across the blue sky.

He'd learned to take this easy stride long ago when he'd walked from Bakersfield to Frisco, but when he left there years later, he'd been able to afford a bus to Los Angeles.

No danger of the local fuzz picking him up today. He had money, so he wasn't a vagrant.

The L.A. police wouldn't be after him. He'd done nothing wrong last night. Carlo Dario's wife had asked him to sleep with her and the money she'd given him was a gift. Her own money, not her husband's . . .

So far he'd only hitched one ride. Most drivers wouldn't stop and he wasn't going to stand at the side of the road and signal for a ride.

That truck had stopped without his asking for a lift. He'd been aware of it creaking behind him, and to his surprise, he'd heard it slowing. When he looked around, he saw it was an old truck taking a bunch of Mexican farm workers to a job. The driver motioned for him to climb aboard.

Two kids had helped him climb into the back.

When they found he spoke Spanish, they told him where

he could cross over to Mexico without being questioned at the border. He'd told them he had a birth certificate—born in the United States—and should have no trouble. Explained he was going to Mexico to look for his father who was half Mexican. He'd ridden less than twenty minutes when the truck slowed at a turnoff to let him jump down, and all the Mexicans waved as he started down the freeway again.

Cars were passing in the slow lanes, but none of them slowed to a stop.

The big commercial trucks never picked anyone up. Several had signs saying they didn't give lifts, but he saw men in others seated beside the drivers. Maybe armed guards protecting valuable cargoes.

He was passing rows of small stucco houses, used-car lots, and stores advertising beer and tequila.

That meant he was getting near the border.

He considered briefly going to one of those used-car dealers and seeing if he could pick up a cheap car for maybe a hundred bucks.

That would be a waste of time.

Better keep walking.

He'd look for a car in Mexico. Not in Tijuana, but in one of the villages.

As he walked he thought about the many times he'd set out like this in the past, walking at the edge of a strange highway.

You saw more scenery walking freeways in New Mexico and Arizona. Ranges of green hills and brown foothills. Mountains with white snow on their tops. Roads cutting through canyons that were old Indian or wagon trails leading to California.

One time he started out from Barstow to walk across the Mojave at night—he couldn't have been more than twelve— and he was picked up almost at once and given a lift all the way to Bakersfield. He'd stayed there three years, working on an orange ranch, before setting off again.

Those times he had no real destination.

He hadn't thought of looking for his father. . . .

Now he was on his way to find Tomas.

With money in his pockets!

What would his father look like?

They hadn't seen each other in twenty-one years.

Would they know each other right away?

He would know Tomas, but there was no way his father could recognize him.

So much he had to tell him, starting with Ella's death . . .

He'd been thinking about both his parents this morning . . .

Especially that last night in Texas. The last time he saw Ella.

He wondered what would've happened if he'd gone south that night. Headed for Mexico, instead of California . . .

His whole life might've been changed if he'd done that. Maybe he would've found Tomas years ago!

He'd been frightened and confused that night because of what happened to his mother.

She had often talked of living in California. Said she would have no trouble finding a job as a waitress. Maybe in Hollywood . . .

She never said anything about looking for Tomas. Only that he would come back someday and they would all be happy again.

He remembered that last night clearly.

His mother had locked him in the cupboard with Satan. She always did that when she expected a visitor. One of her boyfriends . . .

He sat on a blanket, spread across the floor, in the dark with Satan coiled around his arm, listening to what was happening in the bedroom.

Some nights he fell asleep, but most times he stayed awake and listened to them laugh—Ella and the men who came to see her—listened as they had sex.

He hadn't known then what they were doing, hadn't realized until much later.

He'd always been frightened when Sam was with his mother. Sam worked on a ranch outside of town and he was always drunk, arguing and causing trouble.

The first time Ella screamed he had tried to open the door, but it was locked. There was nothing he could do. After Sam left and Ella let him out of the closet, he saw that one of her eyes was bruised. Next morning, it was badly swollen. She explained that Sam drank too much. He hadn't meant to hurt her. Another time Sam broke her arm and a neighbor took her to the hospital in his car.

His mother warned him over and over that no matter what he heard while he was locked in the cupboard, he must never make a sound.

And he never did. None of those men knew he was there.

He realized they gave Ella money because sometimes they argued over the price. She told him the money paid their rent.

He didn't realize until years later that his mother was a whore.

When he heard her crying or when Sam was beating her, he would whisper in the dark cupboard. "I'm here, Momma. I'm here. . . ."

He would tell her the same thing when she finally unlocked the door and let him out. "I'm here, Momma. . . ."

"I know, niño," she would say. "I know you are."

And she would take him in her arms while Satan slipped away across the floor. Sometimes his mother would be crying and he would stroke her red hair. They would hold each other until she stopped sobbing.

"It's all right, lover. Momma's okay now. . . ."

She had been so beautiful with her hazel eyes that changed color and the long red hair.

It was Sam who beat her that last night. Worse than before. He could tell from the way Ella screamed.

When he tried the door, it was locked, as usual, and he could only listen to her sobs. Finally he heard Sam's high-heeled boots tapping a dance across the floor, heard him slam the door in their shack. When he called his mother's name and pounded on the door with his fists, she hadn't answered.

It was a long time before he heard her moaning again, then dragging something across the floor to the cupboard. Heard the key turn in the lock and, when the door didn't open, grasped the nob and opened it himself.

His mother was on the floor, her face covered with blood.

He tried to move her to the bed but didn't have enough strength.

Had to put Satan back in the cupboard before he ran next door to get the old Mexican woman who was Ella's friend.

She screamed when she saw Ella and told him to stay with her while she made a phone call.

The nearest phone was in a cantina two streets away.

He sat on the floor beside Ella, holding her hand, but she didn't answer when he talked to her.

The Mexican woman came back with a towel and a bowl of water from the kitchen. Made him sit on the bed while she wiped the blood off his mother's face.

Ella didn't open her eyes or say anything, even when they put her on a stretcher and two men in white uniforms carried her out to the ambulance.

He and the Mexican woman climbed in to sit beside her while the ambulance, siren screaming, returned to town.

He'd watched them place his mother on a cart and roll her down a long corridor in the hospital.

The Mexican woman sat with him in an empty waiting room. He had gone to sleep until she shook him awake and said they could go home.

Walking down a dark road, under the cold stars, she told him Ella would never come home again. She had gone far away.

He could stay in the shack that night, but tomorrow somebody would come and take him to a nice place where he would live. A foster home or an orphanage.

He hadn't understood what those words meant. Only that his mother had left him and he was alone.

And he hadn't cried.

He'd promised the Mexican woman he would go to bed and have a good night's rest.

After she left he packed his clothes in Ella's old suitcase, placed Satan on top of them, and snapped the lock.

The suitcase was heavy but he managed to carry it.

Turned off all the lights in the shack before he opened the door.

Stepped outside, into the night, closing the door without a sound.

Started north on the road that Ella had told him went to California.

Now he was on his way again. In the opposite direction.

* * *

Lolo was keeping to the slow lanes.

Farrell had to be walking, hoping to hitch a ride.

Drivers didn't pick people up anymore. Too many crimes—even murders—involving hikers.

If Farrell got a lift, he might never catch up with him before he reached the border.

Lolo's eyes stayed on the road ahead, praying he would see him any minute.

If things had gone well for him and he'd been given a ride—which was unlikely—he could be in Tijuana already.

He still thought of him as Don Farrell.

Not the new name—Ed Hannaway—that was on his papers for the Honda.

Which must also be on his driver's license.

No matter! He still thought of him as Farrell. Don Farrell . . .

Pray God he hadn't missed him!

The guy might've gotten a ride that took him west, on one of these side roads, toward the Coast Highway.

He'd only passed two hitchhikers. Both Mexican.

He thought briefly of what that psychiatrist had told him.

The Jogger existed in limbo.

At that point he hadn't known the Jogger liked snakes.

What would a psychiatrist say about that?

He tried to remember what Dr. Clovis had said.

The rapist exists in a state of perpetual limbo. Or something like that. A rapist was frightened by normal sex. Only came alive when he raped.

O'Farrell apparently hadn't been afraid of Carlo Dario's wife.

He wondered if he'd looked at her face.

Clovis claimed a rapist never saw his victim's face.

But then, Mrs. Dario insisted she hadn't been raped. So she wasn't a victim.

Clovis said the rapist was a lost soul, unable to love because nobody had ever loved him.

Poor bastard!

He almost felt sorry for Farrell.

This had happened before when he was closing in on a criminal.

Mustn't forget this was the Midnight Jogger who had raped and killed . . .

He realized his stomach was growling. No time to stop for breakfast.

The air was getting warmer and traffic was heavier in the fast lanes.

He wondered if Morita would be driving north today to have another look at her father's vineyards.

He couldn't imagine himself married to a rich woman.

There'd been several friends back in Samoa who were. Poor boys whose muscular bodies caught the eyes of wealthy women and flew off with them to the mainland. None of those marriages lasted. The boys came home with a lot of money and a document saying they had been divorced. Most of them became alcoholics and never worked again.

Someday he would get married because he would fall in love. He'd always wanted to have kids of his own. But not just yet . . .

Morita had told him soon after they met that she would never have children.

Maybe he and Morita could go on for a while as they were. . . .

Far ahead, at the edge of the road, was a hitchhiker.

He slowed the Plymouth, staring at the distant figure, and felt a shiver of excitement spread through his body.

The guy had a backpack strapped to his shoulders.

As he got closer, he saw that the hiker had brownish blond hair. A strange color that might look bronze in moonlight.

He was wearing a sport shirt, Levi's, and running shoes.

Was there a small cut in one of those rubber heels?

He sighed as he eased the Plymouth to a stop.

Don turned as he heard a car slowing and saw a young guy at the wheel. Maybe in his thirties. Looked Mexican. The guy was smiling.

"Care for a lift?" Lolo studied Farrell's face as he stopped the Plymouth. Much younger looking than he'd expected.

"Thanks! Why not?" He slipped the backpack from his shoulders as he went toward the car. "Kinda warm walkin' now the sun's up."

Lolo saw that the blond hair looked odd, even in the

sunlight, because there were strands of red and brown that made it a color he'd never seen before. His eyes were pale. The pupils, more gray than blue, gave them a faded look. He reached to release the lock and opened the door. "Hop in."

"Thanks." He lowered his backpack to the floor and sank onto the leather seat.

"More room for your feet if you drop that in the back."

"It's okay." He closed the door.

So he didn't want the backpack to get too far away. Maybe there was money in it, the money Dario's wife had given him. As the Plymouth picked up speed, he started a casual conversation. "Goin' far?"

"Mexico."

"Me, too. I'll give you a lift across the border."

"That'll be swell."

"Got friends there?"

"No friends. I'm hopin' to locate my father."

"That so? You don't look Mexican."

"My old man's half Mex, but my mother was Irish. I'm only a quarter Mexican, but I speak the lingo pretty good."

So he was part Mexican! That could be the truth. He was aware that Farrell hadn't faced him as he talked but kept his eyes on the road. "So your father's in Tijuana?"

"Don't know where he is. Gotta find him."

"Mexico's a big place. Good luck."

"Thanks. Are you Mexican?"

"People always think I am. But I'm Samoan. . . ."

"What's that?"

"I was born in the South Pacific. Pago Pago."

"Yeah?"

"American Samoa. Which makes me a U.S. citizen."

"Why you goin' to Mexico?"

"Business."

"Yeah? What kinda business you in?"

"You could say it's an import business." He watched Don come alert at the word import. "Main office in L.A. with branches in Frisco and the South Pacific. Deliveries made to Mexico from all over the world . . ."

"You mean—drugs?"

"You said that, I didn't. You into drugs?"

"Not me! I hate the stuff."

"Good for you."

"I've always kept my body clean. No drugs of any kind. Won't even take an aspirin. Makes me sick in the gut."

Lolo didn't ask any more questions and Farrell remained silent.

They both watched the highway ahead as the Plymouth moved into the fast lane.

Don's mind was occupied with what he would do if a customs officer questioned his birth certificate. His best plan was to act natural. Say he was going to Ensenada for the weekend. Had he told this guy too much? Saying he was looking for his father? The guy seemed okay. If he was dealing in drugs, he wasn't going to report anybody to the police. Maybe they wouldn't question him at the border if he let this guy do the talking. Maybe they wouldn't even look at him. They would probably be friends. The guy must go through every week and they would all know him. . . .

Lolo watched him out of the corner of his right eye. So this was the Midnight Jogger! The Limbo Kid, himself. The border officers would've had several calls from Los Angeles. When he reached the customs booths, every officer on duty would be watching for his Plymouth. All he had to do was flash his ID, motion to Farrell, and the car would be surrounded by officers with guns. Once Farrell was in custody, he would phone L.A. and report he'd caught the Jogger. They would fly Farrell to L.A. with armed guards and he would drive back. But first he would eat a good lunch in Tijuana. A bottle of wine to celebrate his success.

Don was whistling softly to himself.

Lolo saw they had passed through La Jolla and were approaching San Diego.

Don smiled at the thought that Tijuana was just ahead. He would find a quiet spot to have lunch. Real Mexican food. Then he would look for a bus to take him to Mexicali. The first stop on Tomas' map! Check into a motel for the night and move to another one tomorrow. Stay in a different motel every night. Tomorrow morning he would start asking people if they knew Tomas O'Farrill. Stay in Mexicali for a week. Maybe longer. Asking that same question in every cantina.

Careful not to drink too much. One beer in each. Mexican beer . . .

"What's your name, kid?" Lolo asked suddenly.

The question startled him. "My name . . ." He might have to show that birth certificate at the border. "Hannaway. Ed Hannaway . . ."

"Ed Hannaway?" Lolo realized as he increased speed that they would reach the border in less than fifteen minutes.

Don was still thinking about his father. They would have a beer together when they met. Several beers! He smiled at the thought of them standing at a bar together. But what if it took weeks—even months—to find Tomas? No! He would locate him right away. Two or three weeks, at most . . .

Lolo wondered what would happen if he drove straight past the inspectors and across the border. Let Farrell out in the center of Tijuana. Told him to get lost.

Somehow he felt sorry for the guy. Always had this feeling before he made an arrest. Even the most vicious criminal.

Farrell didn't look vicious at all. He was, of course, an animal. A multiple rapist and murderer. Once his picture was on television and in the papers, more victims were sure to be heard from.

Thank God he couldn't set him free in Tijuana if he tried!

The customs inspectors would be waiting for them. They had his license number and a description of this Plymouth.

Don was remembering the mountain overlooking that valley. Was it really a mountain? He would have to find out which part of Mexico had mountains. . . .

Tomas had driven to the top and come to a stop in heavy fog. They slept there all night and next morning the fog was gone. Like today. Burned away by the sun. That was the happiest day of his life, the only completely happy day he ever spent with his parents. A whole day looking down at that peaceful valley. He wanted his father to take him there again. Up to the top of that mountain . . .

Lolo glanced at him, aware of his silence, wondering what was on his mind. He seemed far away. Eyes half closed.

Was he in that limbo where nobody could reach him? What would it be like to exist in limbo? Limbo also meant prison.

The poor bastard would be in limbo the rest of his life.

He slowed the Plymouth as he saw the border ahead.

Don realized the car was moving down an open stretch with marked lanes leading toward the border. He could see the rows of booths where uniformed inspectors waited. Two cars had stopped and their drivers were being questioned.

Soon he would be across the border. Another five minutes . . .

Lolo glanced at Farrell. "You remember a girl named Deborah Kern?"

"Who?" He'd never heard the name before.

"Deborah Kern. You remember her, don't you?"

"Nope." He continued to stare at the halted cars. Saw that both drivers were Mexican.

"Deborah Kern was raped. In Nichols Canyon. You knew she died, didn't you?"

Don felt his muscles tense.

"You've been calling yourself Farrell—Don Farrell—while you lived in Los Angeles. Lived in the Coop . . . But even that's not your real name, is it? What is your name?"

Don didn't move.

"Who are you?"

"I'm—nobody. . . ." He whispered the words, but it was as though somebody else's voice was speaking. "Nobody . . ."

Lolo saw that they were within a few yards of the inspection area and swerved into a lane leading to a free booth. He saw the inspector turn to look at his car.

Don was aware that his mind was no longer controlling his body. It was as though he was doing his mechanical-man act. His pulse was slowed. His flesh was cold.

With his left hand, Lolo slipped the ID card from his inside right pocket, as he talked, and held it ready. "I'm Lieutenant Victor Lolo and I'm arresting you for the murder of Deborah Kern and the rape of those other young women."

Don sat frozen, but his arms and legs were jerking. Out of control.

"You'll be flown back to L.A., where you'll be held for trial." Slowing the Plymouth beside the inspection booth and holding out his ID card to the uniformed inspector. "You were expecting me? Special Investigator Lolo."

"We sure are." The inspector whipped out a revolver as he stepped down from his booth.

"This is the man." Lolo turned to the silent figure beside him. "Pick up that backpack, Farrell." That would keep his hands occupied.

Don leaned down slowly to lift the backpack from the floor but, instead, snapped open the top flaps.

Lolo glanced at a second inspector, who also held a revolver as he joined the first. "Take charge of him. Don't think he'll give you any trouble."

Don snatched Satan from the backpack.

Lolo noticed a change of expression in the faces of the guards and turned to see the snake's thick black body lifted into the air. It was alive! He reached for his revolver, but before he could pull it out, the snake's open jaws were thrust against his cheek and its long coils were whipping around his shoulders. He tried to push it away with one hand as he stared into the lidless eyes.

Don flung the door open and jumped out. Ran toward the Mexican side of the border.

Lolo grasped the writhing snake and tossed it after him, through the open door. Released the door on his side and scrambled out.

Don glanced back as he ran, saw the two inspectors with their drawn guns. He reached into his pockets for the birth certificate that would get him past Mexican customs.

Lolo saw the snake twisting across the marked lanes.

The two inspectors fired their guns.

"No!" Lolo shouted. "Don't shoot him!"

Don heard the shots and felt something hard strike the middle of his back. The impact knocked him forward, off his feet.

There was another fusillade of shots.

One of the inspectors had shot the snake. It wasn't moving forward, but its coils were still thrashing.

Don clawed at the asphalt, releasing the piece of paper he'd taken from his pocket. "I'm here, Tomas. I'm here. . . ." He felt something pouring from his mouth and tasted blood.

Lolo was ahead of the others. He knelt beside the sprawled

figure as he thrust his revolver back into its holster. Turned the body over gently and saw the open eyes. Those pale eyes . . .

Farrell's body was twitching awkwardly.

Lolo looked up as the inspectors joined him, revolvers in hand. "You shouldn't have done that. Wasn't necessary."

"Thought he was pulling a gun," one officer answered defensively. "Put his hand in a pocket."

Lolo got to his feet, eyes on the piece of paper Farrell had dropped from his hand. Crossed the asphalt and picked it up. Saw it was a birth certificate for Edward Hannaway. He thrust it into a pocket.

The inspectors had put their revolvers away and were hurrying back to their booths. One of them picked up a phone.

Lolo sighed.

He would be returning to L.A. alone, with nothing but a birth certificate for Edward Hannaway.

He saw that a circle of people, tourists and Mexicans, were watching him from a safe distance.

And strangely, the dead snake seemed to be inching closer to O'Farrell's body.

In a moment he would have to check the body. Empty Farrell's pockets. See what he was carrying in that backpack . . .

He realized there were tears in his eyes.

Damn fool!

Lolo lifted his head and stared at the blue sky above the hills beyond Tijuana. Not a cloud.

In the silence, far away, he heard a cock crowing.

MORE MYSTERIOUS PLEASURES

HAROLD ADAMS
MURDER
Carl Wilcox debuts in a story of triple murder which exposes the underbelly of corruption in the town of Corden, shattering the respectability of its most dignified citizens. #501 $3.50

THE NAKED LIAR
When a sexy young widow is framed for the murder of her husband, Carl Wilcox comes through to help her fight off cops and big-city goons. #420 $3.95

THE FOURTH WIDOW
Ex-con/private eye Carl Wilcox is back, investigating the death of a "popular" widow in the Depression-era town of Corden, S.D. #502 $3.50

EARL DERR BIGGERS
THE HOUSE WITHOUT A KEY
Charlie Chan debuts in the Honolulu investigation of an expatriate Bostonian's murder. #421 $3.95

THE CHINESE PARROT
Charlie Chan works to find the key to murders seemingly without victims—but which have left a multitude of clues. #503 $3.95

BEHIND THAT CURTAIN
Two murders sixteen years apart, one in London, one in San Francisco, each share a major clue in a pair of velvet Chinese slippers. Chan seeks the connection. #504 $3.95

THE BLACK CAMEL
When movie goddess Sheila Fane is murdered in her Hawaiian pavilion, Chan discovers an interrelated crime in a murky Hollywood mystery from the past. #505 $3.95

CHARLIE CHAN CARRIES ON
An elusive transcontinental killer dogs the heels of the Lofton Round the World Cruise. When the touring party reaches Honolulu, the murderer finally meets his match. #506 $3.95

JAMES M. CAIN
THE ENCHANTED ISLE
A beautiful runaway is involved in a deadly bank robbery in this posthumously published novel.   #415 $3.95

CLOUD NINE
Two brothers—one good, one evil—battle over a million-dollar land deal and a luscious 16-year-old in this posthumously published novel.
                                                           #507 $3.95

ROBERT CAMPBELL
IN LA-LA LAND WE TRUST
Child porn, snuff films, and drunken TV stars in fast cars—that's what makes the L.A. world go 'round. Whistler, a luckless P.I., finds that it's not good to know too much about the porn trade in the City of Angels.
                                                           #508 $3.95

GEORGE C. CHESBRO
VEIL
Clairvoyant artist Veil Kendry volunteers to be tested at the Institute for Human Studies and finds that his life is in deadly peril; is he threatened by the Institute, the Army, or the CIA?   #509 $3.95

WILLIAM L. DeANDREA
THE LUNATIC FRINGE
Police Commissioner Teddy Roosevelt and Officer Dennis Muldoon comb 1896 New York for a missing exotic dancer who holds the key to the murder of a prominent political cartoonist.   #306 $3.95

SNARK
Espionage agent Bellman must locate the missing director of British Intelligence—and elude a master terrorist who has sworn to kill him.
                                                           #510 $3.50

KILLED IN THE ACT
Brash, witty Matt Cobb, TV network troubleshooter, must contend with bizarre crimes connected with a TV spectacular—one of which is a murder committed before 40 million witnesses.   #511 $3.50

KILLED WITH A PASSION
In seeking to clear an old college friend of murder, Matt Cobb must deal with the Mad Karate Killer and the Organic Hit Man, among other eccentric criminals.   #512 $3.50

KILLED ON THE ICE
When a famous psychiatrist is stabbed in a Manhattan skating rink, Matt Cobb finds it necessary to protect a beautiful Olympic skater who appears to be the next victim.   #513 $3.50

JAMES ELLROY
SUICIDE HILL
Brilliant L.A. Police sergeant Lloyd Hopkins teams up with the FBI to solve a series of inside bank robberies—but is he working with or against them?   #514 $3.95

PAUL ENGLEMAN
CATCH A FALLEN ANGEL
Private eye Mark Renzler becomes involved in publishing mayhem and murder when two slick mens' magazines battle for control of the lucrative market.   #515 $3.50

LOREN D. ESTLEMAN
ROSES ARE DEAD
Someone's put a contract out on freelance hit man Peter Macklin. Is he as good as the killers on his trail?   #516 $3.95

ANY MAN'S DEATH
Hit man Peter Macklin is engaged to keep a famous television evangelist *alive*—quite a switch from his normal line.   #517 $3.95

DICK FRANCIS
THE SPORT OF QUEENS
The autobiography of the celebrated race jockey/crime novelist.
#410 $3.95

JOHN GARDNER
THE GARDEN OF WEAPONS
Big Herbie Kruger returns to East Berlin to uncover a double agent. He confronts his own past and life's only certainty—death.
#103 $4.50

BRIAN GARFIELD
DEATH WISH
Paul Benjamin is a modern-day New York vigilante, stalking the rapist-killers who victimized his wife and daughter. The basis for the Charles Bronson movie.   #301 $3.95

DEATH SENTENCE
A riveting sequel to *Death Wish*. The action moves to Chicago as Paul Benjamin continues his heroic (or is it psychotic?) mission to make city streets safe.   #302 $3.95

TRIPWIRE
A crime novel set in the American West of the late 1800s. Boag, a black outlaw, seeks revenge on the white cohorts who left him for dead. "One of the most compelling characters in recent fiction."—Robert Ludlum.   #303 $3.95

FEAR IN A HANDFUL OF DUST
Four psychiatrists, three men and a woman, struggle across the blazing Arizona desert—pursued by a fanatic killer they themselves have judged insane. "Unique and disturbing."—Alfred Coppel.   #304 $3.95

JOE GORES
A TIME OF PREDATORS
When Paula Halstead kills herself after witnessing a horrid crime, her husband vows to avenge her death. Winner of the Edgar Allan Poe Award.   #215 $3.95

COME MORNING
Two million in diamonds are at stake, and the ex-con who knows their whereabouts may have trouble staying alive if he turns them up at the wrong moment.   #518 $3.95

NAT HENTOFF
BLUES FOR CHARLIE DARWIN
Gritty, colorful Greenwich Village sets the scene for Noah Green and Sam McKibbon, two street-wise New York cops who are as at home in jazz clubs as they are at a homicide scene.
                                                  #208 $3.95

THE MAN FROM INTERNAL AFFAIRS
Detective Noah Green wants to know who's stuffing corpses into East Village garbage cans . . . and who's lying about him to the Internal Affairs Division.   #409 $3.95

PATRICIA HIGHSMITH
THE BLUNDERER
An unhappy husband attempts to kill his wife by applying the murderous methods of another man. When things go wrong, he pays a visit to the more successful killer—a dreadful error.   #305 $3.95

DOUG HORNIG
THE DARK SIDE
Insurance detective Loren Swift is called to a rural commune to investigate a carbon-monoxide murder. Are the commune inhabitants as gentle as they seem?   #519 $3.95

P.D. JAMES/T.A. CRITCHLEY
THE MAUL AND THE PEAR TREE
The noted mystery novelist teams up with a police historian to create a fascinating factual account of the 1811 Ratcliffe Highway murders.
                                                  #520 $3.95

STUART KAMINSKY'S "TOBY PETERS" SERIES
NEVER CROSS A VAMPIRE
When Bela Lugosi receives a dead bat in the mail, Toby tries to catch the prankster. But Toby's time is at a premium because he's also trying to clear William Faulkner of a murder charge!   #107 $3.95

HIGH MIDNIGHT

When Gary Cooper and Ernest Hemingway come to Toby for protection, he tries to save them from vicious blackmailers. #106 $3.95

HE DONE HER WRONG

Someone has stolen Mae West's autobiography, and when she asks Toby to come up and see her sometime, he doesn't know how deadly a visit it could be. #105 $3.95

BULLET FOR A STAR

Warner Brothers hires Toby Peters to clear the name of Errol Flynn, a blackmail victim with a penchant for young girls. The first novel in the acclaimed Hollywood-based private eye series. #308 $3.95

THE FALA FACTOR

Toby comes to the rescue of lady-in-distress Eleanor Roosevelt, and must match wits with a right-wing fanatic who is scheming to overthrow the U.S. Government. #309 $3.95

JOSEPH KOENIG
FLOATER

Florida Everglades sheriff Buck White matches wits with a Miami murder-and-larceny team who just may have hidden his ex-wife's corpse in a remote bayou. #521 $3.50

ELMORE LEONARD
THE HUNTED

Long out of print, this 1974 novel by the author of *Glitz* details the attempts of a man to escape killers from his past. #401 $3.95

MR. MAJESTYK

Sometimes bad guys can push a good man too far, and when that good guy is a Special Forces veteran, everyone had better duck. #402 $3.95

THE BIG BOUNCE

Suspense and black comedy are cleverly combined in this tale of a dangerous drifter's affair with a beautiful woman out for kicks. #403 $3.95

ELSA LEWIN
I, ANNA

A recently divorced woman commits murder to avenge her degradation at the hands of a sleazy lothario. #522 $3.50

THOMAS MAXWELL
KISS ME ONCE

An epic *roman noir* which explores the romantic but seamy underworld of New York during the WWII years. When the good guys are off fighting in Europe, the bad guys run amok in America. #523 $3.95

ED McBAIN
ANOTHER PART OF THE CITY
The master of the police procedural moves from the fictional 87th precinct to the gritty reality of Manhattan. "McBain's best in several years."—*San Francisco Chronicle*. #524 $3.95

SNOW WHITE AND ROSE RED
A beautiful heiress confined to a sanitarium engages Matthew Hope to free her—and her $650,000. #414 $3.95

CINDERELLA
A dead detective and a hot young hooker lead Matthew Hope into a multi-layered plot among Miami cocaine dealers. "A gem of sting and countersting."—*Time*. #525 $3.95

PETER O'DONNELL
MODESTY BLAISE
Modesty and Willie Garvin must protect a shipment of diamonds from a gentleman about to murder his lover and an *un*civilized sheik. #216 $3.95

SABRE TOOTH
Modesty faces Willie's apparent betrayal and a modern-day Genghis Khan who wants her for his mercenary army. #217 $3.95

A TASTE FOR DEATH
Modesty and Willie are pitted against a giant enemy in the Sahara, where their only hope of escape is a blind girl whose time is running out. #218 $3.95

I, LUCIFER
Some people carry a nickname too far . . . like the maniac calling himself Lucifer. He's targeted 120 souls, and Modesty and Willie find they have a personal stake in stopping him. #219 $3.95

THE IMPOSSIBLE VIRGIN
Modesty fights for her soul when she and Willie attempt to rescue an albino girl from the evil Brunel, who lusts after the secret power of an idol called the Impossible Virgin. #220 $3.95

DEAD MAN'S HANDLE
Modesty Blaise must deal with a brainwashed—and deadly—Willie Garvin as well as with a host of outré religion-crazed villains.
#526 $3.95

ELIZABETH PETERS
CROCODILE ON THE SANDBANK
Amelia Peabody's trip to Egypt brings her face to face with an ancient mystery. With the help of Radcliffe Emerson, she uncovers a tomb and the solution to a deadly threat. #209 $3.95

THE CURSE OF THE PHAROAHS
Amelia and Radcliffe Emerson head for Egypt to excavate a cursed tomb but must confront the burial ground's evil history before it claims them both. #210 $3.95

THE SEVENTH SINNER
Murder in an ancient subterranean Roman temple sparks Jacqueline Kirby's first recorded case. #411 $3.95

THE MURDERS OF RICHARD III
Death by archaic means haunts the costumed weekend get-together of a group of eccentric Ricardians. #412 $3.95

ANTHONY PRICE
THE LABYRINTH MAKERS
Dr. David Audley does his job too well in his first documented case, embarrassing British Intelligence, the CIA, and the KGB in one swoop. #404 $3.95

THE ALAMUT AMBUSH
Alamut, in Northern Persia, is considered by many to be the original home of terrorism. Audley moves to the Mideast to put the cap on an explosive threat. #405 $3.95

COLONEL BUTLER'S WOLF
The Soviets are recruiting spies from among Oxford's best and brightest; it's up to Dr. Audley to identify the Russian wolf in don's clothing. #527 $3.95

OCTOBER MEN
Dr. Audley's "holiday" in Rome stirs up old Intelligence feuds and echoes of partisan warfare during World War II—and leads him into new danger. #529 $3.95

OTHER PATHS TO GLORY
What can a World War I battlefield in France have in common with a deadly secret of the present? A modern assault on Bouillet Wood leads to the answers. #530 $3.95

SION CROSSING
What does the chairman of a new NATO-like committee have to do with the American Civil War? Audley travels to Georgia in this espionage thriller. #406 $3.95

HERE BE MONSTERS
The assassination of an American veteran forces Dr. David Audley into a confrontation with undercover KGB agents. #528 $3.95

BILL PRONZINI AND JOHN LUTZ
THE EYE
A lunatic watches over the residents of West 98th Street with a powerful telescope. When his "children" displease him, he is swift to mete out deadly punishment. #408 $3.95

PATRICK RUELL
RED CHRISTMAS
Murderers and political terrorists come down the chimney during an old-fashioned Dickensian Christmas at a British country inn.

#531 $3.50

DEATH TAKES THE LOW ROAD
William Hazlitt, a universtiy administrator who moonlights as a Soviet mole, is on the run from both Russian and British agents who want him to assassinate an African general.   #532 $3.50

DELL SHANNON
CASE PENDING
In the first novel in the best-selling series, Lt. Luis Mendoza must solve a series of horrifying Los Angeles mutilation murders.   #211 $3.95

THE ACE OF SPADES
When the police find an overdosed junkie, they're ready to write off the case—until the autopsy reveals that this junkie *wasn't* a junkie.   #212 $3.95

EXTRA KILL
In "The Temple of Mystic Truth," Mendoza discovers idol worship, pornography, murder, and the clue to the death of a Los Angeles patrolman.   #213 $3.95

KNAVE OF HEARTS
Mendoza must clear the name of the L.A.P.D. when it's discovered that an innocent man has been executed and the real killer is still on the loose.   #214 $3.95

DEATH OF A BUSYBODY
When the West Coast's most industrious gossip and meddler turns up dead in a freight yard, Mendoza must work without clues to find the killer of a woman who had offended nearly everyone in Los Angeles.   #315 $3.95

DOUBLE BLUFF
Mendoza goes against the evidence to dissect what looks like an air-tight case against suspected wife-killer Francis Ingram—a man the lieutenant insists is too nice to be a murderer.   #316 $3.95

MARK OF MURDER
Mendoza investigates the near-fatal attack on an old friend as well as trying to track down an insane serial killer.   #417 $3.95

ROOT OF ALL EVIL
The murder of a "nice" girl leads Mendoza to team up with the FBI in the search for her not-so-nice boyfriend—a Soviet agent.   #418 $3.95

JULIE SMITH
TRUE-LIFE ADVENTURE
Paul McDonald earned a meager living ghosting reports for a San Francisco private eye until the gumshoe turned up dead . . . now the killers are after him. #407 $3.95

TOURIST TRAP
A lunatic is out to destroy San Francisco's tourism industry; can feisty lawyer/sleuth Rebecca Schwartz stop him while clearing an innocent man of a murder charge? #533 $3.95

ROSS H. SPENCER
THE MISSING BISHOP
Chicago P.I. Buzz Deckard has a missing person to find. Unfortunately his client has disappeared as well, and no one else seems to be who or what they claim. #416 $3.50

MONASTERY NIGHTMARE
Chicago P.I. Luke Lassiter tries his hand at writing novels, and encounters murder in an abandoned monastery. #534 $3.50

REX STOUT
UNDER THE ANDES
A long-lost 1914 fantasy novel from the creator of the immortal Nero Wolfe series. "The most exciting yarn we have read since *Tarzan of the Apes.*"—*All-Story Magazine*. #419 $3.50

ROSS THOMAS
CAST A YELLOW SHADOW
McCorkle's wife is kidnapped by agents of the South African government. The ransom—his cohort Padillo must assassinate their prime minister. #535 $3.95

THE SINGAPORE WINK
Ex-Hollywood stunt man Ed Cauthorne is offered $25,000 to search for colleague Angelo Sacchetti—a man he thought he'd killed in Singapore two years earlier. #536 $3.95

THE FOOLS IN TOWN ARE ON OUR SIDE
Lucifer Dye, just resigned from a top secret U.S. Intelligence post, accepts a princely fee to undertake the corruption of an entire American city. #537 $3.95

JIM THOMPSON
THE KILL-OFF
Luanne Devore was loathed by everyone in her small New England town. Her plots and designs threatened to destroy them—unless they destroyed her first. #538 $3.95

DONALD E. WESTLAKE
THE HOT ROCK
The unlucky master thief John Dortmunder debuts in this spectacular caper novel. How many times do you have to steal an emerald to make sure it *stays* stolen?   #539 $3.95

BANK SHOT
Dortmunder and company return. A bank is temporarily housed in a trailer, so why not just hook it up and make off with the whole shebang? Too bad nothing is ever that simple.   #540 $3.95

THE BUSY BODY
Aloysius Engel is a gangster, the Big Man's right hand. So when he's ordered to dig a suit loaded with drugs out of a fresh grave, how come the corpse it's wrapped around won't lie still?   #541 $3.95

THE SPY IN THE OINTMENT
Pacifist agitator J. Eugene Raxford is mistakenly listed as a terrorist by the FBI, which leads to his enforced recruitment to a group bent on world domination. Will very good Good triumph over absolutely villainous Evil?   #542 $3.95

GOD SAVE THE MARK
Fred Fitch is the sucker's sucker—con men line up to bilk him. But when he inherits $300,000 from a murdered uncle, he finds it necessary to dodge killers as well as hustlers.   #543 $3.95

TERI WHITE
TIGHTROPE
This second novel featuring L.A. cops Blue Maguire and Spaceman Kowalski takes them into the nooks and crannies of the city's Little Saigon.   #544 $3.95

COLLIN WILCOX
VICTIMS
Lt. Frank Hastings investigates the murder of a police colleague in the home of a powerful—and nasty—San Francisco attorney.
                    #413 $3.95

NIGHT GAMES
Lt. Frank Hastings of the San Francisco Police returns to investigate the at-home death of an unfaithful husband—whose affairs have led to his murder.   #545 $3.95